LIES HE TOLD ME

For a preview of upcoming books and information about the author, visit JamesPatterson.com or find him on Facebook, X, or Instagram.

LIES HE TOLD ME

James Patterson

AND David Ellis

Little, Brown and Company
New York Boston London

Little, Brown and Company
Hachette Book Group
1290 Avenue of the Americas, New York, NY 10104
littlebrown.com

First Edition: September 2024

Little, Brown and Company is a division of Hachette Book Group, Inc. The Little, Brown name and logo are trademarks of Hachette Book Group, Inc.

The publisher is not responsible for websites (or their content) that are not owned by the publisher.

The Hachette Speakers Bureau provides a wide range of authors for speaking events. To find out more, go to hachettespeakersbureau.com or email hachettespeakers@hbgusa.com.

Little, Brown and Company books may be purchased in bulk for business, educational, or promotional use. For information, please contact your local bookseller or the Hachette Book Group Special Markets Department at special.markets@hbgusa.com.

ISBN 9780316403894 (hardcover) / 9780316577861 (large print) / 9780316582414 (Walmart edition)
LCCN 2023945375

Printing 1, 2024

LSC-C

Printed in the United States of America

To Jim and Jill Kopecky,
friends forever

LIES HE TOLD ME

PROLOGUE

ONE

THIS IS HOW I lost David.

It started right here, on the trail near the bank of the Cotton River, late September, as we walked together, David in a shirt and tie, me in a dress but wearing David's suit jacket. I didn't need to tell him I was cold. He shrugged off his jacket the moment the wind whipped up, dropping it like an electric blanket over my shoulders. David always represented warmth to me, a human radiator; I usually had to roll away from him in bed at night.

"What are we doing?" I asked.

To our right, the Cotton River ribboned through our town. It was tranquil this time of year, especially with the unseasonable cold, below fifty, too chilly for even the most ardent Jet Skiers and boaters who refused to acknowledge the end of summer.

"You're taking a walk with your husband on his birthday. Giving an old man his last wish."

"Stop. Forty-two isn't old." I squeezed his arm. "And I have news for you, mate—you don't look old, either."

He laughed that off, but it was true. *Old* is the last word I would ever use to describe David—the picture of health, muscle-bound and trim, quick with that beaming smile.

"It's the bald head," he says. "Hides the receding hairline and the gray."

Neither of which, as far as I could tell, was true. He'd always had that look, ever since the day I met him, thirteen years ago. Not many men can pull off a shaved head, but David could. The day I met him, my first take on him, in his tank top and shorts and running gear, was that he was a gym teacher, maybe a former football player who'd taken up marathon running after retirement.

"Here—stop," he said.

"Right here on the path? Why?"

"What do you mean, why?" he said. "You said we could do whatever I wanted for my birthday."

"Yeah, I did," I said. "I figured it would involve me dressing up in a nurse costume or something. But whatever; it's your call."

David walked ten steps farther, then turned back to face me. Behind him, Anna's Bridge, one of those creaky old truss bridges that always remind me of a carnival ride, though it looked majestic in the late afternoon, backed by a fluorescent orange sky, the river emblazoned with the sun's reflection.

It was like a scene from a postcard.

"This is where we were standing," he said. "The first time I saw you."

I remembered. Of course I remembered. He'd stopped just in that spot, cooling off after a run, looking out over the river. I was jogging from the other direction, toward him, when I stopped right where I was now standing to adjust my music.

"You called out to me."

He said to me then, *What are you jamming on those headphones? Folk music? Polka?* I laughed at the time. He was flirting with me, not particularly well, but I was drawn to his silliness, his confidence in being so playful, like he instantly knew for both of us that we were a match.

I remembered him two weeks later, when I ran into him at the start of a 10K race downtown. We ended up running the race together, clocking a slow time but talking and laughing all the while. It was some of the most enjoyable sixty-one minutes and twenty-eight seconds of my life. We were married within a year.

Now in his crisp dress shirt and purple silk tie, David walked up and touched his forehead to mine. "I knew right then, Marcie, the first time I laid eyes on you right here. I swear I did."

This, *this* was what he wanted to do before our swanky dinner tonight. This was his birthday wish. Not a Bears game or a night in Chicago; not a trip to Vegas. Anything he wanted, I'd told him, just name it, and his choice was to return to the place we first met. That was David, my corny, romantic husband.

He kissed me softly, then whispered, "Now, what was that about a nurse's costume?"

I laughed, bumping teeth with his. Then I looked over

David's shoulder as an SUV sped onto Anna's Bridge, veering wildly, drawing a horn from an oncoming vehicle. The SUV broke sharply to the right, crashing into the truss's side gate with a hideous crunch, the protective railings snapping free, the entire bridge rocking and swaying as the SUV's nose broke free of the bridge and dangled over the edge for just a moment, as if aimed at the river below—

"Oh, no," I whispered.

—before surrendering to gravity, the SUV hitting the water grille-first, bobbing and floating for a moment before sinking below the orange glow of the water.

David threw off his shoes and sprinted toward the bank of the river.

"David, no! No!"

"Find a tree branch or something we can grab!" he shouted as he bounded down the incline, through the tangled foliage by the river's edge.

"You can't go in there!"

"Stay on shore!" he shouted back at me. "You can pull us in! And call 911!"

The lifeguard rules buzzed through my head—*Don't bring victims ashore: keep them afloat until help arrives*—as I called out to David again, pleading with him in vain: "David, don't! David, don't!"

I pulled out my phone as he swam furiously through the water toward the crash site.

Just like that, hardly more than a snap of a finger, and life would never be the same.

TWO

COME UP, DAVID. Come up for air.

Sirens screamed out from a distance. Hemingway Grove police and fire, responding quickly, but it wouldn't be quickly enough.

I'd kicked off my heels, ready to jump in, those lifeguard rules again stopping me. David was right. It was best that I stand by the shore, ready to haul people onto the bank if they could make it that far.

If.

"Come up, David."

The SUV had fallen in the dead center of the river, which was the width of around half a football field, or so it had been described to me when I was a child. David had swum the twenty, maybe thirty yards in no time. That wasn't the problem; he was a strong swimmer, a triathlete. The problem was how long he'd been under once he reached the spot where the SUV had sunk. I tried to keep track of the seconds but couldn't stay calm, couldn't trust my count.

Forty-five seconds? A minute? Maybe it was more like thirty seconds. Maybe he still had time.

I started toward the water, nearly sliding down the incline. I couldn't fathom *not* going in to help David. But one thought kept me on solid ground, and it wasn't the lifeguard rules. It was an ugly but necessary thought.

Our kids, Grace and Lincoln. They couldn't lose two parents in one day.

I couldn't believe I was even thinking such a thing, that David could be gone. He'd come up for air, right? Even if he couldn't pry free the driver and any other passengers, his instincts would force him to the surface for air, right?

People were shouting from the bridge, people behind me, bikers and joggers, stopping and calling out, too. Some of the people on the bridge were taking videos with their phones. All eyes were fixed on the water, waiting helplessly.

The sirens grew closer.

I couldn't believe this was happening. Minutes ago, nuzzling by the place we first met, sharing a treasured memory, remembering how lucky I felt to have him, and suddenly, just like that, David was…no, I couldn't let myself believe it was possible.

It had been more than a minute since he'd been underwater. I was sure of it. My head woozy, I finally remembered to breathe, something my husband could not do.

Then all sound was lost as my vision grew fuzzy with tears. So many thoughts and emotions bombarding me…

—how will I tell the kids; how will it affect them?

—he'll come up for air, of course he will;

—how unfair that he did everything right in life, fol-

lowed the rules, cared for and loved his family, and he has
to be taken away by the actions of some reckless, probably
drunk, driver;

—he'll survive, you know he will, you know David;

—why did today have to be his birthday, why did this
have to be his birthday wish, why did we have to be at this
spot, why couldn't we have been anywhere else, anywhere
else in the world?

And I felt myself but couldn't hear myself screaming,
shouting, pleading—

Then I sensed a *whoosh* overhead, a strong current of air
passing over me. A helicopter, the words HEMINGWAY GROVE
RESCUE on the side, racing through the air toward the crash
site, as people on the bridge waved and pointed toward the
spot in the water.

He'll come up for air, I told myself. *He just will.*

The helicopter hovered over the area, dangerously close
to the bridge. A panel door slid open automatically; a ladder unfolded from a mechanical lever, lowering to the
water's surface.

Jump in, I silently pleaded. *Jump in and rescue him.*

But I could see nobody in the helicopter save the pilot.
The police hadn't had time to scramble a rescue team—
just the copter itself, from wherever it had been nearby.

He'll grab the ladder, I told myself. *They'll fly him to safety.
He'll wave to the crowd a hero, and we will live happily ever
after.*

Believe it will happen. Believe it with all your will.

It will happen. Believe it will happen.

Grab the ladder, David. Please. Please, David, grab the

ladder and come back to us. Don't leave us on your forty-second birthday, not when the kids are so young and need you, not when we have so much time left together.

Grab the ladder, David. Do it. Now.

A hand popped out of the water and grabbed a rung of the ladder.

THREE

DAVID DID THE SMART thing: he didn't try to swim with the unconscious man to the river shore. He stayed right where he was, his left arm wrapped around the ladder's rung, his right arm around the chest of the man he'd pulled from the SUV, bracing himself against the current of the river.

I stood by the riverbank, still in shock, wilting with relief, feeling like a miracle had just been bestowed on me. But he wasn't safe yet. That water was cold, and freezing water saps strength. How long could he hold both himself and a grown man out of the water?

I watched him, never took my eyes off him, while I hit Redial for 911. "A marine unit is on its way, ma'am," I was told.

"Hold on—a boat is coming!" I shouted, but I was certain David couldn't hear me, focusing his energy on staying above water, the harsh splashes from the river's current, which seemed to be picking up, tossing him about while he clung to the ladder. Somehow, he managed to turn his head in my direction and find me. I waved to him and shouted, "I love you!" but he couldn't possibly hear me or read my lips.

I saw it first from the reaction of the people on the bridge, pointing and jumping and shouting—the police rescue boat coming from the east, siren flashing, nearly flying over the water, racing to the scene.

"Get there, get there," I whispered. "Hang on, David. Hang on just a little longer; they're coming."

The boat slowed and pulled up right alongside the ladder. Rescuers opened a side door on the boat and dropped some kind of wide, flat platform onto the water. Two officers crawled out onto it, as if carefully navigating an ice floe. One rescuer grabbed the man and pulled him onto the platform. The other rescuer dragged David onto the boat.

I exhaled the largest breath ever.

The boat sped off, presumably to some meeting point with an ambulance, while rescue workers looked to be performing CPR on the other man.

I ran back to our car, parked by the pub David owns, and drove quickly to the hospital. I called our daughter, Grace, who at age twelve had a phone. Hemingway Grove was a small town in most respects, and I wanted her to hear the news from me first. When I heard her voice, emotion clogged my throat. But I had to minimize the drama, the danger—I just told her that we'd had some excitement and Daddy had rescued a man who fell in the river. *Everybody's fine,* I assured her.

Was I right?

FOUR

BY THE TIME I arrived at St. Benedict's Hospital, several reporters from the local news stations had already gathered. I pushed through them, found the receptionist in the emergency department, and before long was ushered inside.

I pushed open the curtain enough to see David, wrapped in several blankets, an IV in his right forearm. A doctor was examining him. David's eyes began to tear up when they found mine. I rushed over, careful not to mess with anything, and put my hands on his face. "You're okay. Are you? Are you—"

I managed that much before I choked up, bursting into tears.

"I'm okay, Marce," he whispered, his voice hoarse. "God, am I glad to see you."

"Is he okay?" I said to the nurse, a young woman.

"He's being treated for mild hypothermia," she said. "He should be fine. We're keeping him in blankets and giving him a warmed salt-water solution in his veins."

"Hey," David said. "I'm fine."

I pressed my lips against his forehead. I couldn't embrace him, couldn't hold him, swaddled as he was like an infant, other than to gently place an arm around his shoulder. The usual warmth that radiated off him was not there. His skin was discolored and cool to the touch.

"All I could think about…was you," he said, his voice shaky and weak. "You and…the kids…the whole time."

For the next three hours, I didn't leave his side, except to call Grace with updates. *Daddy is fine. Daddy is doing better. Daddy is warmer now. They say Daddy can come home later tonight.* Our babysitter, who had planned on our being out late anyway for David's birthday celebration—boy, did *that* feel like a distant memory—said everything was fine at home, that the kids watched the video over and over on Grace's phone in between Grace texting with her friends and Lincoln, age ten, playing PlayStation 5 on our television.

There was video, apparently, of the incident. I remembered the people on the bridge with their phones out.

I could tell David was improving as time wore on by the wisecracks he made. Telling one of the nurses, who called me Mrs. Bowers, that I wasn't his wife but his mistress. Asking me to go check if they had any extra nurse outfits we could bring home for later.

"Knock, knock." A doctor, a young woman with horn-rimmed glasses, swung the curtain open, then swung it closed behind her. "I'll need to take a look at that arm, Mr. Bowers."

David had punched out the driver's-side window during

the rescue. He used his left hand, his dominant hand, leaving his left forearm and knuckles bloody and raw. There were additional cuts and abrasions on his head, shoulders, and back, incurred when he reached in, unbuckled the unconscious man, and pulled him out. Just imagining it, I had to remind myself to breathe; how he did all that in so short a time, underwater, was almost impossible to fathom.

If I ever doubted the existence of miracles, I no longer would.

"Turns out glass can cut you," David said, his voice stronger now, as the doctor checked the stitches on one particularly bad wound.

"The driver who lost control of the car—he had an epileptic seizure," said the doctor, looking up at us. "We were able to stabilize him. He's going to make it."

"Thanks to the air trapped inside the SUV," said David.

"Mostly thanks to *you*, Mr. Bowers." The doctor nodded at him before resuming her look at his arm. "You know how many reporters are out there waiting for you to come out?"

"Ugh." David's head fell back against the pillow.

"The public relations guy here wants to do a press conference when you're able," she said.

"A press conference?" David scoffed. "For what?"

"You should take a bow," I said.

"Take a bow for doing something anyone would've done?"

The doctor looked back up at him. "I'm not sure just *anyone* would have done what you did. Looked pretty heroic to me."

"You—you saw it?" I asked.

"Oh, the video's gone viral." The doctor chuckled. "You haven't seen it?"

Ah, yes, the video. Our kids had seen it, but we hadn't. David had *lived* it, and I was not in a hurry to revisit those terrifying moments. Still, I looked at my phone. Typed in a few words — **Cotton River Anna's Bridge rescue** — and there was the video, already online in several spots, mostly on social media but apparently even on the local news. David and I watched it together.

The video was taken from the bridge; it began as David swam madly toward the spot where the SUV went under and ran all the way through the arrival of the helicopter (which temporarily blocked the phone's view before the person holding it moved), David's reaching for the rescue ladder, victim in tow, and the marine unit of the Hemingway Grove Police Department coming to their assistance.

"Listen to your wife," said the doctor. "You should be recognized."

David let out a big sigh. "Doctor, you know what I want to do? After you tell me I'm free to leave? I want to go home and be with my family. That's what I've wanted since the moment I hit that water. You think I earned that right?"

The doctor looked at David, then at me, and smiled. "I think you absolutely did."

Around midnight, David was discharged. We were pretty sure that the reporters had gone home, but we left by the rear exit just in case. Walking into our home, normally a routine event, felt like a gift from heaven under the circumstances.

The kids were long asleep but had secured a promise

that Daddy would come in and kiss them when he got home. Ten-year-old Lincoln, buried under his Avengers covers, moaned and mumbled but didn't awaken. Grace, our twelve-year-old, never opened her eyes as David stroked her hair and kissed her cheeks. As we started out of the room, she mumbled, "Daddy's okay. Daddy isn't leaving."

David crouched back down to her, nuzzled her face. "Daddy isn't leaving, Gracie," he said. "Daddy isn't ever leaving."

BOOK I

(One month later)

ONE

THREE, TWO, ONE…BLASTOFF!

Otherwise known as Monday morning at the Bowers home, the machinery slowly groaning and shrugging and clanging into motion.

Starting with my canine alarm clock, Lulu, our Cav, lying on my chest, her wagging tail *whoosh-whooshing* back and forth over our comforter. She *oofs* at me, puppy breath on my face, before graduating to a full-scale whimper-cry.

I trudge downstairs and open the kitchen door. She bounds out into the cool October air. She'll spend the next hour racing around our fenced-in yard, chasing rabbits and squirrels, having no idea what to do if she catches one.

I turn on the coffee grinder and, while it crunches and whirs away, reach for the coffeepot. It's not there, so I try the dishwasher. Nope. I do a 360 around the kitchen but don't see it. Sometimes we take the pot into the living room on a lazy Sunday morning—but no, not there, either.

I'm expected to survive Monday morning without coffee?

Screw it. I head upstairs. David's beaten me into the shower, but he doesn't take long. No hair to wash, at least.

"I can't find the coffeepot," I say to him as he gets out of the shower.

"I'll look for it. I'll get the lunches, too," he mumbles while throwing on a sweater and jeans.

By seven, I'm out of the shower and dressed for court. David is down the hall in Grace's bedroom, engaged in intense negotiations over the process of getting out of bed. David could wake a tiger without being bitten, but Grace knows how to play him.

"Hey, mister." I flip on the light in Lincoln's room, both to help wake him up and to avoid tripping over something on the carpet. Walking through a ten-year-old boy's room is like navigating a minefield, except the consequences of a mistake are not death or dismemberment: they're more along the lines of stubbing a toe or, my favorite, stepping in something of mysterious origin—something squishy or slimy.

On the bed is an Avengers comforter, tucked and nestled into the shape of a boy. I poke my finger into the center mass and hear a moan. I reach under the bottom, find a foot, and tickle it, resulting in a reflexive kick and a protesting groan.

I pull down the top of the comforter and find the face of a boy with messy dark hair, face flushed with heat, who looks like a younger version of the man I married. "Morning, buddy!"

I head over to his dresser and pull out a long-sleeved Blackhawks T-shirt, sweats, and underwear. The sock drawer is empty. Right—I washed them last night and left them in the dryer. "How'd you do in fantasy last night, bud? McCaffrey do okay?"

"McCaffrey's hurt," says Lincoln in his squeaky voice. "He's out for the season."

"How about Lamar Jackson?" And thus I have exhausted my knowledge of fantasy football, a game Lincoln plays with his father in a league of ten-year-olds that David started up. Lincoln loves it, and talking about it is a good way to shake off his morning cobwebs.

"Can I see your phone?" he asks, sitting up, eyes still closed.

"Downstairs you can," I say. "After you get dressed and brush your hair and eat breakfast, including the fruit."

Downstairs, David is looking through the kitchen pantry. "I can't find Grace's lunch box," he says. "Not in her backpack, either."

I look over at the island, where Lincoln's lunch box is open, filled with his food and covered in ice packs. Grace's food—leftover sushi from last night, carrots and ranch, and sliced apples—is out on the island, but no lunch box.

I sigh. "Is she up yet?"

David closes the pantry door. "Depends on what you mean by 'up.'"

"She's not out of bed yet?" I glance at the clock. It's almost twenty past seven.

I take the stairs and march into her room. "Grace, get up, right now."

Grace opens her eyes, sits up, and tosses her covers. *"Fiiiine,"* she says as a three-syllable word.

I pass David, standing in the hallway, who says, "Why can't I get her to do that?"

Because you spoil her, I do not say. *Because you can't discipline a girl with an angelic face like that. Because Grace knows she has you wrapped around her little finger.*

"Grace, did you leave your lunch box at school?" he asks.

"No," she scoffs, as if the question were beneath her, as if she were personally offended at the insinuation.

"Is it in the car?"

"I brought it home on Friday!" She slams closed the bathroom door. Morning is to Grace like rain is to a picnic.

Back downstairs, I make breakfast. Peanut butter toast and veggie sausage for Lincoln, scrambled eggs with green Tabasco for Grace, a bowl of fruit to share. I check Lincoln's backpack while I move around the eggs in the pan. His school iPad is inside.

"Lincoln, did you charge your school iPad?" I ask as he waddles into the kitchen, still half asleep, clothed but barefoot, hair standing on end.

"I don't know." He looks over at me. "Well, obviously, if you're asking, I didn't."

"Obviously. Whose responsibility is that? Is it mine or is it yours?"

He rubs his eyes, declining to answer on the ground that it might incriminate him.

"Where are your socks? Oh, right, the dryer—"

"What the hell?" David says, looking out the back window.

"What?" I walk over to him.

He points to the center of the backyard. "Grace's lunch box."

I do a double take, then focus. "Why is Grace's lunch box in the backyard? For God's sake, Gracie."

I head to the washer-dryer in the mudroom by the garage door to get Lincoln some socks. I hear David calling up to Grace about the lunch box. I can't hear Grace's response per se, but I'm reminded of a growling tiger.

I bend down and pop open the dryer. "What—what the hell?"

"What? What's up?" David calls to me.

I pull the coffeepot out of the dryer. I walk into the kitchen and show it to David.

"Great; you found it."

"In the *dryer.*"

"In the—" He makes a face. "I think we need a family meeting on where things go. Lunch boxes *not* in the backyard, coffeepots *not* in the dryer."

"Seriously," I say. "How did—is today bizarro day?"

He takes the pot from me and kisses my forehead. "No, it's Monday morning. Lincoln, when you're done eating, feed Lulu, would ya, sport?"

"Where's Lulu?"

"The backyard," I say.

"No, she's not."

"Um, yes, she..." I look out the window. Don't see her, but the backyard is bordered with shrubbery on all sides, and she often gets in the bushes when she's chasing small animals.

I step out into the cool air and call out her name. She isn't there. Did we leave the gate open? No, the gate on the chain-link fence is closed, as usual. "Lulu!" I call again. "Lulu!"

I grab Grace's lunch box and bring it inside.

"David, the dog is gone. She's really gone."

"Okay, I'll go find her." David sighs and heads for the door. "Welcome to Monday morning."

TWO

EIGHT TWENTY. THE LAST of the two kids, Lincoln, rides off on his bike with a perfunctory *Bye-love-you* on his way to school, three blocks away. By then, I've already read three texts from David, out looking for our dog, Lulu: **Not by Custers** (the Custers have three Weimaraners whom Lulu loves), **What a fucked up morning** (true enough), and **On way to forest preserve.**

The forest preserve — God help Lulu if she made it that far. She never has. She's been known to chase deer, who retreat to the preserve, but Lulu usually loses interest after they outrun her.

Lulu won't know how to get back from the forest preserve, and she'll get lost within it. It's a good three square miles of woods, trails, streams, deer, to say nothing of the coyotes. Lulu, a harmless puppy, wouldn't stand a chance against a coyote.

Mr. Walters, the third-grade teacher three blocks away,

lost a puppy to a coyote. He now carries a golf club around while he walks his new dog, always on a leash.

I shudder away that thought and head in the opposite direction of David, toward the town square, texting my "mom chain" to be on the lookout for Lulu, attaching a photo for the few of them who wouldn't recognize her. Twenty-two strong, that chain of mothers covers all four directions from our house, on Cedar Lane.

And then I'm off on foot through the neighborhood, zigzagging between front yards and backyards, crunching over the yellow and burnt-orange leaves that dance across the yards in the wind, angling around tombstones and inflatable ghosts and witches and skeletons, pumpkins with evil grins and celebrity faces. Always calling, "Lulu, want a treat?" so she won't think she's in trouble and hide from me, as she's prone to do.

You're not supposed to reward a dog's bad behavior, but I'm past rules. I just want her back. Lulu has been gone a solid hour now. At this point, the odds are not good for a dog. But I stiff-arm that mounting sense of panic.

My mom chain texts back like a hail of gunfire, each vibration bringing me hope:

Oh no! Will be on lookout

Haven't seen her but will look!!

Poor Lulu!

Eight thirty. "Nothing," David tells me by phone, out of breath, jogging through the Hemingway Forest Preserve. "How the hell did she get out? The gate was closed. No way she jumps that fence. We built it high enough a *deer* couldn't jump it."

"I have no idea."

"Maybe the gnomes who moved Grace's lunch box and our coffeepot took Lulu for a walk."

Eight forty. I've hit downtown—the Square, as we call it, remade in cobblestone a few years ago to preserve the old-fashioned small-town theme, as if a town of thirty-six thousand in central Illinois needed that reminder. Some of the stores have played along, with their old-fashioned awnings, retro signage, and brick facades.

In the center of the square is a large statue of our town's founder, a fur trader named Abner Hemingway, there to disappoint any visitors who have a certain literary figure in mind when they detour off I-57 for a bite to eat or an overnight stay. David always quips that we should change our motto from "Small-town charm" to "Sorry, not *that* guy." He estimates that his pub, less than a mile off the interstate, makes around half its annual revenue on a misimpression.

Could Lulu have made it this far? With the passage of more than sixty minutes now, she could have gone in *any* direction. She could be in the preserve, up by the school, dodging traffic on 1st Street—should I get in my Nissan and drive around to cover more ground?

The smell of fresh croissants from Pilsner's Delights. My stomach would ordinarily growl were it not churning in knots. I'm wasting my time. I'm walking around the Square, checking behind and around the mostly quiet storefronts, on the off chance that my dog has made it this far, which seems like such a long shot.

Still, I do it. The general store, no. The barbershop, no. Not by the men's store or the ice cream parlor. The pharmacy, jeweler, karate studio, diner, print shop, sporting-goods store, antiques shop, credit union, Thai restaurant, the other antiques shop, the women's boutique—

Five minutes to nine. I have court at nine thirty. David already has suppliers waiting for him at the pub. We're running out of time before that moment—that dreaded, ugly moment of resignation—when we throw up our hands and decide to stop searching, to go to work and resort to putting up signs all over town. I already know the outcome if it comes to that. We'll never see that sweet little face again.

"Lost your dog?"

I turn and see a man with red hair, dressed in workout clothes, wearing sunglasses, sitting on one of the benches with a paper cup of coffee in hand. I don't recognize him, but the town's just big enough, thank God, that not everyone knows everyone. Someone like me, born and raised here, probably knows almost everyone in the street. But not this guy. He's probably a visitor making a stopover on his way to Memphis or Florida, staying at Hemingway's Inn, over on Iroquois, thinking there will be memorabilia from Ernest himself (there is) and rooms named with cheesy references to *For Whom the Bell Tolls* and *The Sun Also Rises* (there are).

"She's a Cavalier King Charles," I tell him. "Twenty pounds, white with big brown spots."

"Haven't seen her, but I'll keep a lookout."

"Her tag has my phone number."

"Sure thing. I wouldn't worry. She'll probably find her way back home. It'll be like she never left." He gives me a big toothy smile before getting up and walking away.

Like she never left? I highly doubt that, strange red-headed guy. But he doesn't know Lulu. She could get lost inside a car. There is zero-point-zero chance Lulu will come back on her own. Either we find her or someone else does and calls us.

Or she's lost forever.

At nine, I shake my head. I have to head home, get in my car, and drive to court.

"Where are you, sweet girl?" I whisper, my voice trembling. "I won't give up looking. I promise."

THREE

I DON'T FIND LULU on my walk back to the house. But I have to get this court appearance out of the way so I can come back home and keep searching.

"Nobody took her," David reassures me through my earbuds after I suggest the possibility while driving to court. David's on his way to the pub.

"That happens, you know," I say, gripping the steering wheel. "Dogfighters like to use little dogs for practice for the big dogs. They steal them and—"

"Marcie, don't—don't go there. She dug a hole under the fence or slipped through the bars or something. I don't know. She's running around the neighborhood somewhere, and we're gonna find her. I'll get done with this meeting and go back and spend the whole day looking for her if I have to."

I try to let those words calm me, but we both know things are getting worse as every minute passes. And now we're not even out there looking for her. She could be back in our neighborhood, trotting around, tail wagging, looking for us, and we're not there—

I slam on my brakes to avoid the car in front of me, stopping suddenly on 2nd Street. I reach for the horn, but it was my fault, didn't see the red light.

Get a grip, Marcie. Get a grip.

I make it to the courthouse, in the town next to ours, three minutes before the nine thirty call. It's a dumb status hearing on discovery, meaningless. I'd skip it, but Judge Grimsley dismisses any case in which the plaintiff fails to show up for a hearing. This, *this* I'm doing instead of looking for Lulu.

I reach into my bag for my court ID to skip the line and the metal detector. But it's—it's not there. My ID isn't there. Huh?

I look inside my bag. The ID is always inside the front compartment, attached to a clip for this very reason, so I *can't* misplace it. But the clip dangles nakedly.

I drop the bag to the floor, squat down, and riffle through the entire bag. My case file, notes, laptop, pens, hand sanitizer, breath mints, lint brush—no court ID.

I grip my hair. What's going on? What circle of hell has engulfed us this morning? The lunch box, the coffeepot, Lulu, now my court ID—

I see my client, a woman named Rina Lorenzo, standing down the hall outside the courtroom. She comes to every hearing, even the meaningless ones. I wave to her as I get in line with the others for the metal detector.

I'm not back in my gray Nissan SUV, heading home, until well after ten.

"I'm driving around 1st Street," David tells me, finished with his supplier at the pub. "Maybe you could look south of the house."

"It's been close to three hours," I say. Our sweet, harmless little dog, who has no clue how to help herself. I check text messages and update my mom chain, saying that no, we still haven't found Lulu; please keep looking. I search through photos of Lulu on my phone, looking for the best one to put on the signs that will go up all over town. Lulu going down the slide with Lincoln, my son clutching the three-month-old puppy in his hand. Lulu in a bath, a puff of soap on her head. Wearing a tiara Grace put on her, her head cocked as she stares at the camera. Numerous close-ups that Grace takes all the time around the house. Those big brown eyes, framed by coffee-colored spots, the thin snout with the button nose—

A dull pain in my stomach as I park in the driveway. David pulls his car up alongside mine.

"What a morning," he says when he gets out. "I forgot my inventory list at home. I had to go look it up on my computer at work."

"Tell me about it—I couldn't find my court ID. If I lose that—"

"Your court ID's right there on the dash," he says, pointing inside my car.

"It's—seriously?" I look through the window. Yes, there it is. I let out air. "I'm losing my mind this morning, I swear."

"You're focused on Lulu."

"What if she made it to the forest preserve after all?" I ask. "And she's walking around, so scared, and those coyotes—"

"Hey, hey." David puts his hand on my shoulder. "We can only do what we can do. And that's think and search."

He's right, of course. I lean against the warm SUV. "Okay. Right. Well, what makes the most sense—"

We both hear it—the familiar high-pitched bark. We look at each other, then race to the backyard. Coming up to the fence, from inside the yard, is Lulu, her tail wagging eagerly, her bark more like a whine.

"Oh, my God, honey." I open the gate and squat down, relief flooding through me as Lulu jumps all over me, knocking me back to a seated position.

"What—what the hell happened?" David looks around. "The gate's still closed. How'd she get back in?"

I don't know, and I don't care. Not for now, at least, as Lulu burrows her head in my lap and continues whining.

"Is it possible she was in the yard all along, behind a bush or something?"

I don't know, and I don't care. Then I look up, as Lulu rushes over to David and gives him the same treatment she gave me.

"It's like she never left," I whisper.

FOUR

NEAR BEDTIME FOR THE kiddos—at least this day can't get any worse.

"Fourteen times twelve," says David, sitting on the couch in the family room off the kitchen, the *Monday Night Football* game on but muted.

"One sixty-eight." Grace answers almost immediately, while texting on her phone.

"How?"

"Fourteen times ten is 140; fourteen times two is 28; 140 plus 28 is 168."

"Sixteen times thirteen."

Like David, Grace is a math whiz, taking double-advanced math this year with the seventh graders, a year above her. She takes after me in looks—fair-haired, green eyes—but has David's brain. David does complex math in his head all the time, for fun, he says, geek stuff, but no ordinary brain is drawn to such mental machinations.

Lincoln has returned to the kitchen table, a long string

of cheese stretching off his bite of take-out pizza. Yep, I bailed on dinner. (I have a gremlin on my shoulder I call Chill Mom, who assured me it was okay that I had to work late and pick up food to go.)

"Whoever invented math was not a nice person," my son says.

David leans his head back on the couch cushion, turned toward Lincoln. "Don't think of it as an invention. Think of it as a discovery. Math is part of our world, like nature. Somebody just figured out how it operates. It's how we explain the world, like science."

"Why you own a pub is beyond me," I say, as I often do. He'd be a perfect math teacher—the enthusiasm, cornball humor, wicked knowledge—or a perfect financial whiz, playing the market and inventing algorithms. But since the day when, eight months after I met him, he saw that vacant property located four blocks off the interstate and decided to open a pub—Hemingway's Pub, natch—it's all he's done.

David seems content, but watching him light up when he enters the world of numbers, I wonder if he's following his true calling. Life's short, after all. Money's great, but as they say, if you do what you love, you won't work a day in your life.

(As if I'm one to talk.)

David bounces off the couch and picks up a Nerf football, drops back to pass. "Be honest," he says. "Do you think it's too late for me to try out for quarterback for the Bears?"

"Yes," the kids reply in unison.

"You're too old, Daddy," Grace notes. "You're forty-two. That means you've turned three thirteen times."

"Well, yes—wait—how many times?"

"Fourteen times," Grace says, correcting herself. *"Fourteen."* She smacks her forehead. Grace doesn't like being wrong. She scored 99 out of 100 on a science test last week and stewed all weekend about the one question she got wrong. I'll need to keep an eye on that perfectionist trait as she grows older; it could be as much of an albatross as an asset.

"Okay, fine." David drops the football. "There's always my dream of being a singer and dancer." He does a bit of Astaire, complete with the nimble footwork. "What do you think?"

"I think you should never do that in front of my friends," Grace deadpans.

"I'm gonna do it tomorrow," he says, walking over to her, tickling her. "I'm going to follow you to school dancing and singing. I'm going to announce, 'I am Grace Bowers's father, and I'm sorry, but I just *gotta dance!*' "

"All right, bed, now," I say, ready to put this bizarro day behind us.

A half hour later, Lincoln nestles into bed under the covers. David strokes his hair. "Excited for the Justin Fields costume Mommy got you?"

I'm lucky he has a costume at all. Consumed as I was over the last two weeks with a trial before Judge Donnelly, my professional–family life balance askew during that time, I desperately searched the internet last Friday night for a youth-size Justin Fields jersey, finally finding one that would arrive before Halloween for the low, low rush delivery price of $39.99. I threw in mini shoulder pads and pants for good measure to appease my maternal guilt. Turns out you *can* put a price on love.

"Tomorrow will be fun, buddy." I tuck him in and kiss him on the cheek.

"Daddy?" he says, as David pulls away. "Do you remember your mommy and daddy?"

Ever since David pulled that man out of the Cotton River, we've had variations of this conversation at night. I wonder if David's brush with death affected the kids more than I realize, the notion of their father's mortality.

"Oh, a little bit," says David.

David's parents died in a house fire in Youngstown, Ohio, when he was four years old. Having no siblings or next of kin, David was placed in foster care. He had three "families," so to speak, before he turned eighteen.

"Were you scared in the water?"

"In the river when Mr. Peterson's car went in? Yeah, sure, Linc, I was scared. But you know what kept me going?"

Lincoln shakes his head.

"Knowing that you and Grace and Mommy were waiting for me. Knowing that I'd never leave you guys." He gives Lincoln another kiss on the cheek. "Never, ever."

Careful, warns Cautious Mom, the gremlin on my other shoulder, who competes with Chill Mom. *Don't make promises you can't keep. What if you have a brain aneurysm or get hit by a truck and* poof, *you're gone?*

But David doesn't go to such dark places. He sees the world in bright, vivid colors.

I walk into the master bedroom. David comes in, too. I

hear the click of the lock on the bedroom door. I know what that means.

"Grace isn't down yet," I say.

"She'll be in her bathroom for half an hour at least." His hands slide underneath my shirt. I feel myself reacting. David gets me. He gets me like no man ever has. "Say yes," he says, "and I'll give you the best ninety seconds of your day."

"Oh, the faux modesty." But he's right about one thing — if we wait for optimal conditions, we'll be too tired to do it. Lock the door, make it quick and quiet, and if Grace knocks, make up an excuse. "Okay, sailor," I say, whipping down the comforter to climb into bed.

We both see it, to his left and my right, through the bedroom window overlooking the backyard. A burst of flickering light. A flame.

Fire.

FIVE

"STAY WITH THE KIDS," David says, rushing out the bedroom door, but I'm right behind him down the stairs.

When we hit the first floor, we see the flames outside, on the patio leading into the backyard, the wispy orange threads just sneaking into our view through the glass french doors. Exactly what's on fire back there? A tree? A bush? The deck railing? If it's the deck railing, the whole thing will be in flames in a matter of seconds—

I'm racing through options—we don't have a fire extinguisher, *Why don't we have a fire extinguisher,* there's a hose out back attached to a sprinkler, we could unhook it and use that, where's my phone, I left it upstairs, we have to call the fire department—

David whips open the doors and bounds onto the patio, looking to his left, doing a double take. Just as I'm reaching the patio myself, David says, "What the fuck?"

I look to my left. The grill. Our Weber grill, the old-fashioned, egg-shaped, charcoal-burning kind David prefers over the fancy gas ones. The oval lid is popped open, and flames billow out from the core—charcoal, freshly lit on fire. Like...

Like someone's starting a cookout.

"What the fuck is right," I whisper.

David jogs down the rear walkway of our house, then pivots and heads into the backyard. Me, I can't take my eyes off the grill, the flames already subsiding as the charcoal begins its slow sizzle to a white-hot char.

David hustles back to the patio, out of breath. "Whoever did it took off," he says.

"But why—who would..." I look at him. "Should we call the police?"

David shrugs. "And say what? Someone snuck behind our house and started a barbecue?"

"It's a trespass," I say, but David's right. The cops would chalk it up to a teenage prank, a modern-day version of the ding dong ditch game we used to play as kids, ringing someone's doorbell and running. And they'd probably be right.

"Well, I'm sure Kyle would be happy to rush right over," says David.

"Oh, stop. Seriously, what is this—just stupid teenagers?"

"I mean, I guess so." David paces around the patio, our table and chairs still intact, undisturbed. He walks along the rear walkway again, returns to the backyard. "It's kind of...hostile, though, y'know?"

"I was going to say creepy. We're upstairs putting down the kids, and they're out here dumping charcoal into the grill, pouring lighter fluid, and lighting a match?"

"Weird and hostile and creepy, all of the above," he says. "But at least—I mean, at least it was never a threat. It's a fire, but it's contained inside the grill. It's not like it was going to set the patio on fire or anything."

That's true. It wasn't malevolent in *that* way. "So...what do we do?"

He shrugs. "You hungry? I could throw some burgers on."

I shoot him a look. "It was meant to spook us, David. And as far as I'm concerned, it worked."

David plays with that thought and checks his phone. "Well, it's only two and a half hours till Halloween. Maybe someone was just getting a head start on the creepy, spooky stuff. I'm sure that's all it was."

But his face reads otherwise. That brain of his is turning over and over, trying to connect all the bizarre things that happened today. None of them, individually, cause for alarm. Collectively, maybe another story.

But if something has come to mind, David doesn't say so. Maybe he has no answers, and maybe there's nothing *to* answer.

Or maybe he does, and there is.

We all have our secrets, after all. Spouses don't tell each other *everything*.

SIX

FINALLY, AS I STAND before my vanity, toothbrush working, I'm ready to put this ridiculous day behind us. The dog alone—did she leave and return through a closed gate? Was she in our yard all along in the bushes and we missed her? Or did someone take her and return her?

Not to mention the fire and the coffeepot and lunch box and court ID—

My phone buzzes with a text message. The message is from an old acquaintance, a coworker, Howard Shimkus. Well, not so much a coworker as one of the senior partners and top trial lawyers at Millard Halloway in Chicago. The text reads:

Today's the day. 15th anniversary!

Oh. That's right. Fifteen years ago. I'd rather forget. I usually do forget, actually, my previous life a more distant memory every year, but then Howard sends me a text on this date, the day before Halloween, as if it's an annual tradition.

He is correct that today is the day, though the whole thing became public news the following morning, leading the press to label it the Halloween Massacre. Three witnesses in total, all scheduled to testify against mob boss Michael Cagnina at his upcoming racketeering trial.

A debt collector—an enforcer for Cagnina.

A racetrack owner who had helped Cagnina launder money and run a gambling ring.

And Howard's and my client Silas Renfrow, Michael Cagnina's top assassin.

All three—along with half a dozen federal marshals— found burned beyond recognition, nothing but torched skeletons, inside the detention center where they were being kept as protected witnesses.

Now close to seventy years old, Howard is in the twilight of his career as one of the top white-shoe defense lawyers in Chicago, and here I am, far removed from those high-powered cases, back living in the town where I was born, chasing deadbeat husbands, handling adoptions and divorces. I am long forgotten to Howard, yet he thinks of me this one time every year.

Maybe that's because I'm the only other person who knows the truth.

"Who's that on the phone?" David asks, grabbing some dental floss.

I scoop away my phone. "Nobody," I say. "Just a nervous client."

SEVEN

"QUESTION: WHY DOES A woman who graduates summa cum laude from one of the best law schools in the country, then lands a job at one of the top law firms in Chicago, come back to Hemingway freakin' Grove to live and practice small-town family law?"

Tommy Malone clicks off his handheld recorder and taps the brake as the car in front of his, a green Jeep driven by Darlene Farraday, comes to a stop on the road outside Hemingway's Pub, left turn signal blinking. The parking lot is pretty full, impressive for a Monday night near midnight. The pub itself is done up well for tonight's pre-Halloween party. The giant statue of Ernest Hemingway stands front and center on the lawn overlooking the street, a giant witch's hat propped atop Ernie's head, the statue surrounded by ornate backlit tombstones and pumpkins.

Fun, he thinks, without being too cheesy. Pretty damn expensive, too.

Darlene's car turns into the lot. Tommy follows in with his rental. Darlene drives her car around to the rear of the building. Tommy stops much sooner, along the street side of the paved lot.

He kills the engine and waits for Darlene. While waiting, he raises the recorder to his mouth again.

"Question: How do a lawyer with individual one-time clients and a bar owner with small profit margins manage to build a new house that must have set them back a million dollars? In cash, no less—no mortgage?"

He hears the door slam on Darlene's car. He reaches under his seat and removes the hammer.

Darlene takes the walkway up to the pub's side entrance, adjusting the purse strap over her shoulder. She's tall and fit at age forty, roughly the same build as Marcie Bowers, who is the same age. Pretty, too, he thinks as Darlene enters the pub.

Not like Marcie, though. Marcie is...striking. Not just those eyes, those sculpted features, but the way she carried herself this morning as she hustled around the town square searching for her dog, surely stressed and hurried but burying all that under an implacable expression, even managing to be polite to Tommy, seated on the bench.

Formidable, Tommy thinks. That's the word. Marcie Bowers is formidable.

Tommy reaches into the glove compartment and removes a long rusty nail he found at a construction site down the street. He gets out of his rental car, hearing the vague sounds of music, the Red Hot Chili Peppers, from the pub. He walks over to Darlene's Jeep in the rear of the lot, looking around for anyone else, but they're all inside booz-ing it up and socializing.

He stops at Darlene's Jeep. Glances around again. Then he squats down and hammers the nail into the rear driver's-side tire.

EIGHT

DARLENE FARRADAY BURSTS INTO a laugh, liking Tommy's wisecrack, though her amusement is probably fueled more by alcohol than by Tommy's sense of humor.

"I haven't done this since...wow, since college," she says. "Getting food after the bars."

Tommy and Darlene are at a truck-stop diner just off the interstate, only a few blocks away from Hemingway's Pub. Darlene's Jeep and Tommy's rental sedan are the only vehicles in the lot that don't have at least eight wheels.

"I'm not keeping you up, I hope?"

"The salon opens late on Tuesdays," she says. "So a Monday night is like a Saturday night to me."

"A salon? You do hair?"

Darlene Farraday is the co-owner of A Hair Out of Place, a salon she opened fourteen years ago. But Tommy's not supposed to know that.

"Sure do. I could give you a free haircut before you leave

town if you'd like. I'd offer to color it, too, but I wouldn't dream of changing that hair of yours."

"Ah, yes, the carrot top. A curse more than a blessing."

"Do you have any idea how many of my clients would kill to have red hair? It's distinctive. Especially on a man."

Flirting with me, Darlene? Tommy can't tell. She's divorced, another thing he isn't supposed to know. He wouldn't mind going a round or two with her, especially if it would loosen her tongue.

"Well, I lucked out tonight," he says. "I can't find much for background on Marcie Bowers or David Bowers. And here I run into a sorority sister of Marcie's."

"I think I'm the one who lucked out," she says. "I wouldn't have the first idea how to change a tire."

"Oh, that was nothing."

"It wasn't nothing to me. Not at one in the morning. But I'm not sure I've been much help about Marcie. We aren't in touch as much as we used to be. All I can tell you is what I already said. She was super smart and serious, and she wanted out of HG."

Right, but the way Darlene's saying it—same way she said it earlier, when they first discussed Marcie—suggests resentment. Like Marcie thought she was too good for the town or something.

"But she *got* out," he says. "And then she came back."

"She came back because her mother was dying and her father was already gone. Basically, hospice care for her mother."

"Right, but then she stayed. That's what I find interesting. She didn't go back to Chicago. She stayed in Heming-way Grove."

Darlene shrugs. "Lot of people end up back here after exploring the world for a while. It's a good place to raise kids."

Tommy sits back in his chair. "Unfortunately, that's not interesting."

"It's not . . . interesting?"

"I mean, my editors want a human-interest piece, right? Everybody knows David rescued that man from the river. Everyone's seen that video. For my profile to have any legs, I need something personal."

"You mean, like . . . scandalous?" she asks. She looks away, a mischievous curl to her lips.

Now we're getting somewhere. Darlene has a thought. He can tell. And he can tell she wants to tell him.

"Was there something that happened at her law firm in Chicago, maybe?" he asks. "She represented a lot of white-collar criminals . . ."

Darlene shakes her head. She seems to have lost touch with Marcie around that time, after college. She stares into her coffee cup. She's thinking. Considering.

The best thing Tommy can do is stay quiet.

Finally, Darlene looks up at him. "Would this be off the record or whatever?"

"Whatever you want."

She nods, eager, he thinks, to spill. "Well, some people thought she came back for Kyle."

She means Kyle Janowski, Marcie's old flame, her high

school sweetheart, currently a cop in Hemingway Grove. But Tommy plays dumb.

"But some of us," says Darlene, "we thought it had something to do with her job at the fancy law firm. She said it was time for a change, but isn't that what you say when something went wrong? I mean, Marcie was so ambitious, and she was in this big-time law firm doing big-time things, and suddenly she drops everything. But she wouldn't talk about it."

Tommy nods.

I'll bet she wouldn't, he thinks.

NINE

HAPPY HALLOWEEN, I GUESS. No missing dogs or lunch boxes or coffeepots, at least. I watch Lincoln leave, the obligatory *Bye-love-you* as he rides off on his bike to school. I watch him pedal along the street—no sidewalks around here—and turn right until he's out of sight, with that ever-present niggling worry that something bad will happen, a stranger danger offering him a ride, a car blowing a stop sign and smacking my ten-year-old biker. The constantly raging battle between Cautious Mom and Chill Mom, the latter of whom whispers to me in her soothing voice that the kids are going to have to learn how to live in the world sooner or later, and sooner is better.

Before I leave, I set the house alarm, something I've never done because, y'know, this is Hemingway Grove. But after yesterday, it feels like a good idea.

I have court all morning. The last of the hearings involves my client Diane Worley, who sits in the front row while I stand at the bench before the Honorable George Slattery. Standing next to me, my opposing counsel argues in favor of his client, Diane's ex-husband, an asshole radiologist who left Diane and their three kids after he started making big money, trading Diane in for a younger, prettier model and moving to Chicago.

When it's my turn, I say, "Let's rewind the clock, Your Honor."

I remind him that Diane worked two jobs to support her husband, Ron, and two young kids while he completed med school and residency. That Ron divorced her two years after joining his lucrative radiology group, running off to Chicago with his pretty new girlfriend while their youngest, their third, was only eighteen months old. That he agreed to the standard 28 percent of his income for child support. That since he started raking in the dough, Ron doesn't think she and the kids need 28 percent, even though he knew his income would fluctuate. That he's breaking his word after the fact.

That Diane stopped working after Ron got into that radiology group. That she's long out of the workforce now and would have a hard time getting work as an accountant, at least at the level she once held. That their middle child's speech and occupational therapy bills are going up every month.

The judge, with his bald white head, with his wildly unkempt gray eyebrows and deep circles under his eyes, which make him vaguely resemble a raccoon, turns to me when I'm done and says, "I'm going to grant the husband's petition. I don't think the wife deserves a windfall for her husband's success."

"A *windfall*?" I almost come out of my skin. "This isn't maintenance. This is child support — for the *kids*."

"Counsel!" The judge turns on me. "I'm making my ruling. I'm not going to punish the husband for his success."

"Sharing your newfound wealth with your children is not *punishment*, Your Honor."

The judge leans forward. "I am making my ruling, Ms. Bowers. Would you like to be held in contempt?"

I look away but remain silent. These old men — they have no idea what it's like for women in Diane's situation, women who have sacrificed their prime employment years to raise children and later find themselves beholden to their ex-husbands' generosity. My hands ball into fists, but there's nothing I can do that won't make matters worse.

My phone buzzes. I slip it out of my pocket and peek at the face. Caller ID says it's my home-alarm company. Probably a low battery on one of the sensors. Since we never turn on the alarm, a battery's probably gone dead and we didn't even know it.

"...get a date from the clerk," the judge finishes. "That's all."

My phone buzzes a second time. Same number. That can only mean one thing.

As I look at a distraught Diane, shaking her head and holding back tears, I answer the phone.

"Hello, this is Marcie."

"This is Jade with Secure Alarm. We're registering a breach on the patio door."

"I'm not home. Nobody's home," I say.

"Would you like us to contact the police?"

Somebody's . . . breaking into our home?

"Call the police," I say. "I'll be right there."

TEN

SERGEANT KYLE JANOWSKI ROLLS his cruiser along-side another squad car on Prairie Drive, aimed in the opposite direction. In the car are two patrol officers, Blatt and Stevens.

"How's diaper training?" Kyle asks Blatt, a senior patrol officer now, who was assigned to Stevens, the rookie. "You let him drive, I see. Has he killed anyone yet?"

"No, but the day ain't over." Blatt works the toothpick in his mouth. Mark Blatt always viewed himself as a cowboy, Kyle thinks. Always hoping today will be the day he pulls his service weapon in the line of duty. He should have picked a different town to serve and protect.

"Stevens," Kyle says. "Has Blatt told you the story of when he chased the streaker across the high school football field?"

"Not yet, Sergeant."

"Well, he will. If you wanna know what really happened, buy me a beer sometime."

"He was resisting," says Blatt.

"Yeah, sure." Kyle smirks at the memory and nods at Blatt. "Tell him the one about the guy we curbed the night before Easter, the Range Rover. Think it was 2018."

Blatt chuckles. "Yeah, Kyle and I see this car that's weaving on Old Anna Road. It's, like, two in the morning. So we curb him, and Kyle has the driver's side, asks the guy where he's going. Guy says, 'I'm going to a lecture about the dangers of alcohol abuse, smoking, and staying out late.' Kyle says, 'Who's giving a lecture at two in the morning?' The guy says, 'My wife.'"

Kyle is laughing at the memory before the story's over. "All right, ladies, go serve and protect. And Stevens, don't let Blatt give you shit about your sideburns."

Stevens touches the side of his face. "My...sideburns?" He looks at Blatt. "What about my sideburns?"

A call cackles through the radio. *"All units, we have a home-alarm distress signal at 343 Cedar, patio door. 343 Cedar."*

Kyle looks at the officers. "I know that address."

"That's two blocks away," says Stevens.

"Unit 12 responding," says Blatt to dispatch.

343 Cedar is Marcie's house.

"Unit 19 responding," Kyle says.

ELEVEN

THE KIDS AREN'T HOME, I keep reminding myself, my chest burning with dread while I drive. *Whatever the burglars steal, they steal. It's all replaceable. My family is not.*

But our dog. Lulu will be freaked with the alarm going off. Whoever broke in—they wouldn't hurt Lulu, would they?

"I can come home," David says into my earbuds.

"Where are you?" I ask him, not hearing the crowd noise I'd usually expect from the lunch rush.

"The pub," he says. "Out back taking out the trash. It's a madhouse. All hands on deck. Do you want me to come?"

"Just wait," I say as I turn my car onto Cedar, within sight of our house. "The police are here. Two cars."

"Be careful, Marce. Let them do the heavy lifting. And call me."

I park in the driveway and get out of my car, shaky, unnerved. A police officer, a large man, comes around from the side of the house. "You're the homeowner? Mrs. Bowers?"

"Yes."

"We don't see any outward sign of forced entry. We have officers by the patio door."

"Hey, Marce." It's Kyle, walking through my backyard.

I haven't seen him in over a year. Every once in a while, we run into each other. It's become less awkward over the years, but still — it's awkward.

"Oh — hey," I say.

"Doesn't look like anyone forced their way in," Kyle says. "Okay if I enter and look around?"

"God, please do," I say.

"Okay. Officer Blatt here is going to keep watch over the front of the house."

In case whoever's inside runs out the front to escape, though he doesn't want to say that to me.

"Why don't you stay out here, just in case?" he says. "Maybe across the street."

In case someone really *is* inside and there's a confrontation. I shudder at the thought of someone creeping through our house, our things.

My nerves jangling, I follow him to the patio door. There's another cop, skinny and young, shifting his weight from one foot to the other, hand on his holster. Closer to the door, I can hear the whooping siren, the burglar alarm going haywire inside.

"I'm going in, too," I say.

"That's not a good idea. Let us do our jobs."

"My dog's in there. I'm going in."

Kyle pauses but says nothing. He reaches for the door handle. Grips it and turns it. The door opens, the sound of the burglar alarm piercing now.

He turns back to me. "This door's normally locked, I assume?"

"Yes. I mean, it should be."

Especially last night, after the unexplained barbecue on our back patio at nine thirty at night. David slept near this door the rest of the night. No way he left it unlocked.

"The alarm probably scared him off," says Kyle. "He's probably a mile away from here by now. Probably never even got inside."

But that doesn't stop Kyle from drawing his service weapon off his hip holster. The other cop does the same. Kyle puts a protective hand on the other officer's gun and gently pushes it downward. "Gun stays down unless, Stevens, right?"

"Roger that, Sergeant."

Kyle nods. "Okay, let's have a look."

TWELVE

I FOLLOW THE OFFICERS inside, heart pounding, adrenaline racing, as the alarm bellows out its *woo-OOP, woo-OOP* cry. I reach over to the alarm pad, type in the key code to turn it off. The house rings from the sudden silence.

For a moment, none of us moves, listening for sounds.

"Police officers!" Kyle calls out with a reassuring authority. Whatever else, I can't deny that I'm glad he's here. "Announce where you are and have your hands showing!"

I look around. The dining room, overlooking the patio, seems undisturbed. There are a few nice things in this room, including an ornate chandelier, but nothing you'd expect a burglar to snatch and grab.

"Lulu!" I call out. "Lulu, honey, c'mere!"

Kyle puts out a hand. "Marcie, step back onto the patio. You can't be inside. We'll look for your dog, I promise. Big dog? Small?"

"Small. A Cavalier King Charles. Wouldn't hurt a flea."

"Okay. Now please go outside."

This time, I obey. I head back onto the patio not far from the barbecue grill, the lid now closed after last night's impromptu cookout from who-knows-who.

I hear voices in the backyard, a man and a woman in conversation. Two more cops, I see, as they come into view, joining in the search inside the house. "You probably shouldn't be so close," the female officer says to me. "Why don't you go back to your car?"

They head inside, radioing their presence to the other officers. I stay where I am.

Someone was inside our house. Someone walked through our house, touched our things, invaded our private space.

With nothing else to do but make myself crazy, I check my phone. Diane, my client, has texted me, saying she hopes everything's okay at my house and asking about next steps in the dispute with her ex. She must feel like that old white male judge has no idea what her and her kids' lives are really like. She's right about that. Now we'll have to appeal, which will cost Diane more money, even after I cut my fee, which I always seem to be doing—

The patio door opens, causing me to jump. I realize how nerve-racked I am.

Kyle steps out, holding Lulu in his arms. She breaks into a combination whine and yodel as I take her, her whole body trembling.

"She was down in the basement by the boiler," he says. "Trying to get away from the sound of the alarm, I think. It's all clear inside, Marcie. Nothing taken, as far as we can see. Nothing disturbed, either. Your boy has an iPad on his bed. Your daughter has a laptop in her room. There's jewelry in your walk-in closet. Those are the first things a burglar would take. My guess, nobody ever got inside. Not past the door. They heard the alarm and decided to try another house. They want something quick and easy."

"But how did they get in?"

"Door must have been unlocked."

"Could they have picked it?" I ask.

Kyle makes a face. "Picking a lock takes a lot of effort and time. If the door was locked and they really wanted in, they probably would've smashed one of the door windows, reached inside, and unlocked the door. My guess, this is some random guy who was going around trying doors till he found one that opened."

I look at him, start to speak but don't.

"What?" he asks.

I shudder at the weight of the statement that was on the tip of my tongue. Saying it aloud makes it seem more real.

"I don't think this was random," I say.

THIRTEEN

THE OTHER OFFICERS FILE out. I profusely thank each of them. You take cops for granted until you need one. Kyle stays, especially after my last comment to him.

I walk back into the house, putting down Lulu, who follows me. Kyle follows me inside, too, stays by me as I do a check of the entire house. My nerves are still rattled, but the sense of danger is gone, replaced with a mounting sense of violation. I enter every room, the kids' bedrooms, these sacred, safe, warm places where they sleep and play and study and dream of their lives. Wondering if some creepster invaded their private space, touched things, wanting to disinfect every nook and cranny to remove the taint. I check for anything amiss, anything moved, anything disturbed, anything missing.

All the while feeling ever so grateful that an armed police officer—that Kyle, in particular—is escorting me.

We end in the last room upstairs, the master bedroom.

Nothing out of place, no reason to think the creepster invaded this private area.

"You said you don't think this was random," says Kyle.

"Some...weird things have been happening," I say.

I give him the rundown. Kyle doesn't speak, but his facial reactions to the various odd and borderline disturbing things only reinforce my concerns.

"You think of them individually, and how inconsequential they are, and you blow them off. I mean, my coffeepot in my dryer? Who would go to the trouble of sneaking into my house to do that? And Lulu—maybe somehow she got out and back in."

"But now you think differently," he says.

"Wouldn't you?"

"Well..."

"Seriously—unless I've started hallucinating or sleepwalking, how *did* my coffeepot get inside the dryer overnight? It didn't walk over there by itself. God, I sound like my mother."

"Your house alarm wasn't set?"

"We don't set it usually. Today was the first day. We had one installed when we built this house, but we never—I mean, look where we live, Kyle! Who robs houses in Hemingway Grove?"

I bring a hand to my face, shake my head. "I'm beginning to think that somebody's doing something. I don't know who, I don't know why—"

"Okay, okay." His warmth against me, his arms around me, so seamless and natural that I don't know if I fell into his arms or he came to me. Of course, this is innocent. Of course, this is wrong, but so familiar, so comforting, so—

His hand slowly runs up my back.

"No." I release myself, step back. "Um, I—"

"Yeah, no, I'm—right. Right, right. Obviously." His face flushed, Kyle steps back, puts his hands on his hips, nods his head toward the door. "Yeah. So I'll... probably go back downstairs?"

"Sure, sure."

He leaves the bedroom and heads downstairs. He opens the french doors and steps onto the patio before turning back, now at a safe distance, cooler heads having prevailed.

"So we should pass a car by your house on a regular basis for a while," he says, regaining his balance, returning to the business at hand. "Think about installing cameras. They're a good deterrent."

"Good idea. And thanks, Kyle. Thanks for doing this. It was... it was good seeing you."

His eyes meet mine and stay there for a beat too long. Then he blinks away the eye contact. "Just doing my job." He turns and walks through the backyard without another word.

FOURTEEN

"OH, THE MANDALORIAN! I *love* that guy!" I drop a couple of "fun-size" candy bars into Ethan's pillowcase and wave to his parents, Greta and Tyler, standing on the sidewalk.

Ethan, in that Star Wars costume, is only five. I remember vividly when both Grace and Lincoln were that age, when I stood on those sidewalks watching them shuffle up walkways asking homeowners for candy, when my kids wouldn't dream of doing anything without their mommy or daddy nearby. And now Lincoln, after begging and pleading, has gone trick-or-treating without me.

All for the best, Chill Mom tells me. *You don't want to raise a mama's boy.*

The sun has long set. The trick-or-treaters are dwindling now, our bowl of candy less than half full.

I check my phone. "Ten after seven," I say. "Lincoln said he'd be home by seven."

"Lemme call him." David looks at his phone, digs up

the number for Lincoln's Gizmo Watch as I walk into the kitchen to check on the chili in the pot.

We both hear the buzzing in the kitchen drawer. David, phone against his ear, walks over and pulls open the drawer. He punches out his phone. "Gizmo Watch is in the drawer."

So we have no way of contacting Lincoln. "He said he'd wear it."

"I should've double-checked." David turns to me. "I'm sure it's fine. He's out with Will."

I stir the chili. Take note of the bottle of green Tabasco sauce on the counter. David always sneaks some of that in when I'm not looking.

"Somebody could've done all these things that have been happening," I say. "Our alarm wasn't set. They could've walked in, moved around Grace's lunch box and the coffeepot, maybe gone into the garage and moved my court ID onto the dashboard."

"I know, but that's crazy."

"Maybe it is," I say, "but it's less crazy than any other explanation. Nobody's been hurt, right? It's all ultimately harmless. They move around the lunch box and coffeepot. They take Lulu but bring her back. They start a fire but only in our grill to contain it. They break into our house but don't take anything."

"Just for kicks? Like you said, ultimately harmless." David comes over and rubs my shoulders. This isn't bothering him as much as as it's bothering me.

I wiggle away from his touch. "But that's the thing. Whoever it is—he's risking criminal charges. He's broken into our house *twice*. Just to do harmless stuff? Just having fun? Someone who wants to have fun wouldn't take that kind of risk. It's as if...they're messing with us, David. Trying to send us a message or something."

I walk over to the front door and look out. On the street, Grace says goodbye to her three friends, Monica, Ellie, and Rainey—a ladybug, Rey from Star Wars, and a waitress from a 1950s diner, respectively—and bounds up the walkway to the door.

Still no Lincoln.

"Well, good evening, Your Honor!" I say to my daughter, in her black robe and lace collar, the Notorious RBG.

"Yeah," she says in her typical understated way.

We are raising a very serious girl, apparently. David thinks it comes from me.

"Food's ready. Veggie chili and salad. Did you see Lincoln out there?"

"No. Lincoln's not home yet?"

"Not yet. Wash your hands, honey."

"Can I lay out the candy?" She holds up a swollen pillowcase. She and Lincoln will set out their candy and make trades.

"Hey, there she is, the Notorious RBG!" David kisses Grace on the forehead. "Or am I supposed to bow to you?"

Grace holds out her hand. "Bow to me, good sir," she says with a British accent. And of course, David complies in grand fashion. David can bring out the playful in Grace in a way that I can't.

"Seven twenty," I say to him as Grace races into the family room to lay out her candy.

David nods. "Maybe he went to Will's house."

"That wasn't the plan."

"I know, but it's Halloween. Maybe—maybe I should call over there."

I let out a nervous sigh. "I wouldn't—it's just that with all this weird stuff, y'know."

"I know. I'll go out and look for him. And I'll call Will's house on the way."

"Good. That would be good."

Then I hear that squeaky prepubescent voice. I almost jump as the door pops open, cool air rushing in, and there's my miniature Chicago Bears quarterback, beaming.

"Hey, it's Justin Fields!" David says, putting his hand on my shoulder, preempting me, trying to defuse the tension. He doesn't want me to bark at Lincoln, doesn't want him seeing our nerves. He's right about that, I guess. Lincoln was just a little late. And he didn't have his Gizmo Watch. He lost track of time. He's not used to keeping track of time.

So I just muss his hair and watch him and David head into the family room, recounting where he and Will went, the "huge candy bars" the Lindermans gave out, the smoke machine the Wrights had on their lawn, and I breathe an enormous sigh of relief.

"Let the trade talks begin!" David announces. I'm in the kitchen now, getting the chili ready to be served, warming milk for the hot cocoa after dinner. Grace will eat anything with honey and hates vanilla. Lincoln likes nuts and cara-mel the most.

"—biggest candy bar I've ever seen—"

"—looks like a special treat—"

"—I should get two small bars for this one—"

"—no way—"

"What's this? That's more like a gift—"

"Can you open it?"

I look through the kitchen into the family room. David is trying to unwrap a small purple bag tied with a bow, while Lincoln predicts it's "probably something chocolate—"

"Oh, my God!" David drops the open bag, then puts out his arm. "Stay—back up, back up, back up, get away!"

"What?" I rush into the family room as both kids get to their feet.

David turns the bag over, the contents falling out.

A…mouse. Not a fake one, not plastic or rubber—a real one. A little shriveled gray rodent with its tail wrapped around it. Not moving. Dead.

"What the—" David looks up at me.

"That's so cool!" says Lincoln. "A mouse!"

Somebody gave Lincoln a dead *mouse*?

"That's not a mouse," says Grace. "Look at the tail."

I get up close for a better look. She's right. It's not a mouse.

It's a rat.

FIFTEEN

"IF WE HEAR OF any other reports, we'll let you know," says the police officer, a young man in uniform, standing in our foyer.

"Thanks, Officer." David closes the door behind the officer, sets the house alarm, and turns to me. "Okay. All the candy's in the trash."

"All *Lincoln's* candy." It was a point of contention. I wanted to toss every piece of candy both kids got. David persuaded me to leave Grace's candy. She wasn't with Lincoln, didn't hit that corner where Lincoln got his candy. And bless her heart, Grace volunteered to split her haul with Lincoln, probably sensing her parents' tension.

What a disastrous end to the night.

For the third time, I go through Grace's candy, checking that the wrappers are still sealed, looking for puncture holes, any evidence of tampering.

"They'll never find the guy," says David, moving to the kitchen, looking out the window into the backyard.

"Someone wearing a Darth Vader costume, standing on the corner by the Buseys' house, handing out candy?"

That was the best description we could get from Lincoln, who became more upset the more we pressed him. "Are we still clinging to the possibility that this was a prank and Lincoln just happened to be the victim?"

"A coincidence? No." David stuffs his hands in his pockets. "Not with everything else going on."

"I talked to Kyle about this," I say.

"Kyle?" David's head snaps in my direction, but I see him try to moderate his response. "When?"

"He was one of the officers who responded to the house alarm today."

David's eyebrows lift. "You didn't mention that before."

"It was hardly important."

David doesn't seem to think it was unimportant, but he doesn't press the matter. "You told him everything that's been happening?"

I nod. "He said they would drive patrols around the house during the day. And overnight, for that matter. That seems like a good idea, doesn't it?"

"It does. Yeah, it definitely does." He turns back to the window.

"You're upset with me."

"I'm—" He throws up his hands. "I'm upset about all of this."

"The bigger question," I say, "is who's doing this and why."

"I know, I know." He turns to me again. "Got any clients pissed off at you? Or other lawyers' clients you beat in court?"

That had never occurred to me. "I—I can think about that. Anyone pissed off at you?"

"Who gets pissed off at a tavern owner? Maybe some drunk we eighty-sixed? I can't imagine. But you're right, none of this is random. Someone is trying to get our attention without actually hurting us."

"Yet," I say as I gather up Grace's candy. "Without hurting us *yet*."

SIXTEEN

I REMEMBER HIS EYES more than anything. Probably because that's the only part of his face I ever saw.

By the time he hired Howard Shimkus (and, by extension, me, as Howard's young associate) to be his lawyer, Silas Renfrow had been taken into custody by federal authorities as part of the investigation into mob boss Michael Cagnina. He had had plastic surgery to alter his facial features. And he didn't want anyone—not even his lawyers—to see his new face.

The whole thing was cloak-and-dagger. "Unlike anything I've ever seen," said Howard, a highly respected attorney with twenty years' experience prosecuting and then defending white-collar and violent criminals.

We were picked up in downtown Chicago by undercover federal marshals and placed in the back of a van without windows. We didn't know where we traveled, only that it was two hours away from downtown. We were led directly into a building, presumably an old government office re-inforced to house important government witnesses.

Inside, it was a fortress, with concrete barriers, remote-locking doors, bulletproof glass, and federal marshals armed with rifles and automatic weapons.

We were led past a series of cells, which we were told were empty, before we reached the one housing Silas Renfrow. The door was solid metal with a single slot, a long rectangular peephole at approximately waist level, so guards could see Silas's position inside the cell before entering, preventing an ambush.

Two chairs were put out for Howard and me just outside the cell, with a desk in between.

"This isn't private enough," said Howard to the marshal.

"It's what your client wanted," the marshal snapped.

I looked at the opaque metal door, then the rectangular peephole, where I saw a pair of eyes, ocean blue, looking back at me. I almost jumped in my seat.

"I know Howard already," said Silas from behind the door. "What's your name?"

His voice sounded robotic: he was using a voice-altering microphone, as if this whole thing weren't surreal enough.

"Um, hello, Mr. Renfrow, I'm Marcie Dietrich," I said. "I'm an associate of Howard."

"My compliments, Howard," he said, his blue eyes turning to Howard, one eye winking. I was eye candy, in other words, not a serious attorney. The curse of any young female lawyer trying to break in.

Howard said, "Nice to see you again, Silas."

But Silas's eyes were back on me. "Marcie, tell me what you know about me."

I wasn't expecting to do much of the talking. But I'd surely done my homework.

"You're Michael Cagnina's reputed assassin," I said. "You've been accused or suspected in the alleged murders of—"

"No, no, no," he said. "You can do away with 'reputed' and 'accused' and 'suspected' and 'alleged.' Everything they say about me is true."

I glanced over at Howard. But the client was directing the questions to me, so it was up to me to answer.

"How many people have I killed, Marcie?"

I swallowed hard. "Fourteen," I say. "Fourteen that they know of."

"Excellent," he said. "Excellent qualifier. Fourteen that they know of. Do you want to know what the real number is?"

However intimidated I felt, I couldn't back down. "If you'd like to tell me," I said.

"Thirty-two, Marcie. I've killed thirty-two people. Do you know what I felt about those murders? Each and every one of them?"

"Silas," said Howard, reasserting himself, "why don't we—"

"I'd like an answer to my question," said Silas. "And then we can proceed as you wish, Howard. Marcie? My question."

I looked into those piercing eyes, focused on me. In that moment, I felt like I could see him better just by looking at those eyes than if I'd been able to study his entire face.

"Nothing," I said. "You felt nothing."

His eyes narrowed a bit. I was pretty sure he was smiling.

SEVENTEEN

MY EYES POP OPEN, fear seizing me, though the tendrils of the nightmare have faded from my memory. My heart pounding, my eyes stinging from perspiration, I turn to David's side of the bed, which is empty, the covers pulled down, the indentation of his head on the pillow.

I pat the bed for my phone and find it. The phone glows back at me with a time of 2:38 in the morning. Lulu, sleeping at the foot of the bed, lets out a loud sigh but otherwise doesn't move.

I hear movement downstairs, footfalls, as if pacing. The faint murmur of David's voice, low and deep.

I don't have my contacts in but fumble for my cheater glasses on the nightstand. Then I send him a quick text message: **Everything ok?** I hit Send.

A *ping* sounds from inside the bedroom. David's phone, resting on his nightstand, a power cord stuck inside it.

He doesn't have his phone with him? Then who is he talking to and...how?

My feet drop onto the rug. My head swims in fogginess. I've tossed and turned all night, with all the craziness happening. I've hardly slept. Though I somehow managed to miss David's getting out of bed.

I walk into the hallway, lean on the banister that spirals down to the foyer by the front door.

"It's not that simple, okay?" David whispers, almost a hiss.

I take the stairs down, my hand on the railing, as I hear David say something quickly that I can't make out.

"Hey, Marce. You okay?" David, who must have heard me, walks into the foyer as I'm halfway down the stairs.

"Who were you talking to?" I whisper.

"Just...a private security company," he says.

"At two thirty in the morning?"

"Those places have 24-7 service. I was thinking about hiring somebody." He meets me on the stairs. "Maybe I'm overreacting, getting creeped out in the middle of the night. I just wanted to talk to them at least."

"Okay. But...how?" I ask. "Your phone's on the nightstand."

"Oh, yeah, I know—the landline."

"The landline?" I ask as we head back up the stairs. We never use the landline phone. We debated even installing one when we built this house.

"My phone was dying."

"You were—you were saying it's not that simple? What's not that simple?"

David falls into our bed. "They're going to call back later today. We'll see if it makes sense to have someone stay around here for a while."

I climb into bed. "Okay." But it feels like it's not okay.

"I need sleep," he says. "I'm exhausted."

I put my head on the pillow and stare at the ceiling, thinking about the words I heard him say, the tone of his voice. Feeling like I'm missing something.

David rolls over, facing me, touching my arm. "I was just explaining to the guy on the phone that I had been thinking all these things happening to us were silly coincidences, but maybe it's not that simple. That's all it was."

That doesn't land well with me. That's not what it sounded like. It sounded like the resolution of an argument, something more emotional, more personal, more intimate. He was snapping at someone. He was flustered, upset.

It's not that simple, okay?

I look at him but don't say anything.

What's not that simple?

David closes his eyes and goes silent. I stay silent, too, but don't close my eyes for hours.

EIGHTEEN

CAMILLE LOOKS OUT THE window of her fifth-floor apartment on 1st Street, the day after Halloween. The snow is beginning to fall, and in Hemingway Grove, it usually sticks.

"Day sixty-three," she whispers.

She checks her phone for the time. Quarter after eleven. She can just barely squeeze it in. She moves the coffee table against the couch, pushes back the love seat to give herself some room.

She starts with stretching. Lunges and leg swings, cactus and eagle arms, spinal twists and bridges.

Then she walks over to the bathroom, jumps up, and grabs the pull-up bar mounted over the bathroom door. Locks her legs at forty-five degrees and bangs out twenty-five pull-ups in rapid succession. She drops to the floor for push-ups, twenty-five of them at a gunshot pace, her nose touching the carpet each time, back straight as a ruler.

She repeats the routine, spent when she's finished. Not

the longest or greatest workout, but it will have to do for now.

She checks her phone again for the time.

She showers, good and hot, letting the water scald her face. She towels off and wipes a circle on the steamy mirror to look at herself.

Staring back at her is a forty-year-old woman, physically in the best shape of her life, muscles toned and taut, only six months removed from her third triathlon. Maybe a few new lines on her face, some softening of the skin beneath the eyes, but her dark hair still isn't showing gray.

She was never much for glamour, never cared much for the opinions of others. She wants to look good for herself. Wants to feel young and vibrant, not old and creaky.

Day sixty-three.

She doesn't look any different. She doesn't feel any different. Not physically at least.

This is what you get, she thinks. *This is what you get when you fall in love with a married man.*

She dresses and heads to the window again. Sees his car pass on 1st Street. There is a parking lot for the building, but he won't turn in. He will park at least a block away and approach the building by an indirect route. He will be bundled up, a watch cap pulled low over his forehead, his coat collar high around his neck. He will do everything he can to avoid notice, to conceal his appearance.

Hemingway Grove is a small town, after all. It's hard to stay anonymous.

Especially if you own a popular bar and restaurant. Even

more so if a video of you performing a dramatic river rescue just went viral.

Fifteen minutes later, a knock at her door. She looks through the peephole. David, though inside the apartment building now, still wears his cap and jacket, the last remnants of melting snow dripping off him.

Camille removes the chain guard and opens the door.

NINETEEN

IT'S NOT THAT SIMPLE, okay?

The words won't leave my brain, no matter how force-fully I try to evict them. Unable to stay seated behind my desk, pacing my office, trying to focus on some motions and an interlocutory appeal I have to draft, but always returning to those words David spoke over the phone when he didn't think I could hear him.

It's not that simple, okay?

By noon, I'm losing my concentration. I want to see him. Sometimes I'll drive to the pub for lunch, but usually I wait until after the rush, after one o'clock. Today, I'm not in the mood to wait.

I reach the pub at a quarter past noon. The lot is half full. A good crowd, but nothing crazy. Inside, the bar area—with its exposed brick, shiny oak tabletops, booths with leather seats, and brushed-nickel overhanging lamps—is busy but not slammed. The bartender is Gwinne, an Italian beauty. She has looks that would qualify for a magazine cover, a cup size that would make any woman envious—I'm guessing they're fake—and silky dark hair that bobs around in a ponytail. There isn't a man in the bar who isn't ogling her.

She gives me a little wave while she draws on the tap, pouring a beer. She's never been particularly friendly and seems even less so now. The male customers sure love her, though.

"Is David here?" I ask.

"No, he's not. I'm not sure where," she says.

The dining area in the back is humming with activity. Most of the staff recognizes me with quick waves or nods, but they don't have time to chat, buzzing between tables for orders or going back and forth from the dining area to the kitchen.

"Marcie, hi!" One of the assistant managers, Dennis, touches my shoulder as he passes.

"Hi, Dennis—is he in the back?"

"Oh, David had to step out. Said he'd be a few hours."

"Oh—okay." Shoot. He's not here. That's what I get for an unannounced pop-in.

I pull out my phone and type a text:

Stopped by to say hi but missed you. Returning soon?

I poise my finger over the green Send button. But I don't send it.

Instead I pause. Take a breath.

It's not that simple, okay?

I hit the Backspace button and erase the entire text. I type this one instead:

Thinking of stopping by for quick lunch. Are you free?

This time, I hit Send.

I stand outside his office door, listening to the familiar symphony of the kitchen, burgers sizzling, pots scraping, hot oil hissing, people calling out to each other in English and Spanish, until my phone buzzes. A response from David:

We are crushed right now all hands on deck maybe later?

I read that text over and over, searching for any conceivable interpretation that isn't a flat-out lie.

What…what possible reason could he have to lie to me about where he is?

I won't…I can't let my mind go there.

With a burning in my chest, I put the phone in my purse and head for the exit. Out the window, it has started to snow, the wet, slushy kind. A waiter, a thirtysomething guy named Jesse who's been with David for years, calls out to me.

"Careful out there, Mrs. B.," he says. "Something bad's coming our way."

I look at him and nod, force a smile.

"Or it's already here," I mumble.

TWENTY

"I KNOW, CAM, I know; I get it," David says inside Camille's apartment, hands in the air, as if surrendering. He drops into the love seat, hands covering his face.

"If you know, then do it." Camille keeps her distance.

David's phone buzzes. He fishes it out of his pocket and reads it, groaning. His thumbs type a response.

"Who's that?" she asks. "Marcie?"

David nods. "She wants to stop by the pub for a quick lunch."

"And what are you telling her?"

"That we're slammed right now. It's a bad time." He hits a button, sending the text, then tosses the phone on the love seat.

"More lies," says Camille.

He looks up at her. "What do you *expect* me to tell her?"

She walks over to the window overlooking 1st Street. The snowfall is picking up. They're predicting three to four inches.

"You have to tell Marcie," she says. "It's long past time."

David bounces off the love seat, scooping up his phone with a sweep. "It's not that simple, Cam." He shakes his head with a fury, blows out air, looks up at the ceiling.

It's not that simple. The same answer he gave to her last night on the phone.

"Do it now, David," she says. "Or I promise you, it will get worse."

TWENTY-ONE

SERGEANT KYLE JANOWSKI READS the intake reports from last night over lunch. Part of the paperwork that comes with his rank, though it's his least favorite part of the job. He does it over a late lunch, a tuna sub with chips.

The intake was higher than usual last night, given that it was Halloween, which usually spawns overactive imaginations and worried neighbors, even in a quiet town like Hemingway Grove—

Wait.

The Bowers house. Officer Dunleavy took the call last night. Kyle reads it, does a double take.

"A *dead rat*?" he whispers.

Someone put a dead rat in the Bowers kid's trick-or-treat bag? Wrapped it up and everything?

Kyle puts down the reports, spins around in his chair, and goes to his computer. He types in a search and pulls up a news video from thirteen years ago, a reporter from channel 7 news in Chicago, a woman whose hair flaps in the wind as she speaks.

"We are live outside the federal courthouse in downtown Chicago, where reputed organized crime boss Michael Cagnina was just sentenced to over sixteen years in prison following his conviction on multiple counts of tax evasion."

Right. Kyle remembers. The feds "Al Caponed" Cagnina. Couldn't get him on the violence or extortion, so they got him on tax evasion.

"Cagnina, who was believed to run the crime family that dominated organized crime from Chicago to Kansas City, was suspected in the Halloween Massacre of two years ago, when three witnesses scheduled to testify against him were assassinated, all in the same day."

Right. Kyle remembers *that* well, too. Everybody heard about it. It happened not long before Marcie came back to Hemingway Grove for good. He always wondered if her representation of one of those dead witnesses had something to do with her return to HG.

He pulls up what he can on the witness whom Marcie represented, Silas Renfrow. He finds a documentary on PBS from around that same time, well over a decade ago. A narrator with a baritone voice tells the story as photographs and video of mob boss Michael Cagnina move on and off of the screen.

"Little is known of Silas Renfrow, the man long believed to be the mysterious gunman who carried out the execution orders given by Cagnina during the violent reign of the Cagnina crime family. Though authorities long suspected him, Renfrow was rarely photographed and kept such a low profile that he was

often referred to as Silent Silas. Renfrow never paid taxes, never held a job, never put his name on a mortgage or lease or utility bill. That didn't stop the FBI, ultimately, from apprehending him after months of surveillance.

"*Renfrow was one of the three witnesses killed in the so-called Halloween Massacre after gunmen stormed a secret detention center outside of Rockford, Illinois, murdering half a dozen federal marshals before killing the three witnesses scheduled to testify against Cagnina. Though they could never prove their claims, the FBI has long suspected that Cagnina was behind the execution of these three witnesses.*"

For his final search, he clicks on another video, this one from not long ago—also from a Chicago news station, but the reporting is taking place hundreds of miles west of there, outside a federal supermax prison.

"*Joan, any minute now, former mob boss Michael Cagnina will be released from federal custody in Florence, Colorado, after serving over thirteen years of his sixteen-year sentence for tax evasion...*"

Kyle shakes his head. Jesus. Michael Cagnina got sprung this past May, only five months ago.

And now Marcie's having all this trouble.

It can't be a coincidence.

TWENTY-TWO

SPECIAL AGENT FRANCIS BLAIR, at his desk in the FBI field office in Chicago, leans back in his chair, eyes closed, as he listens to the contents of the wiretap through his earbuds, two men talking.

"I got three tickets to the show tonight."

"What time does it start?"

"I'll probably get there about six thirty."

The "ticket" is a pound of meth. The "show" is the meet, the drop-off from the manufacturer to the distributors.

Blair doesn't work narcotics; he's still in Organized Crime. And the conversation on the audio recording isn't taking place in Chicago but nearly twelve hundred miles away in Tampa, Florida, a city far removed from Blair's jurisdiction, a city that otherwise would hold no importance for him other than this simple fact:

It is now the home of Michael Cagnina, the mob boss released from prison only five months ago. And these two men on the wiretap? Former associates of Cagnina.

He takes out the earbuds just as his supervisor walks past his office and stops, greets Blair with a how-ya-doin'.

"How's the task force treating you?" asks the supervisor.

The task force that Blair got roped into, he means—an operation run by US Customs to catch a ring of cargo thieves.

"I'm going in for the initial meet today," he says.

"Is that what you're listening to?" His supervisor nods, gestures toward the earbuds Blair just tossed. "They've got wires up?"

"No, this isn't the task force shit. These are from DEA out of Tampa."

Blair's supervisor, only a year from retirement now, makes a face. "DEA? Tampa? The hell are you doing listen—oh. Oh, don't tell me this is about Cagnina."

Blair lifts a shoulder. "Just checking to see if he's getting back in the game."

"And is he?"

"Not as far as I can tell," Blair concedes.

"You gotta let Cagnina go," says his supervisor. "What's done is done. He's down in Florida now, and he's retired."

"Right, right, I know," says Blair. "I took my shot and missed."

"Missed? Thirteen years in the pen isn't 'missing,' Frankie. Who cares if it was tax evasion? You put him out of business."

"Yeah, maybe, but not for the shit that would've put him away for life. Guy murders three witnesses, and nobody lays a glove on him for that."

"Well, hey, least you're not bitter." His supervisor taps the door but points at him before leaving. "Frankie," he says, "leave Michael Cagnina alone."

TWENTY-THREE

IF ONLY I KNEW fifteen years ago what I know now. If only the partner I worked for, Howard Shimkus, hadn't been so busy with other cases.

You don't have to go alone, Howard told me in his spacious partner's office as paralegals and assistants packed his trial bags. *Really, Marcie. Silas can wait until this trial's over, and then I'll go with you. The trial should be over in three weeks.*

The feds had just made their formal plea offer to Silas in return for testifying against mob boss Michael Cagnina, and normally Howard and I would have delivered that plea offer to Silas personally. No phone calls or emails were allowed—those were traceable forms of communication, and the government was determined to keep Silas's whereabouts a secret. Only clandestine in-person visits were permitted. But Howard, in demand as a high-profile defense lawyer, had a fraud trial about to start in federal court in

97

southern Illinois, so he couldn't afford the full day it took to visit Silas—two-hour blind drives to and from the undisclosed location where Silas was held, plus the visit itself.

Howard sensed it, I knew—sensed that Silas had gotten under my skin the first time, the only time we'd met up to that point. But the last thing a young associate like me wanted to do was confirm as much, make the senior partner think I couldn't handle my stint in the big leagues.

No problem, I assured Howard. *I can handle it solo.*

Sitting in the windowless rear compartment of the van, driven by federal marshals, I didn't even know which direction we were traveling in. All I knew was that it had to be far from downtown Chicago. I had nothing to do for two hours but occupy myself with work, reviewing Silas's file and the plea offer.

Thirty-two kills, he'd told me the first and only time I'd met him. Suspected in fourteen murders, but the real number was more than twice that.

By the time I was out of the van, two hours later, I was nauseated, motion sick. I tried to enjoy a few seconds of fresh air between the van and the fortified entrance to the building where the feds held my client.

Or maybe I was just feeling nerves.

I walked past the barriers, the automated doors, the bulletproof glass, through the maze of hallways, reaching my chair placed in the hallway outside his holding cell.

"Hello, Marcie Dietrich."

Through the slot in the metal door, Silas's deep blue eyes. The bionic voice, with the voice scrambler he used. I tried to picture him but couldn't; nobody had photographs of him. He had managed to obscure his identity entirely. If the feds had photos of him, they didn't share them with us. Anyway, Silas had helped himself to substantial plastic surgery before he surrendered to the authorities, so however he used to look would bear little resemblance to his current appearance, even if I had the X-ray vision to penetrate the metal door.

"Mr. Renfrow, Howard sends his—"

"I told you last time to call me Silas, Marcie. And yes, I know Howard couldn't make it. He is very much in demand, that one."

"He is," I said, feeling the tension in my voice. I straightened my posture and took a deep breath.

"You'd like to be like Howard, I assume? An attorney everyone wants to hire? Prominent and wealthy?"

I'd never thought about it that way. I wanted out, I knew that much—out of Hemingway Grove, on to a challenging career in the law in the big city. Where it would lead I hadn't forecasted.

"It could be you're taking a job with a big law firm just to pay off your law-school debt. Many people in your position do that. Or maybe you want the acclaim of working for a prestigious firm like Millard Halloway. A tremendous stepping stone, if nothing else. A stamp of approval."

I raised a shoulder. "I suppose I'm just trying to learn as much as I can for right now. What comes down the road, I don't—"

"No, no, no," he said. "Marcie, you undoubtedly had

several offers out of law school. The top of your class from University of Chicago? Any number of law firms would have taken you and put you in some department representing the large corporations that pay those princely legal fees. One robber baron suing another. But you didn't choose them. You joined a firm with a substantial criminal-defense practice. You wanted to work for Howard Shimkus. Why criminal law, Marcie? Of all the things available to you?"

I sat back in my chair, feeling stripped bare. A simple question, one that I'd never really asked myself. He was right. I was drawn to criminal law. I'd lived a prim and proper life. I'd followed the rules. I was the high school valedictorian who dated the varsity quarterback, the sorority girl and honor student, the editor of the law review at U of C, always serious and straight. Little Miss Perfect.

I'd stayed right down the middle, and I wanted to explore the extremes. I wanted to represent the people who broke the rules, who took incalculable risks, who spat in the face of convention, who did things I'd never have dreamed of doing myself.

"You want to live vicariously through people like me," Silas said. "Take a walk on the wild side without getting *too* wild."

I'd spent all of one hour with this man, and he was dissecting me.

"So how do you like it?" he asked. "You know what I've done. All the people I've killed. Do you simply tolerate representing me? Or do you enjoy it?"

"I look at it professionally," I said. "I don't judge my clients."

"Of course you do, Marcie. You may be too polished to say so. But you either enjoy it or you don't. And you certainly judge me. You wouldn't be human if you didn't."

"Mr. Renfrow, I think our time would be—"

"If I'm making you uncomfortable, Marcie, I'll stop. I didn't mean to rattle a nice young lady like you—"

"You didn't rattle me—"

"I realize how intimidated you must be."

I looked down. He was baiting me, trying to piss me off. It was working.

I looked back up at him.

"I think you're a monster," I said.

The hallway went quiet. Silas kept his eyes on me. I kept mine on him. I considered the possibility that I had just committed career suicide.

His eyes narrowed, which again made me think he was smiling. But he waited me out. Probably wondering if I would fill in the silence with a profuse apology. But I was playing his game now. I wasn't going to back down.

"And yet you're representing me," he said.

"Yes."

"The thought of representing me thrills you, doesn't it?"

"Yes."

"If I decided to go to trial, you'd represent me to your fullest, wouldn't you?"

"Yes."

"You think you could actually win, don't—"

"I know I could."

The sound of Silas chuckling through voice alteration sounded like something from a movie, like a hideous robotic monster, Darth Vader on laughing gas.

"Now we're getting somewhere, Marcie," he said.

TWENTY-FOUR

SPECIAL AGENT FRANCIS BLAIR runs his hand over his unshaved face. Looking the part in his puffy red vest, unbuttoned flannel shirt with a black T-shirt underneath, ratty jeans, and work boots.

Inside the van with him is the technical team and the head of this task force, Agent Neary with US Customs, a career government guy, gray-haired and wrinkled, a smoker's gravelly voice.

"You're a long way from mobsters and Organized Crime," he says to Blair by way of apology. "Appreciate your help on this."

Blair looks at his watch. "So we know nothing about who's showing up?"

"No idea," says Neary. "They say you'll know. And then you'll ask the question."

"Any chance I can bum a smoke off ya?" Blair says.

"Exactly. And then he'll say..."

"Think I can spare one."

That's the code. Then the contact will show Blair the crates holding the stolen video-game consoles.

"We won't have eyes or ears inside, you understand," says Neary. "Once you get past the gate, you're flying without a net."

Blair already knows that, of course; the task force is following ass-covering protocol by making sure they reiterate to their agent that he's about to go in cold, so if this whole thing goes to shit, they can say they warned him.

He has to go solo because of the security guards, who are corrupt, part of the theft ring. They pat down everyone entering the freight area, ostensibly looking for contraband and weapons, but they're really searching for wires and hidden body cameras. So the FBI can't sneak in there and install surveillance. And Blair can't go in miked up. No wire, no body cam, no badge, no weapon, no backup.

Flying without a net, as Neary said.

"I get it," says Blair. "If they make me, I'm toast."

Blair pops out of the van, a block down from the freight company's main entrance. The whipping winds off nearby Lake Michigan lift Blair's hair as he approaches the gate and the guard station.

A beefy guard steps out from the booth. Checks Blair's papers—Blair's fake name, front company. The guard pats Blair down and runs a wand over him. Satisfied, he hands Blair a hard hat and a lanyard bearing Blair's fake name.

Blair heads to cargo area C, where he's supposed to meet his contact, a person with a pack of cigarettes showing, leading to the confirmation code. *Any chance I can bum a smoke off ya? Think I can spare one.*

He is surrounded by huge drums, crates stacked high, large rectangular containers the size of boats, men and women in hard hats and colored jackets buzzing back and forth.

He passes twenty people at least, mostly men, all in hard hats, ID's dangling from lanyards on their chests. He scans each of them, their shirts and pants, looking for a pack of cigarettes. That's all he has to go on. The contact, on the other hand, knows Blair's fake name—Pete Martin—and will see it on the ID around Blair's neck. He also knows that Blair will be wearing a puffy red vest and flannel shirt.

More men pass, including one holding the hand of a small child, which rules him out—

"You lost? Need help finding something?"

Blair turns back. It's the man with the small child. The name Joe Driscoll on his ID. A pack of smokes sticking out from his front pocket.

Blair tries not to be too obvious about checking the man out so he can remember his features later, when the bust goes down. The man is Black, bald, maybe six foot two, 180 pounds, maybe midthirties, wearing a haggard expression, raccoon eyes. The little girl, probably no more than age four, in her own little hard hat, has a distinctive look to her that Blair immediately flags as Down syndrome.

"Uh, no," says Blair, recovering from his surprise. "But any chance I could bum a smoke off ya?"

The man, Joe Driscoll, nods. "Think I can spare one."

Jackpot.

Driscoll removes the pack of cigarettes and hands it to

Blair. "Here," he says, "I can show you where you need to go." Driscoll starts walking, his young daughter alongside him. Blair keeps pace, the little girl between the two men.

"I'm Jody," the little girl says to Blair.

"Nice to meet you, Jody."

"Had to bring her with me today," says Driscoll.

"My mommy's in the hospital," says the girl.

Blair looks down at her. "Oh, gosh, sorry about that."

"She's getting radiation."

Radiation. Cancer. Oof.

"Okay, sugar, that's private stuff, remember?" says Driscoll. "Right down this way."

They turn down a row of stacks, twenty feet high at least, nearly blocking the midday sun, leaving them in cool shadows.

Driscoll turns to Blair, holds out a key. "Go ahead and check it out."

Blair will now take the key, open the crate, and confirm that it contains the video-game consoles before closing it back up. But first, he looks into the eyes of this man, Driscoll.

"Take care," Blair says quietly. "Rough business you're in."

The man chuckles, though it sounds more like a grunt. "Like I have a choice," he says.

Blair watches Driscoll leave with his daughter. *Christ,* he thinks. Driscoll's wife has cancer, his daughter Down syndrome. And now he'll go down on a federal conspiracy charge for this theft ring, no matter how small his role — five years minimum in the pen.

A few minutes later, Blair has left the freight yard, heading back down the street, looking out over Lake Michigan's rippling waters. The van is waiting for him as expected. He climbs in.

"How'd we do?" asks his superior, Agent Neary.

Blair shows him the key. "The goods are ready to go," he says. "We're in play."

"Yeah, and who was the contact?"

The contact was a bit player, not a ringleader. A guy doing a minor job for a few needed bucks for his struggling family.

Joe Driscoll. Black, bald, six two, 180 pounds, midthirties.

"I didn't get a name," says Blair. "His lanyard was twisted around. Couldn't see it. I tried. But I didn't want to be too obvious about it. He was a short white guy, overweight, gray hair, wore a goatee, probably late forties."

Neary nods. "Think you could recognize him again?"

"Maybe," says Blair. "Hard to say."

TWENTY-FIVE

I STAGGER OUT OF the pub like a zombie, my chest burning, still stinging with disbelief as I read, for the tenth time, the text exchange I just had with David.

Me: Thinking of stopping by for quick lunch. Are you free?

David: We are crushed right now all hands on deck maybe later?

And yet David is not inside the pub. A flat-out, undeniable lie.

It's not that simple, okay? he said to someone on the phone last night, whispering downstairs on the landline. And his explanation didn't ring true.

I sit in my car, shaking, unable to bring myself to turn on the ignition. I pick up my phone and start typing a search: *How to tell*

The first prompt is: *if your spouse is cheating*

God, am I that much of a cliché? I put down the phone. No. I'm not going to be that woman. If I have a question, I'll ask it, no matter how crushing the answer might be. This isn't me, harboring doubts, afraid to speak my mind. I will just ask him.

Why, David? Why did you lie about being busy at work when you weren't actually at work? Where were you?

Does this have something to do with all these things happening to our family?

Yes, I decide as I drive back to the office for my appointment. I will just ask him.

At the office, I meet with my client Diane Worley, who has just reviewed a draft of the appeal I will file in the case where the judge let her ex-husband off the hook for additional child support.

"This is so good, Marcie." Diane sets down the document on my desk. "And you did it so fast."

It took me more than six hours to get it into shape, but as always, I will cut my bill in half for a client like Diane, who can't afford high legal fees. "It was fresh in my mind," I say. "And the sooner we file, the sooner we overturn that ruling."

"You think there's a chance?"

"I do, yes. A decent chance. You never know with judges."

I look around my office. Nothing fancy. Diplomas on the walls, family photos on my desk, a glamorous view of the parking lot through my window. But it's mine. I may not enjoy matrimonial law as much as criminal defense, but at least I feel good about my clients now. And at least I call my own shots now.

I don't know if the appellate court will overturn this decision. How teeth-gnashingly frustrating it must be for

Diane, knowing that the fate of her and her children's financial well-being rests in the hands of a selfish ex-husband, blessed by a trial judge. And her husband off with another life, a young trophy wife at his side.

"Diane, can I—oh, you know what? Never mind," I say.

"What? You can ask me anything."

"Well…" I drum my fingers on the desk. "How did you know? When did you first—"

"How did I know my husband was cheating on me?" She allows a bitter smile. "Oh, well—probably the first sign was that he was exercising more."

Not an issue. David works out almost every day I've known him.

"Later on, I learned he'd opened a separate bank account and thrown some money in it and attached a debit card to it. He had the bills sent to work so I'd never see them."

A separate bank account. Okay.

She leans forward. "But the real kicker for me was the burner phone."

"A burner phone. A prepaid phone?"

It's not that simple, okay?

Was David really talking on the landline when he whispered those words? Or did he have a second phone?

Diane nods. "When I caught him using another phone, I knew. Unless you're a drug dealer or a terrorist, why else would you have a separate prepaid phone?"

TWENTY-SIX

HAPPY HOUR AT HEMINGWAY'S Pub. It's the third time this week Tommy Malone has been here, always between the hours of four and seven. He's kept to himself, sitting alone in a booth in the bar, wearing a baseball cap to downplay his memorable red hair.

He lays out some work in front of him — sales numbers and graphs and charts that are utterly meaningless. And he has earbuds in, synced to his phone. He looks like someone getting a little work done but enjoying a few cocktails while doing so. Between the work laid out and the earbuds, he figures nobody will bother him. So far, it's worked, all three days.

In reality, Tommy is counting. Counting the drinks the bartenders pour and the finger food they serve, counting the number of times the bartenders use the cash register or credit card machine. He already knows the prices they're charging for wine, straight liquor, martinis, draft beers, premium draft beers, bottled beer, and mixed drinks, plus the appetizers.

"Two mixed drinks, one wine," he says into the microphone on his earbuds, his words transcribed onto his phone.

"Cash register, five thirty-eight."

"Credit card, six twenty-two."

"Four drafts, nonpremium."

Like that all night, or at least between the hours of four and seven.

He knows he won't catch every single transaction. Or he might confuse a draft beer for a premium or miss the fact that a Jack and Coke was a double. But he's pretty damn close. And the overall count is the most important thing.

The late, great Jimmy Buffett is wasting away in Margaritaville over the speakers blasting in the corners. There are currently twenty-five people spread out among the long bar, the high-top tables, and the booths. Off to the right is the dining area, reachable only by walking past a hostess station. Tommy's not bothering with the food. Drinks are easier to catalog. And a sample is all he needs anyway.

Tommy's seen more than his share of taverns, and Hemingway's Pub is cleaner, classier than most. Well lit, fresh paint on the walls, new flat-screen TVs, an impressive and colorful collection of bourbons and vodkas and tequilas and rums behind the bar.

The stone statue of Hemingway outside the pub is a nice touch—a replica, or so it says on a plate at its base, of a statue of Hemingway in Pamplona, Spain. Beckoning tourists and travelers to come have a drink with Papa.

The security system is surprisingly low-rent, purchased through a local vendor. Alarm pads by each of the three entrances, plus a motion detector and glass-break sensor.

David Bowers is here, got back to the pub midafternoon, though Tommy waited until four to come in. No chance David would talk to Tommy, not if Tommy introduced himself as a freelance reporter for *USA Today*. David has declined all interview requests about the heroic river rescue.

From what Tommy's seen over the last three days, David Bowers is all about the receipts. He chats up the customers a bit but otherwise seems to leave the management to one of his people. David collects the receipts from the cash register at the bar; he collects the receipts from the register by the dining room; he disappears into some back office.

Tommy would really, really like to see that back office where David works.

Tommy walks up to the bar for a refill from the busty bartender, Gwinne, who has a face he'd expect to find on a Miss Italy contestant. She knows how to work it, too, dressed just provocatively enough but leaving something to the imagination, those tight leather pants, a revealing skin-tight white shirt with a flannel hanging loosely over it.

"In town on business?" she says to Tommy as she puts a second bourbon in front of him. "Can't really hide that red hair."

"Don't I know it. Hey, is what I'm hearing true? Your owner over there—he's the guy that rescued the man from the river, like, a month ago?"

"That's him." Gwinne looks over at David, who has reappeared behind the bar with a bunch of receipts in his hand. "Our resident hero. Not that he'd admit that."

"Let me buy him a drink," says Tommy. "Pour us a Baker's."

"Oh, David doesn't drink."

"No? He owns a bar and doesn't drink?"

She shrugs. "Never has, as far as I know."

Interesting.

"My girlfriend went nuts over that video of him rescuing that man," Tommy says. "Me, I've never seen anything so brave. No way I'd have the guts to do what he did. Any chance — any chance I could take a picture with him and send it to her?"

"David," Gwinne says as she walks away, attending to another customer. "Customer wants a picture with the Cotton River hero."

David walks over and greets Tommy with an extended hand, lighting up with a smile.

Could be an act for the customer, sure, but Tommy senses otherwise. That's David's default position, Tommy figures, happy and positive energy and all that shit.

"Having a good time tonight?" he asks Tommy. "Everything good?"

"Yeah, great. Nice selection of bourbon. So . . . any chance at a photo? So I can impress my girlfriend?"

"Nah, nah, I'm not into that stuff. How about a drink on the house instead?" David manages to blow him off without seeming like he's blowing him off.

"Ah, okay. Hey, could you sign something?"

He laughs. "Like an autograph?" David shakes his head but ultimately shrugs. "I guess that's fine." He grabs the back of a blank receipt, poises his left hand over it with a pen. "Actually, I'd feel like a pompous jerk signing an autograph."

Tommy decides not to push it and returns to the booth. He didn't really want the autograph anyway. He just wanted to see which hand David would use to write.

Left. He used his left hand.

Tommy leaves at seven and walks around to the rear of the restaurant, where his rental car is parked and where, not coincidentally, the supply entrance to the restaurant is located.

The entrance is surrounded by a tall wooden fence, but for purely cosmetic reasons—concealing the dumpsters and air conditioner—not security. It's easy enough to open the swinging gate to gain access to the entrance, which is protected by a knobless metal door that looks quite thick. Next to it, an alarm pad.

Tommy turns back to the swinging gate. He reaches up and removes his "eye" device, a small motion-sensitive contraption he stuck high up on the interior of the gate two days ago. The device, facing the metal door and alarm pad, surely has picked up the alarm code by now, because this is the entrance used by the manager who opens the restaurant every morning.

Tommy drops the device into his pocket, walks to his car, and drives away.

"See you tomorrow night, David," he says to himself.

TWENTY-SEVEN

AGENT BLAIR TAKES THE elevator to the fourth floor, shows his credentials at the front desk, and heads down the hallway. Rebecca Crandall is on the phone when he walks in. She gives him a surprised-happy look when she sees him and motions for him to sit.

"Well, don't *I* feel honored!" she says, hanging up the phone, pushing herself out of her chair, and giving Blair a hug. "A visit from no less than Special Agent Francis Xavier Blair." She pats him on the chest. "How ya doin', Frankie?"

"Never had it so good," he says, his standard line.

Blair goes way back with Becky Crandall, back to their days together at the Bureau, before Becky moved over to a different part of the alphabet-soup club, becoming a supervisor in the criminal division of the IRS's Chicago office.

They play some quick catch-up. Becky's on her second marriage and has three kids, all in their teens. Blair's personal life, on the other hand, is not much of a story—one divorce, nobody since, and no kids to show for it.

"You're still in OC, I hear," she says.

Blair makes a face. "Yeah, but I got roped into a task force with Customs. Cargo theft. Real exciting stuff. Anyway, OC isn't the Organized Crime it used to be. Now it means street gangs and drugs, maybe a few small-time extortion rings."

"No more Michael Cagninas. Hey, you know," she says, snapping her fingers, "I thought of you—what, five, six months ago?—when Cagnina got sprung."

Blair makes a face. "What a world, right? Thirteen years he gets. All the rackets he ran, the people he terrorized and killed—not to mention killing the three witnesses who would've nailed him on all that. And all he goes down for is a paper crime."

Becky nods, gets serious, checking him out. "Somebody needs to let the past go," she says. "Yeah, he only went down for tax evasion, but that's something, at least. That's thirteen years inside."

Every damn person says that. But Blair can't let it go. He won't let it go.

"That's why you've stayed in the Bureau, in Organized Crime, no less, all this time," says Becky. "Am I right? I mean, you're the only one left. Everyone else on that team moved on from the Bureau after that debacle with the witnesses. Not you, though. What, you're hoping Cagnina will reopen for business so you can catch him?"

Blair waves her off. "Nothing like that. I'm just a glutton for punishment is all."

Becky isn't buying it. She gives him a sidelong glance, a smirk on her face. "Seriously, Francis Xavier—get Michael Cagnina out of your head."

She drops her hands on the desk. "So why the visit? Looking to move over to Revenue so you can see my smiling face every day?"

Blair tosses a file on her desk. She picks it up.

"Let me guess," she says. "You want the IRS to give you the what—to dig up whatever we can on some person of interest—but you won't give us the why."

Blair smiles. "That about covers it. Sorry; it's sensitive stuff."

"So who's the lucky person of interest?" She opens the file. "Bowers," she reads. "Hemingway Grove?"

Blair nods. "And I need it right away," he says.

TWENTY-EIGHT

"A FRESH START," SILAS Renfrow said to me through his bionic voice, his blue eyes visible through the slot of the holding cell. "You don't ever think about that? Fresh starts?"

It was the fourth time I'd met with Silas over the course of three weeks, while the partner from my firm, Howard Shimkus, was on a trial downstate. It was the second Monday of October, Columbus Day, a day when all the courts were closed, so I had time freed up to make the trek here with my federal escort.

Ostensibly, Silas and I were still debating whether to accept the plea deal the government had offered him. We could also make a counteroffer or reject the deal and prepare for trial. But Silas was always changing the subject, always turning it away from the case and on to me—or even to current events, as best he could follow them from this solitary lockup. I had the real sense that Silas was lonely.

"Oh, what am I saying—you're so young," he said,

correcting himself. "Your life right now *is* a fresh start. You haven't lived long enough to have regrets yet."

That wasn't entirely true. There was Kyle, my boyfriend through high school and college and most of law school. I wasn't sure I would've logged our breakup under the category of regret, because my diagnosis was correct—Kyle was born and raised in Hemingway Grove and wanted to live his whole life there. Me, I wanted out. I wanted Chicago or some other big city—or some adventure at least. So I was confident I'd made the right decision in breaking things off. But that didn't make it sting any less.

"Maybe I should just pull a heron, say goodbye to this place," Silas said. "But I'd hate to deprive you of my company."

Whimsy and sarcasm did not translate well when delivered through a voice-altering microphone—human feelings expressed in a robot's voice. Nor did I understand what Silas meant by a "heron," which as far as I knew was a long-necked bird. But it sure seemed like he was talking about suicide.

"We should get back to the plea offer," I said, lifting a packet of papers from my lap as I sat in the chair outside his cell. "Or decide whether we should take our chances at trial."

"Trial," he said, in apparent mockery—again, hard to discern in his altered voice. "Do you really think Mickey Two Guns will stand trial for what he's done?"

Mickey Two Guns, one of the many nicknames for Michael Cagnina, apparently the one Silas favored.

"Why wouldn't he?" I asked. "You think he'll take a plea?"

He laughed, or at least it sounded like a laugh. "No, Marcie, I do not think he will take a plea. Not in a million years."

As best as I could discern with that voice, he was talking down to me, stating the obvious. I didn't understand what was so obvious.

"You really are young," he said.

"Then explain, please." I didn't hide my irritation. Condescension was my Achilles' heel—I'd rather someone spit in my face than patronize me.

"I have a better chance of becoming pope," Silas said, "than surviving in here long enough to testify against Michael Cagnina."

TWENTY-NINE

SEVEN O'CLOCK. THE KIDS are back from their various activities—Grace's dance lesson, Lincoln's indoor soccer practice—and they're eating noodles with red sauce and broccoli the way Grace likes it.

We all look up as David comes in from the garage through the mudroom. I feel a twinge as I see him, looking sleep-deprived, dark circles beneath his eyes, as he forces a smile. "How we doing, gang? Sorry—things have been crazy."

"There's pasta," I tell him.

"I nibbled on something at work." He rubs his hands while he looks out the kitchen window into the backyard.

"Grace had a question on math," I say.

"Sure, yeah. I just—let me make one phone call." He disappears from the kitchen not two minutes after arriving.

Dinner is almost over, then the kids will help me—or at least they're supposed to help me—clean up.

"Grace, put away your phone," I say, catching her while

she's supposed to be wiping the table. "Did you practice piano?"

"Yes."

"No, she didn't," says Lincoln.

"Hey—"

"Yes, I did, *genius*."

"Hey!"

I jump at the sound of David's voice, surprised both by his reappearance and by the harshness of his voice. He points a finger at Grace. "No 'genius' comment."

"Calling someone a genius is an insult?" she protests.

"When you say it like that, of course it is, and you know it! Cut it out, Grace!"

"Fine." She puts down her phone. "Next time I'll call him an idiot. Would that be better?"

"Grace," I say.

"Don't get cute, young lady." David slams his hand down on the kitchen island with a *whomp*. "I'm *not* in the mood for cute!"

"Okay, wow, okay," I say. "I think we've covered it."

David turns to me. We've made a point of not stepping on each other when addressing the kids, not undermining the other's authority. But he's never been physical with his anger. I don't think I've ever seen him hit or slap something when he's mad. And over this? The kids have pushed things way further than this before.

"Grace," I say, "apologize to Lincoln for calling him genius. Do it now."

David takes a step back, blows out a breath of air, glancing at me again. "Whatever," he snaps. He turns and walks out of the kitchen again.

While Grace fumbles out an apology to Lincoln, I follow David, about to climb the stairs. "Let's go get some air," I say. "Go for a walk."

He turns back to me. "Now? It's, like—there's at least three inches of snow outside."

"Yes, now," I say. "You and I need to talk."

"It's...not a great time, Marce."

"No, David," I say, steeling myself against the shiver running through me. "It's long past time."

THIRTY

CAMILLE HOLDS A CUP of ginger tea as she stands by the picture window in her fifth-floor apartment, overlooking the downtown. She is careful not to brush against the telescope mounted on a tripod by the window, positioned just so.

She carefully moves her eye to the eyepiece. David's house, a good half mile away, looks peaceful right now, a few inches of freshly fallen snow clinging to the rooftop, the snow in his yard glistening in the landscape lighting. Most of the downstairs is lit up. She catches a glimpse of the son, Lincoln, passing by a window, tossing a football in the air.

She adjusts the focus, looking through David's bedroom window, then zooms the focus back out to the entire house, even most of the yard.

This morning, David left before six. Marcie got the kids out the door and went to work, setting the house alarm before doing so. After school, Grace had her dance lesson,

Lincoln his soccer practice. David just got home a half hour ago.

Camille puts down the tea and pulls a blanket over her shoulders. The heat in this apartment isn't great, and some cold air escapes by this window. Her phone buzzes. It's her best friend, Zoe. She considers not answering but punches the green button.

"Feeling any better?" Zoe asks.

"The ginger tea helps. Haven't vomited in five hours." Camille peers again through the telescope. The house looks relatively still, quiet.

"What's the latest?" Zoe asks. "Let me guess. He's still not going to leave his wife."

"I hate it when you say it like that. They're married on paper only. They don't even sleep in the same bedroom."

"Says him," Zoe replies. "How do you know he's telling you the truth? Oh, that's right—you don't!"

"You're making me feel like a home-wrecker, Z. He doesn't love her, and she doesn't love him. He just doesn't want to rock the boat. He's—"

"Waiting for the right time, I know, I know."

God, Camille thinks, is she becoming that predictable? Is she just rationalizing? But everything she's telling Zoe is true. He doesn't love his wife. She doesn't love him. Zoe doesn't believe that, but Zoe doesn't know him.

"Well, so have you told him?" Zoe asks.

"Have I told him...what? That I'm pregnant?"

"Uh, yeah, Camille. Have you told him you're pregnant? Kind of an important piece of information, don't ya think? It might make a difference."

She breathes out. "I told him, yes."

"And?"

"He's going to tell his wife. He's going to leave her. We're going to get married and raise our child together."

Camille looks back through the telescope, tensing as she sees David and Marcie leaving out the front door.

"Gotta go, Z. Talk soon." She punches out the phone.

She focuses in on them. Marcie, not looking happy, walking in front of David as they move down the porch. David, with his coat collar up, cap on his head, looks even less happy—worried, even.

The expressions on their faces, the body language— distant, unaffectionate.

"Did she confront you, David?" Camille whispers. "Is this the moment of truth?"

THIRTY-ONE

JUST BLURT IT OUT, I tell myself as the cold air stings me on the front porch of our house. *Just say it. Then it will be over. Then whatever happens happens. No matter how horrible.*

"Marcie, let's at least stay close to home," David says to me as we head down our front walk to the street. "With all the weird stuff happening lately."

I reach the street and turn around. "We can stop right here if you want."

"Uh—okay, sure. What's—what's going on?"

I swallow over the lump in my throat, try to even out my breathing. He's looking at me intently but, it seems, also with apprehension.

"Today, I went to see you at the pub. For lunch. You said you were too busy. But the pub wasn't busy, and, more important, you weren't there."

"You..." His eyes narrow. "When you texted me today, you were already at the pub? You were, what, testing me or something?"

"No," I say, my voice trembling, "you are not going to turn this around on me. Yes, I was testing you. I was seeing if you'd lie to me. And guess what? You did. Why?"

"Why did you test me?"

My mouth drops open. "You're really going to play that game? Misdirect, distract, avoid the question? Okay, David, y'know what?"

I catch myself raising my voice. Nobody else is dumb enough to be out here in the cold right now, but voices carry. No matter the rage and hurt I'm feeling, I will not make a spectacle out here. I will not do that to our children.

"Okay, fine," I say. "I'll play the game. I tested you because you lied to me the other night, when you were downstairs on the phone, whispering in the middle of the night. 'It's not that simple, okay?' Remember those words? You said you were talking to a security company. That wasn't true, was it?"

David lets out a sigh, looks away, shaking his head.

"Two lies," I say. "And all these strange things happening to us. Why, David?"

David puts out his hands, like he's trying to frame an answer, trying to pinpoint how to begin. I never thought that communicating with me, his wife, his life partner, his soulmate, would require such effort.

"Are you having an affair?" I ask, and despite myself, all my efforts, my eyes well up, my throat chokes up.

"Oh, for God's sake, no." He moves toward me, arms out. "Marcie, of course not."

But I step back. I'm not that easy. No matter how desperately I want him to deny an affair, to hear those words from him—I'm not that easy. "Then what?"

"Oh, God." His head falls back a moment. Then he says, "We're having money problems." He lowers his head, eyes closed.

"Money problems?"

"The pub isn't doing well lately," he says, a hand shielding his eyes. "The economy and everything. I'm trying to make it work. I'm talking to the bank about refinancing the loan on the building."

"This is all…all about *money*?" I say, cocking my head.

"Well, I don't know about 'all.' All that weird stuff with the dog and the lunch box and the coffeepot and breaking into our house—I have no idea. But yesterday, for example, when I wasn't at the pub, and I wasn't honest with you? I was at the bank, working on a loan refi. I didn't want you to know."

Replace one piece of bad news with another. But nothing compares to the thought of your spouse giving himself to another woman. I feel relief flood through me.

"And the phone call? 'It's not that simple, okay?' What was that—"

"Same thing. I was talking to one of my managers, the one who takes the early morning deliveries?"

"Yes?"

"We've fallen…" He shakes his head. "We've fallen behind on payments. Our produce delivery didn't come. That's a killer for us. He told me to start laying off some people, but—it's not that simple, okay? You lay off employees, you can't stay open, you sink even deeper into debt. Anyway, I—I didn't want you to know. I didn't want you to know any of it, Marce."

"Why? Why wouldn't you want me to—"

"Because I promised I'd always provide for you and our family, that's why," he says. "I made that promise to you."

"I never *asked* you to make me that promise, if you'll recall. I always planned on maintaining a law practice. I don't need to be 'taken care of.' We're a team. If we're having problems, then we deal with them together."

"I know, I know, I know. I…" He looks up at me. "I know."

"Don't ever lie to me again, David," I say.

"I…" He puts his hand to his chest. "I won't." He walks over, leans his forehead against mine. "Marcie Dietrich Bowers, how could you think for one second that I was cheating on you? Really? Me?"

He presses his lips to mine. Money problems, they're money problems—we can figure something out. There is only one David. There is only one Bowers family.

"You and the kids are the only things that matter to me in this world," he whispers. "You're it. You're everything."

THIRTY-TWO

I LOCK THE BEDROOM door after Grace and Lincoln are down for the night. David and I tear at each other's clothes. I want him with a desperation I've never felt, a sense of urgency born of relief. Yes, times are tough for us, financial problems. But we can handle that. David is still mine. He always was.

He throws me on the bed and climbs on top of me. I wrap my legs around his waist. Everything is okay. Everything that matters is okay.

David knows me; he knows the buttons to punch, my buttons. The first time, I cry out in spite of trying to keep quiet with the kids down the hall, David putting his hand over my mouth and chuckling, sweat from his brow trickling onto my face. My body on fire as David thrusts inside me, two animals going at it as we used to when we first started dating, when we realized that this thing was more than just a thing, it was real, it was forever —

The second time, I mute myself, folding my lips inside

my mouth while I let out a slow guttural moan. David can no longer hold back. This time, it's my hand over his mouth, his jaw clenched, while his body shudders.

He collapses on me, all but smothering me in a way that would feel like smothering if it were anyone else, but it's David. It's my husband.

"No, don't move," I whisper as he starts to pull out. "Stay here. Stay with me."

This is it. This is what I want.

We can handle anything if we're together.

"Money's just money," I whisper. "We can figure something out if we have to. We could take out a mortgage. We could sell the house and get something smaller."

"I could sell the restaurant," he says, still catching his breath. "We could move to freakin' Hawaii and start over."

"You could teach math," I say.

"You could go back to criminal defense."

"Whatever we want," I say, still coming down from the high.

"Whatever we want," he says. "A fresh start."

I don't know how serious we are, but there's a certain thrill to envisioning it. It is possible. We can do it.

"If you believe it hard enough, you can make it be true," David whispers.

THIRTY-THREE

I STILL REMEMBER THAT morning fifteen years ago, Halloween morning. I was in my law office, sipping a Starbucks coffee and getting ready to draft an appellate brief, when my secretary buzzed me on the intercom with two breathless messages: Howard Shimkus was on the phone, needing to speak with me "urgently," and two FBI agents were in the outer office, demanding to see me.

Taking a call from one of our senior partners took priority. "You're not gonna believe this, Marcie," Howard said. "Silas Renfrow is dead."

"Silas is . . . he's—"

"All three witnesses in that secret detention center. They got to all three witnesses. They're all dead. They stormed the place, killed all the marshals, then the three witnesses, then torched the place. Burned everything and everyone to a crisp."

I remembered Silas's words to me only weeks earlier—there was no chance he'd survive long enough to testify against Michael Cagnina.

"The FBI just paid me a visit, some guys from the Springfield office," said Howard.

"What a coincidence. I have two FBI agents waiting outside my office right now."

Those agents, to say the least, were agitated. Even more so when they questioned me about everything I knew, to which I politely but firmly replied that anything Silas and I discussed was protected by attorney-client privilege.

"Lady, half a dozen US marshals were killed along with the three witnesses," said the lead FBI agent, a guy named Francis Blair, as if that fact allowed me to make an exception to the most sacred rule a lawyer follows.

And besides, what could I tell them? That Silas predicted that Cagnina would somehow discover the location of the secret detention center and rub out the people testifying against him? I didn't see how that would help anyway.

Eventually the agents left, and I read online about what was being called the Halloween Massacre. It had taken place up north in a suburb of Rockford, a town called Roscoe, where the detention center was located. The three witnesses shot, decapitated—decapitated!—and set on fire. A half dozen US marshals killed in a gunfight. The whole detention center torched.

It wasn't until a week later, when Howard finally completed his long fraud trial in downstate Illinois, that he and I had a chance to talk about the whole thing at length. We were at the bar at the Union League Club, Howard drinking Scotch, me a glass of wine. By then, the shock had worn off. The Halloween Massacre had taken on celebrity status, and no lawyer enjoyed notoriety more than Howard.

He'd even started to have a sense of humor about it. "To Silas," he said, raising his glass—not his first—of Scotch. "We hardly knew ye. Literally. We never saw your face; we never heard your real voice; and we had no fucking idea where we were when we visited you. Now." He patted my arm. "Give me stories. A blow-by-blow of everything you discussed."

So I did. How Silas preferred talking about anything other than the charges against him. How he tried to get to know me personally and talk about myself. How he even started getting a little too personal, including what I took to be a reference to suicide. "He said something about 'pulling a heron' or something and saying goodbye."

Howard's round head whipped in my direction. "He said what? Say that again."

"He said if he could 'pull a heron' and say good—"

"Oh, shit. Sweet holy motherfuck." Howard fell back against his chair, losing the color in his face. Then he reached for my arm. "Who have you—wait, you didn't— tell me you didn't say this to the FBI."

"No, of course not," I said. "It was a privileged conversation. But what does it mean? I thought a heron was some bird that looks like a goose. This is some old-fashioned figure of speech or something?"

But Howard wasn't listening to my question. He was looking up at the ceiling. "Oh, Jesus Christ," he whispered as his eyes closed.

He sat there for a while like that, eyes shut, head back, as if in meditation. He always had a flair for drama; it's probably what made him a good trial lawyer.

"It sounded like he was talking about killing himself," I said.

Howard let out a small sound but otherwise didn't react.

"I'm in the dark here, Howard," I said. "Help me out."

"No. Stay in the dark. The dark is good. The dark is your friend."

"But you can't leave me hanging—"

"Marcie, I want you to listen to me. You can't ever, ever repeat that to anyone else. Anyone, ever." He opened his eyes, rejoining planet earth, and leveled his stare on me. "And as far as I'm concerned, you never told *me*, either."

Howard wouldn't explain any further or give me any idea what that cryptic phrase meant. But me being me, I couldn't let it go. I thought about it, then started searching the internet. It took some time. A lot of trial and error. But eventually, I discovered the meaning of "pulling a heron."

I wish I hadn't. I wish I'd let it go. Because what I discovered changed my life forever.

THIRTY-FOUR

TOMMY MALONE WALKS THROUGH the frigid darkness, returning to Hemingway's Pub on foot, not a terrible walk from the hotel where he's staying, toting a bag over his shoulder. The parking lot is empty at two in the morning and well shoveled from the snowfall, but he watches out for the possibility of ice.

At the back entrance, he types six numbers into the alarm pad, the same six numbers his "eye" device captured the early morning manager typing into the pad the last few mornings. Sure enough, the thick metal door pops open, allowing Tommy inside.

Tommy figures he has until five in the morning—three hours from now—before anyone shows up at this place. That's been the routine over the last several days of his surveillance, at least; you never really know.

He keeps his flashlight low to the floor, just enough to allow him to navigate through the supply room and the kitchen, which smells strongly of disinfectant, until he reaches the back office. This is where he will know for sure.

The door is locked but not, thank God, with a code. Just a straightforward single-cylinder deadbolt lock. In his business, you learn how to get past these things pretty quickly.

And he does. Less than two minutes with the tension tool and jiggler, and he's inside David's office. He risks flipping on a light, figuring that an interior room, with the door closed, won't emit any light outside the restaurant to any patrol officer or lookie-loo who might be driving by.

David's office is military-level neat, with three stacks of paper on the desk, shelves filled with folders labeled clearly. He notes a bit of dust on the desk, which tells him that whoever is charged with cleaning up the restaurant isn't allowed in this office.

"Only *you're* allowed in here," Tommy whispers. "Isn't that right, David?"

He needs the receipts—the receipts from the last three nights, taken from the cash registers between the hours of 4:00 p.m. and 7:00 p.m., when Tommy was here watching. He finds the folder for the receipts from this week and looks them over. For each day, there are three stacks of receipts.

Three stacks. But there are only two cash registers.

Maybe the third stack is for credit card receipts? But no, Tommy finds as he leafs through the receipts for yesterday. The credit card slips are included along with the cash receipts.

What's this third stack?

That's when he sees it. Hell, it's sitting right there in front of him, right next to the computer: a third cash register. A cash register inside David's office?

He smiles. His job just got much easier.

He doesn't bother with the dining-room register—he didn't pay attention to food, only to drinks. He riffles through the bar receipts, doing math on his phone's calculator, counting all the beverages purchased at the bar yesterday between the hours of 4:00 p.m. and 7:00 p.m. He does the count quickly once, then repeats it. Each time, he gets the same number: 127 drinks of various kinds were purchased during that three-hour window and rung up at the bar.

That sounds right. Tommy, watching from the booth yesterday, had a count of 124. He was off by a handful, which he figured might happen no matter how careful he tried to be.

Wait. He realizes he didn't count his own drinks, *dumbass,* in the calculation. He had three bourbons. So the count of 127 beverages matches exactly.

Leaving aside the receipts from the dining room, that leaves the mysterious third stack, from the cash register so close to Tommy right now that he could reach out and touch it. He riffles through the stack quickly, counting the number of drinks purchased according to these receipts. He does it once, then again, and because his two counts are different, he counts a third time, more slowly and meticulously. Finally, he's sure of the number.

Fifty-eight. The receipts from the mysterious third register record fifty-eight additional drinks purchased between

4:00 p.m. and 7:00 p.m. yesterday. Drinks, of course, that were never actually purchased.

And every one, every single one of these phantom drink purchases—every single damn one of them—was rung up as a cash purchase. Of course they were.

Tommy sits back in his chair. "I fucking knew it," he whispers.

He pulls the receipts for the two days before yesterday from the three-ring binder and repeats the process, comparing them to the counts he made while watching from his booth in the bar. And the results aren't much different.

Three days ago, David's mysterious third cash register showed sixty-two additional purchases of booze—again, all in cash. Two days ago, the inflated number was fifty-one additional drinks. And yes, all in cash.

Sixty-two, fifty-one, fifty-eight—David's mixing the numbers up from day to day, keeping it relatively level, because he's not an idiot. That would be the smart play. Keep a nice, fairly steady total from day to day of fake purchases. Nothing that would jump out to a bank looking at your daily deposits.

And this is just for the sale of drinks—alcohol and mixers that have long shelf lives. Imagine what David could do with the food, some of which inevitably goes bad before it gets used and has to be tossed. Every item of food the pub throws out David could pretend was sold and consumed and ring up a cash transaction for it.

Tommy closes the binder and puts it back where he found it. He takes a deep breath and releases it.

To review: David Bowers is the town hero, an internet sensation, after diving into a river to save a drowning man.

He's a local business owner who has operated a popular restaurant for more than a decade.

He's left-handed. He doesn't drink.

And he's one hell of a money launderer.

THIRTY-FIVE

THE FOG SO THICK I can't see anything before me but faint shadows, the ground beneath me uneven and treacherous, while I search for him, call out, David, David, *and then I feel a pressure in my chest, my breathing growing shallow,* David, David, David—

My eyes open into the large brown eyes of Lulu, lying on my chest, her nose sniffing my mouth, small whines escaping her. I hear the growls and churns within her skinny midsection. She's always had a sensitive stomach. She does this to me a lot. She needs to go outside in the middle of the night.

I pat the bed for my phone and squint at it, not having my contacts in. It's just past three thirty in the morning. David's body rises and falls in a soothing rhythm next to me. The house is quiet with the exception of my little dog's whines.

"Okay, already," I whisper, causing Lulu to pop to attention and hop off the bed. I clutch my phone while my feet find my slippers, basically fuzzy sandals, on the floor.

Down the stairs we go, my right hand on the railing, my left shining the phone's flashlight on the stairs while the remnants of the dream cling to me like cobwebs. At the turn of the staircase, I glance out the large picture window overlooking the intersection of Cedar and Wilbur. The trees quiver in the wind. Shadows move about.

I can't put my finger on it. But something feels wrong.

I'm wearing only a long pajama top, wishing immediately that I'd thrown on something else, because the downstairs feels drafty. I punch in the alarm code to deactivate the alarm and open the back door for Lulu to go out. The harsh air smacks me, so I step back, praying this will be the only time tonight that Lulu has an emergency.

I glance over to the living room, where the halogen light we installed over the baby grand piano is on, something I've talked to Grace about. And the piano's fallboard is up; I've told Grace time and again to pull it down over the keys when she's done practicing to avoid dust buildup.

I close the fallboard gently over the keys and walk over by the window to flip off the light switch. The little corner of the room falls dark. I startle when I see, through the window, a car parked up the street on Wilbur.

Nothing unusual about people parking their cars along the street, but this car, some kind of boxy SUV, is clearly running. Its headlights are off, but there's no missing the fumes from the exhaust. On a night like this, with temperatures below freezing, it would be impossible to sit in a car without the heat running.

I check my phone again to make sure I have this right — it's half past three in the morning. So this isn't a parent picking up a kid for before-school athletic practice or a music lesson. This isn't even someone doing a paper route.

This is a car trying to minimize its presence with the lights off, a person sitting idly in a car that is directly facing my house.

Lulu barks to be let in. I rush to the door, let her back in, close the door and lock it, and punch in the code to reactivate the alarm.

Then I return to the window, this time pulling back the curtain entirely so I have a clear look. I can't possibly make out the license plate or the make or model of the vehicle, much less see the occupants.

I think of shouting upstairs to David, but the kids might hear. I don't want to leave this spot at the window again. I somehow feel safer with my eyes on that car.

So I decide on a compromise.

On my phone, I find David on my favorites list and punch the link, then bring the lit-up phone to my ear, making sure that my actions are clear and visible to the driver up the street as the phone rings.

In an instant, the SUV whips backward, does a 180, then heads north on Wilbur, away from me.

I don't come close to getting a license plate. I don't know what kind of car it was or have any identifiers. I don't know who was inside the car or what they want. I only know one thing for certain.

That car was definitely watching our house.

THIRTY-SIX

DAVID PEERS THROUGH THE window, grimacing. "And tell them what?" he asks. "That a car was parked up the street, and then it left? You can't say anything about the car other than that it was an SUV."

"It left when the driver saw me making a phone call. It peeled away as soon as I put my phone against my ear."

David nods. "So you couldn't make out anything at all about the car except that it was boxy? You couldn't see the driver at all, but the driver could clearly see *you* through the living-room window?"

"He probably could. Maybe he had binoculars."

"Which we can't prove."

"Well, if he was watching our house—"

"Which we can't prove, either—"

"—he probably *did* have binoculars."

He gives me a look of exasperation.

"Why are you fighting me on this?" I shout, catching the volume of my voice. "Don't you care about all the strange stuff happening to us?"

"Of course—of course I do, Marce. You're the lawyer here. Think like one. We have nothing to tell the police. I mean, go ahead." He flips his hand. "If you want to call them, call them."

He drops into a chair, rubbing his eyes.

"What's going on, David?"

"I..." He looks up at me. "I don't know."

"Your financial problems," I say. "How bad are they?"

"Well, they're...I mean, how am I supposed to—"

"Did you borrow money from someone? Do you owe money to someone who won't take it so well if you don't pay it back?"

"What? Did I borrow money from a loan shark?" He laughs. "Are you serious?"

"Then what the hell is happening to us? We're being targeted, David. So far, it hasn't been violent. But who's to say it won't escalate? Meanwhile, you're sitting over there playing the fiddle while Rome is burning."

He pushes himself out of his chair and lets out a breath. He picks up his phone, dials three digits, and puts the phone against his ear. "Hi, this is David Bowers at 343 Cedar Lane in Hemingway Grove. I'd like to report a suspicious car sitting outside our house. It just left. But we're afraid it will come back. Great—thank you."

He kills the phone. "We'll hire security. Around-the-clock security."

"With what money?" I ask.

"We're not broke, Marce. The business is struggling, yes. But we have money in the bank. Let's do it. Around the clock. Maybe that will scare off whoever's doing this."

THIRTY-SEVEN

AT HALF PAST FIVE, Kyle Janowski is already awake and showered, preparing to throw on his uniform, when his phone buzzes. He reaches the Bowers home at six.

The sun is still over an hour from showing its face as he pulls along the curb. The cold hits him hard when he steps out of his ride.

Officer Virginia Risely is there, standing by her squadrol, wearing her uniform jacket, hands on her hips, when he pulls up. "Sorry to bother you, Sarge, but you had a flag on any incident involving the Bowers—"

"Yeah, I did, Ginny. Glad you called."

"You go back with Mr. Bowers?" she asks.

"I grew up with Marcie Bowers," he says. "Hardly know David."

He leaves out the part about Marcie dumping him because, she claimed, she didn't want to settle down in HG—only to later do that very thing, settle down in HG with another man.

"Well, Mr. Bowers had to leave for work. Mrs. Bowers's daughter has to get up now for music before school. So we're pretty much done. We told her we'd increase the patrols around her house."

"That's fine," says Kyle. "I don't need to talk to them. Just tell me what I need to know."

Ginny exhales, frosty air leaving her mouth as she gives him the brief rundown.

"Okay, so let's look at the ALPRs for the northeast quad," says Kyle. "Call Ramona over at town services and tell her I want them ASAP. Kind of time window we're looking at, around three thirty in the morning, can't be too much data."

"Okay, boss." Ginny gives him a look. "Something concerning you here?"

"Oh, they've had some strange stuff happen," he says. "She's a lawyer, and he owns Hemingway's Pub—maybe someone has a grudge or something. Who knows these days?" He puts his hand on Ginny's shoulder. "Get the information right away and let me see it the minute you do."

"Sure thing, Sarge. Hey, you're up and in uniform pretty early."

Kyle nods. "Got an out-of-town meeting this morning," he says.

"Where you headed?"

"Chatsworth," he says.

"Chatsworth? What, did someone steal a cow or something?"

Kyle obligingly smiles. He wishes his meeting were that frivolous. It may be his best chance to figure out what the hell is going on with the Bowers family.

THIRTY-EIGHT

"SERGEANT JANOWSKI, IS IT?" Oliver Grafton raises a hand to Kyle.

"It's Kyle, Agent Grafton. Thanks for seeing me."

"Call me Ollie. Everyone always did. Never had much time for the formality myself. Everyone else at the Bureau, they—well, they sort of got off on it, if you know what I mean; the whole 'special agent' crap. I always preferred plain old Ollie. Or Graf if not."

Grafton is more than ten years removed from the FBI now, retired at age sixty-nine and living alone in a house around fifty miles from Hemingway Grove in a town called Chatsworth. Kyle's great-uncle lived out here; Kyle tries out the name to Grafton, who says it rings a bell.

"You grew up here, then," says Kyle, sitting at the kitchen table across from Grafton.

Grafton nods. "Born and raised in this house. Never thought I'd come back. Joined up with the Bureau, the central district—y'know, Springfield—after law school and transferred to Chicago in the late nineties. After I retired and then my wife passed, and the house was just sitting here, I figured, why not? It's not a bad place to retire, actually." He looks at Kyle. "But you didn't come out here to hear about my life. You wanna hear about Mikey the Knife."

Kyle smiles at the nickname, one of many he's heard.

"Or Mickey Two Guns." Grafton chuckles. "Michael Cagnina. You probably heard he got out not long ago. Heard he's down in Tampa–St. Pete."

"You worked that case," says Kyle.

"Back in the day, yeah, I did. Don't remind me, the way everything went south. The bitch of it was, it wasn't the Bureau's fault, those witnesses getting killed. That was on the marshals' office. But we all knew when the case against him went in the sewer that it would be us front and center in the shitstorm." He waves a hand. "Well, we got him anyway, even if it was on a tax charge."

"I'm looking at something going on in my town," says Kyle. "One of the people in my town was a defense attorney for Silas Renfrow in that case."

Grafton purses his lips, nods for a long time, almost as if showing respect. "Silent Silas," he says. "He was a ghost. We looked for him for months until he surrendered to us. One of the most cold-blooded, ruthless killers ever born. As much as we hated to lose him as a witness against Cagnina, it seemed like there was some rough justice in seeing him get lit on fire and burned to a crisp."

"I understand." Kyle plays with his hands. "Some strange things are happening to this woman, Silas's former lawyer.

People are messing with her. Broke into her home, moved things around, put a dead rat in her kid's Halloween bag—"

"A dead rat. Huh." That seems to get Grafton's attention. "But why would Cagnina have a beef with her? I mean, lawyers annoy all of us, but we don't—we don't blame them for what their clients do."

"That's what I can't figure," says Kyle. "It's just that all this weird stuff is happening to her all of a sudden, and Cagnina just got out of prison five months ago. Seems like it might be connected."

Grafton's eyes narrow. *"Silas's* lawyer," he mumbles. "Silas, of all people."

"Why do you say that?"

"Oh, well, it's probably nothing. Really just an old wives' tale."

"Tell me, please," says Kyle, feeling like he's getting some traction.

"Hell, it's not even an old wives' tale. Just something one of the agents said once. After the whole thing was over. After Cags was convicted on tax evasion and we had at least *something* to show for years of hard work."

"Yeah? What did this agent say?"

"And he was half in the bag, at that. Most of us were. A big blowout after the conviction. You know how cops can drink. Thing was, I was on some medication at the time, so I had to watch myself." He shakes his head. "Yeah, Frankie Blair, one of the lead agents. That boy could drink back in the day."

Kyle is about to come out of his skin. "What did Agent Blair say, Ollie?"

"He said, and I'm pretty sure this is a quote, it stuck with me so much. He said, 'Are we really sure that Silas is dead?'"

Kyle draws back. "I'm not...I'm not following."

"Like he faked his own death," says Grafton. "Put another body in his place and escaped. Could you even imagine? And where would a guy like that even go?"

Kyle tries with all his might to maintain a poker face. Where, indeed, would a guy like that go?

Probably someplace nondescript. A small town where you could live anonymously. Until something thrusts you into the spotlight.

Something like a heroic rescue of a drowning man in a choppy river, all captured on a video that goes viral.

No, Kyle thinks. *It can't be.*

Did Silas Renfrow move to Hemingway Grove and marry his former lawyer?

THIRTY-NINE

WHEN I WALKED INTO the office of the senior partner, Howard Shimkus, fifteen years ago, I didn't realize that my legal career in Chicago was about to end. It was almost two weeks since the federal government had notified us of Silas Renfrow's death but only days since Howard and I had talked about it.

"Oh, good, the motion to dismiss?" he asked when I walked in holding a document in my hand. When I put it down on his desk, he took one look at it and immediately knew it wasn't the pleading he'd been expecting. "Jesus, Marcie, what are you doing?"

"Liam Herrin," I said, pointing at the printout of the online article I'd just handed him. "Escaped from a maximum-security prison in Northern Ireland in 1971. Lured a guard into a laundry shack, killed him, changed clothes with him, then set fire to the shack. Prison officials thought it was Herrin who died. By the time they learned otherwise, Herrin was long gone."

Howard kept a poker face, nodding carefully.

"That's what it means, Howard. 'Pulling a Herrin.' He wasn't talking about a bird. He was talking about killing a prison guard and changing places with him. Escaping."

Howard was good. A trial lawyer of his experience was long adept at handling surprises, at holding still amid a hurricane. He brought his hands together in a steeple.

"That's why you were so upset when I mentioned that phrase," I said. "Because it means Silas Renfrow escaped—"

"We don't know that Silas did any such thing," he said, his voice a strange mixture of calm and aggression. "Do we? Do you have some special insight into what happened in that detention facility that no one else seems to have?"

I didn't, and he knew I didn't. I had no proof. What I had, however, was Howard's reaction that night when I mentioned Silas's Herrin reference, swearing me to secrecy, praying with all his might that I hadn't mentioned it to the FBI.

"To say nothing of the attorney-client privilege," said Howard. "Ever heard of that?"

"I've also heard of rule 11," I said. "Committing a fraud on the court."

"Whoa, whoa, whoa. Close that door. Close it." Howard got to his feet as I shut his office door.

"You're waiting for me to draft the motion to dismiss," I said. "We have to file a suggestion of death to get the criminal charges against Silas dropped. We have to tell the court in writing that he's dead. But he's not."

"We can say in writing that the government has *informed* us he's dead. We know *that* part's true." He seemed proud of himself for that very lawyerly distinction.

But inside, I felt something snap. I knew it then, as sure as I ever knew anything. Howard knew what Silas had done. He knew in advance what Silas was planning. That's why he didn't want to be around for any meetings with Silas, why he sent me instead, using his other trial as an excuse. He wanted to create as much distance from Silas as possible, so he could plead ignorance when it happened. And I was just a young associate who could be manipulated, bossed around if I became a problem.

"This firm doesn't sell out its clients," he said. "We get that reputation, we're as good as dead in the legal community."

"There's a difference," I countered, "between selling out a client and being part of the client's fraud."

Howard's face turned a shade of purple. He darted a finger in my direction. "I don't want to hear that word again from you. Get that motion to dismiss on file today. I don't even need to see it."

"I can't sign it," I said.

"Of course you can. It's the most routine of routine motions. It will be granted without any—"

"No," I said. "I mean I *won't* sign it. I'm not going to say he's dead. Because I no longer believe he is."

It felt like the ground was shaking beneath me. Howard let out a small chuckle, though he was far from amused. He mentioned something about my future at the firm, my future as a lawyer, but all that was now moot. I knew I could never work for Howard Shimkus again, and thus I was done at Millard Halloway. I'd flamed out at one of the top-tier Chicago law firms within a couple of years.

I could've made a big deal of this, I guess. I could have run to the ARDC, our attorney disciplinary commission, or gone to the FBI with my speculation. But it felt, suddenly, as if I were an alien on the planet they call the practice of law. I had to leave. I had to go somewhere else entirely—wipe the stink off myself and reboot.

I went home to HG. I needed a break, and my mother was quite ill. Three months became six, six became nine, and then she was in hospice care, waiting out the last months of her life from a hospital bed in her home. I mostly cared for her, caught up on light reading, and went for long runs along the Cotton River.

A little more than a year later, during one of those long runs along the river, I met another jogger.

His name was David Bowers.

FORTY

CAMILLE TOSSES HERSELF OVER on the bed, unable to sleep. The afternoon sun beams through the blinds in stripes. She looks at the clock. Almost 3:00 p.m. She needs to get up anyway.

She's beyond exhausted and nauseated but on edge, too. It wasn't hard to tell what happened last night, watching David and Marcie through her telescope while they stood outside their home. They went from squaring off and accusatory to embracing, lovey-dovey, walking arm in arm back into the house. David somehow deceived Marcie into thinking everything was okay.

What on earth is he waiting for? He's making it more difficult for everyone involved by not breaking the news to Marcie sooner rather than later.

She hears a knock at her door. She pops up in bed, instantly alert. Who the hell would be knocking on her door?

She moves to the door slowly, staying off to the side. "Who is it?"

"Police, ma'am," comes the reply.

She checks through the peephole. Sure enough. A man on the younger side, handsome and well built, wearing the police coat with furry collar. A local.

She opens the door but leaves the chain on.

"Camille Striker? I'm Sergeant Kyle Janowski, Hemingway Grove PD," he says. "Mind if I come in a second?"

"I do mind, actually."

That seems to surprise the sergeant, who blinks hard. "You won't let me come in?"

"Do you have a warrant, Officer?"

He's not an officer. He called himself a sergeant. But she's in a pissy mood.

"No, I do not have a warrant."

"Then no, you can't come in."

He takes a breath, trying to be civil. "We're going to have a conversation with you behind that door chain and me out in the hallway?"

"Looks that way," she says. "You can start by telling me what this is about."

"I think you know what this is about, Ms. Striker."

She gives him a chilly smile. She's pregnant, nauseated, tired, and grumpy. Not a good combination. But she has to be careful, too. No sense in aggravating the local cops.

After a few more moments of awkward silence, the sergeant clears his throat. "The reason I'm here," he says, "is that I want to know what you were doing outside the Bowers home at three thirty in the morning."

FORTY-ONE

"WE HAVE A LICENSE plate reader that captured your plate crossing the intersection of Wilbur and Front Street at 3:41 a.m.," Sergeant Janowski tells Camille.

"Is that a crime?" she asks. "Driving at 3:41 a.m.? I'm not familiar with the local laws."

He doesn't think she's cute. "What are you doing in Hemingway Grove, ma'am?"

"Is *that* a crime—being in Hemingway Grove?"

The sergeant frowns. "There's no reason to make this difficult."

"Make what difficult? This conversation we're having? I could end it at any time. I'm under no obligation to talk to you. But I haven't closed the door yet, so if—"

"The Bowers family called 911 last night," says the sergeant. "After seeing a car idling outside their house in the middle of the night."

David called the police on her? That doesn't make sense. Marcie, she thinks. It must have been Marcie.

This is what happens, David, when you keep secrets. It always gets messy.

"What reason do you have to be watching the Bowers house, Ms. Striker?"

"Who said I was watching the Bowers house?"

"Are you saying you weren't?"

"I'm just wondering why you think that."

Yeah, she's needlessly egging him on. Annoying a cop who's asking the right questions. The only problem is, she won't answer them.

"What are you doing in HG?" he asks for the second time. "You don't live here. You don't work here. You live in Chicago."

But I didn't always live in Chicago, Sergeant. You've done your homework, but you haven't dug that deep.

Camille makes a point of checking her watch. "Anything else, Officer?"

"Okay, you won't answer my questions. That's ... that's your prerogative."

"Thank you," she says. "We done?"

She starts to close the door, but he puts a hand out to stop it.

"One more question," he says. "Do you know the name Silas Renfrow?"

Her heart skips a beat. "Bye, now," she says, closing the door.

She falls against the wall and draws a deep breath. The nausea inside her is rising. Whoever named it morning sickness didn't give away the complete story. But it's more than that. It's her nerves, too. The cops have noticed her now. She's no longer invisible.

And yes, she most certainly knows the name Silas Renfrow.

FORTY-TWO

SPECIAL AGENT FRANCIS BLAIR walks into Becky Crandall's office at the IRS's criminal division in Chicago. "Hope I'm not stopping by too late," he says. "I know you Revenue folks like to call it a day about four."

"Fuck off, Francis." She removes her glasses, tucks her hair behind her ears. "Nice scruff, by the way."

The facial hair—three days' growth of beard. "I'm undercover. A task force with Customs. Might've mentioned to you. A sting op. Cargo theft. Been working it about a year now."

"Well, don't you live the exciting life?"

"Yeah, don't I? Tell me you have something good for me, Beck."

"You tell *me* something first," she says. "Does this have anything to do with Michael Cagnina?"

He takes a seat across from her. "Why do you ask that?"

"Oh-kay." She leans back in her leather chair. "The runaround. Answer a question with a question. I don't 'need to know,' right? Never mind our history. Never mind I worked that fucking Cagnina case with you back in the day."

Blair throws up his hands. "Not my call, Becky."

She pushes a file across the desk to him. "Hemingway's Pub is owned by DCB Enterprises. His initials, David Christopher Bowers. An offshore corporation."

"Offshore. Hmph."

"Yeah, hmph. Not illegal, though. Anyway, you know much about the place? The pub?"

He shrugs. "Not really. Why?"

"It's done really, really well as a business. Very strong revenues. Very strong. It serves food and sells booze. But it must be really popular with revenues like that."

"It's located right off the interstate. I know that much." Blair opens the file. "So I suppose with a name like that, it probably draws a lot of one-off customers — travelers. Plus the local town regulars. Shit, what do I know about restaurants?"

"Well, I don't know much, either," says Becky. "But I do look at a lot of financials. This place is doing better than most."

Blair looks over the numbers. "Yeah, seems like it. You're thinking, what, he's laundering money?"

She shrugs. "It's an ideal vehicle. Personally, if I were going to launder money, a restaurant would be my first choice. A combo restaurant and bar, actually. Drinks are so easy to fudge. But I can't tell if there's laundering just by looking at financials."

"Got it."

"You see who's preparing his tax returns, though?"

"No. Who?"

She sighs. "Down in the corner, dumbass."

He finds it. "David Bowers is doing his own corporate tax returns?"

"He sure is. Now, that's not anything *necessarily* suspicious, either. But if I were laundering money, I wouldn't just pick a restaurant and bar—I'd also do the tax returns myself."

"Okay, what else?"

"David Bowers is paying himself at least a half a mil a year. Pretty nice coin for a place like Hemingway Grove."

"Shit, I'd take that up here in Chicago."

"Me, too, pal. One year it was as high as seven fifty. He varies it. But never less than five hundred a year. Awfully good pay for a guy running a bar and restaurant. Just sayin'. That's probably how he was able to build his house with cash." She looks at Blair. "Did you know that? That he has no mortgage on his new house, paid for it in cash?"

"Yeah, I know that," says Blair.

Her eyes narrow. "You know that. So you've been looking at this guy already."

He lifts a shoulder. "Need-to-know, Beck."

She wags a finger at him, getting more comfortable with her thought. "I googled this guy David Bowers. Took me two seconds to find about a thousand videos of him making that dramatic river rescue. Pretty freakin' heroic stuff."

"It was, sure." No sense in being disagreeable on that point.

"Made his face go viral," says Becky. "I'm thinking maybe some facial recognition technology with the Bureau might have picked something up."

Blair blinks and tries to keep a straight face.

"Meaning you think you know who this guy is," she adds. "Not that you'll tell me."

"Not that I *could*," he counters. "I mean, even if, hypothetically, you were right."

She smiles, shakes her head. "And you're still gonna pretend this isn't about Michael Cagnina?"

"Beck, I never — I never said one way or the other."

"For fuck's sake, Frankie. I'm, like, seven months from retirement. I'm not looking to get in on anything that's gonna get me whacked. I don't even carry a service weapon anymore. I got one foot out the door. I'm gonna take a consulting job with a bank and live the good life any day now." She leans forward. "I won't tell anyone. Just let me live vicariously through a former partner."

"Okay, fine, Beck. But tell me first—what makes you ask?"

She chuckles. "You mean besides the fact that you have Cagnina on the brain? That he's your white whale? Besides that?"

"Yeah, besides that."

"Okay. Besides that. Because I remember, and so do you, Frankie, that we always thought Cagnina managed to stash away some dough before we closed in on him. Right? Didn't we always think that? Like, sixteen, seventeen million dollars?"

"Course I remember."

"So I've got nothing exciting to do here in this gig," says Becky. "And maybe my imagination is getting the better of me. Or maybe it's just my advanced age. But I'm thinking if Michael Cagnina stowed that money away, about the only way he'd ever be able to spend it is if somebody cleaned it for him first."

Blair smiles. Becky was always a smart one.

"I fucking knew it." She slaps her hand down on her desk. "You've found Cagnina's money launderer, haven't you?"

FORTY-THREE

TOMMY MALONE DRIVES BY the Bowers home for the second time. It's past ten in the morning. Nobody should be home. David and Marcie at work, Lincoln and Grace at school.

The snow is a problem. The temperatures have eased slightly around here, starting the thawing process, but there are still plenty of patches of crispy snow on the ground. He'll have to be careful about footprints.

He parks two blocks away and walks. Checks his phone first, the app for his "eye." First time he broke into the Bowers home, before they started setting their intruder alarm, he installed the small device in their mudroom high above the washer and dryer. To the homeowner, a tiny thing hardly noticeable alongside the carbon monoxide detector, barely worth a second glance. But for the intruder, miles away with a remote laptop, there's a nice view of the alarm pad every time someone punches in the code. It's worked for Tommy every time, just as it worked for him when he got inside Hemingway's Pub through the rear door.

He walks slowly, casually, his breath still showing in the air before him—it hasn't warmed up *that* much—and he thinks about how far he's come. From snatching their dog, Lulu, to tossing their coffeepot in the clothes dryer to dropping a dead rat in the boy's Halloween bag to seeing David washing money through that restaurant.

And now this. This will decide it once and for all.

He walks up the driveway, adjusting the neon-orange vest that village workers wear—sanitation, electrical, whatever. The vest and denim jeans and tool belt make everybody think "municipal employee." Without missing a beat, he lifts the latch on the gate and enters the backyard. There are patches of snow on the ground but a clear, if wet, path to the back door.

He gets through the lock easily enough and hears the intruder alarm. He has the code memorized by now; no need to check the app. He punches in the numbers, and the alarm goes silent. He tosses a few dog biscuits to the floor to satiate the yapping dog, Lulu, who remembers him and isn't a fan. More where that came from. This shouldn't take too long.

He pulls the can of spray paint off his tool belt. Red spray paint is a nice touch.

It only takes him thirty seconds to finish the message on the bright white wall.

Lulu is just finishing up the doggie treats when Tommy returns to the alarm pad. He sets the alarm once more, giving him forty-five seconds to close the door behind him before the alarm will turn to a loud shrill.

But he doesn't close the back door behind him. He leaves it wide open.

It won't take long now before he knows for sure.

FORTY-FOUR

KYLE JANOWSKI PULLS HIS car into the Bowers's driveway, the second police vehicle to arrive. He checks the time before he bounces from the car. Coming up on eleven in the morning. The sun has decided to make a cameo appearance, causing him to squint.

Officer Ginny Risely is waiting for him on the driveway. She's probably sorry that the Bowers family lives in her assigned district.

"Everything okay?" he asks her.

"Everything stable," she says. "Okay might be a different story."

"Tell me." Kyle puts his hands on his hips.

"Normal home-intruder alarm call," she says. "Hatch and I respond."

Hatch, meaning Lee Hatcher, her partner.

"We beat the homeowner to the house. Mr. Bowers."

"*Mr.* Bowers," says Kyle. "David?"

"Right. So we're first on the scene. The back door's wide open," she continues.

The door was left open? That's odd.

"So we enter, right? An open door like that, we're gonna go in every time." She looks at him for approval.

"That's right, Ginny. Keep going."

"Well, Mr. Bowers is not far behind us. He walks in, and he's pissed. Or maybe that's too harsh. He's *upset* that we're inside. He couldn't get us out of that house fast enough, Sarge. He didn't even want us to secure the interior. Most people, y'know, they're spooked as hell—they want us to do a walk-through and make sure the bad guys aren't hiding in a closet or something."

"Right, right."

Just then, Kyle can hear them coming around from the rear of the house through the backyard—Officer Hatcher and David Bowers.

Ginny hears them, too. She leans in closer to Kyle. "I saw something in there," she says as Hatch and David come through the gate.

Kyle steels himself. It's been a long time. It shouldn't still affect him.

"Kyle, right?" David extends a hand.

"Hey, David. Good to see you."

"Yeah, good to see you, too. I want to thank your two officers here, getting here so quickly. Totally professional."

"Sure, sure. Just doing their jobs. Two of our best," Kyle adds.

David rubs his hands together. "I can probably take it

from here. No harm, no foul. No real damage. A little spray paint, some dumb kids."

Spray paint. Kyle glances at Ginny. He's getting the same vibe as she did. David seems awfully eager for them to leave. "Well, I'm glad to hear it was nothing serious," he says. He turns to Ginny. "We have enough for a police report?"

"Well, that's the thing," Ginny starts.

"Oh, no need for a police report," says David.

Huh? That doesn't make sense. "Well, for insurance, if nothing else—"

"Nah, I won't bother with insurance. To clean up some spray paint? The hike in premiums isn't worth it. You guys have been great." David starts to backpedal. "Really, thanks for everything. I can take it from here."

And with that, David disappears through the backyard.

"Weird, right?" Ginny says to Kyle.

"Very." Kyle looks at his two officers. "What, did they force entry? That damage alone is worth insurance—"

"If they forced entry, it was a pick," says Ginny. "No damage."

"And they spray-painted."

"Yeah, they spray-painted," says Hatch. "But what I think? What Ginny and I think?" He looks at Ginny. She nods. "We think he knew the alarm code. We think he picked the lock, disarmed the code. Then he reset it when he left."

"Why do you think that?" Kyle asks.

Ginny this time. "An alarm's going off, you know you

don't have much time inside, right? The cops will be coming quickly. And he took the time to write a note in spray paint. That doesn't seem like something you do if you're in a hurry to take off."

"Oh, they wrote a note? They didn't just spray around?"

"No, they didn't. It was a note. But here's the thing, Sarge. He disarms the alarm and leaves a note, spray-paints it on the wall. Right?"

"Okay..."

"Yeah, but then before he leaves, he resets the alarm—but leaves the back door wide open."

Oh. Right. Kyle's tracking their thinking now. "He resets the alarm but keeps the door wide open. So after a brief grace period—like thirty seconds, a minute, whatever—that alarm is set, and it will detect the open door and go off again, full bore."

"Right, and the cops will come. Just like we did."

"Whoever did this," says Hatch, "we think he wanted us to come."

"But...why would he want the cops to come?"

They both raise their shoulders. It doesn't make sense.

"Okay, well—what does the note say?"

Ginny smirks. She pulls out her phone. "I'll text you the picture I took," she says.

FORTY-FIVE

TOMMY MALONE SITS AT a restaurant a mile away from the Bowers house. His earbud is in as he listens to the sounds from the police scanner. Listening in a town like Hemingway Grove is a lot easier than listening to the chatter in a place like Chicago.

"All units, we have a home-alarm distress signal at 343 Cedar, patio door. That's 343 Cedar."

"Unit 14 responding."

"Copy that, 14."

Tommy takes a sip of his soda, pulls the lettuce out of his turkey BLT.

"Unit 14 to Dispatch. The patio door is open. We've announced our office with no response. We're heading inside."

"Copy that, 14."

"Dispatch, contact Sergeant Janowski per his direction."

Tommy perks up. Sergeant Janowski. Per his direction? Sergeant Janowski has some special interest in the Bowers family?

"Dispatch to unit 19. Dispatch to unit 19."

"Dispatch, this is unit 19."

"Sergeant, Officer Risely is responding to a home-alarm distress call at 343 Cedar and requested you be notified."

"Copy that, Dispatch. Unit 19 responding."

The plot thickens. He finishes the fries, the only thing on his plate worth eating, and sips his Coke.

"Dispatch, this is unit 14 at 343 Cedar Lane. The homeowner advises he does not wish to file a report. We're terminating."

Checkmate.

Tommy closes his eyes. He knew it. He knew it all along.

David Bowers didn't want to report this. He wanted to downplay what happened. He didn't want them to see the note. He probably wanted the cops out of that house as soon as possible.

He picks up the cell phone and dials the number.

"It's him, boss," he says. "We fucking found him."

FORTY-SIX

KYLE JANOWSKI DRIVES AWAY from the Bowers house with more questions than answers. Who is doing this to the Bowers family? Is he right about David? And how does Camille Striker fit into the equation?

And what about Marcie? How much does she know?

His phone rings. Officer Risely, whom he just left at the Bowers house. He puts it on speakerphone. "Hey, Ginny. Everything okay?"

"Yeah, Sarge, I just forgot to tell you. You asked me to look into that lease at the apartment building? Camille Striker?"

"Right."

"Turns out David Bowers is paying for it. Month to month. Told the landlord she was his cousin."

"Thanks, Ginny." Kyle punches out the phone.

Who the hell is Camille Striker? She lived in Chicago most of her life. He knows her professional background but not much more.

But what she does—or at least did—for a living can't

be a coincidence. That and the fact that ever since she arrived in town, strange things have been happening to the Bowers family.

He finds the number and dials it, still on speakerphone.

"This is Ollie."

"Agent Grafton, it's Sergeant Janowski from the Hemingway Grove PD."

"Sure, Sergeant. Remember, it's Ollie. Or Graf."

"Right, sorry. Ollie. Ollie, can I bother you with another question on that same topic we discussed?"

"Silas Renfrow, you mean."

"Yes, exactly," says Kyle. "Would you happen to remember if Silas Renfrow had a girlfriend or wife?"

FORTY-SEVEN

"WELL, YOU'RE IN GOOD health, no question. You're doing everything right. You're taking the prenatal vitamins. Your diet is the right one, and you're exercising just the appropriate amount. But we know it's still very early." Dr. Morales, a middle-aged woman herself, looks over her glasses at Camille. "So we keep our expectations at an even keel, right?"

"Right. Sure." Camille hears herself saying the words but isn't sure she believes them. At age forty, she didn't think she'd ever have a child. She wasn't planning to have one, either. But ever since she got the news from the at-home test, waiting those agonizing five minutes and then finding two pink lines, not one, on the tiny face of the tester—ever since then, the idea of being a mother has slowly grown and taken shape, just like the child itself, to the point where she can't imagine being anything *but* a mother now.

But she knows the risks at her age. And she isn't quite at

three months, even. It is way too early for her to have her hopes this high. The good doctor is right.

"Do you have help?" Dr. Morales asks. "Is the father in the picture?"

Camille lets out a small laugh. "How much time do you have?"

"None of my business. Just wondering in terms of help—"

"I would say he's in the picture." Camille rocks her head from side to side. "How much in the picture is the real question."

"Okay. Got it."

"He's married. Not to me."

Camille catches herself. Why did she just say that? Why would she volunteer that information to someone who, if not a complete stranger, certainly isn't a close friend?

Probably *because* she isn't a close friend. And she's sworn to secrecy.

Or maybe pregnancy does something to your social filters. Her moods lately. Though she's kind of enjoyed losing the filters.

"I see. Well." The doctor puts down her laptop. "I'd just like you to have a support network—that's the only reason I ask."

"I'm good." She's not sure why she said that, either. *Good* is probably not the right word. *Scared, uncertain, shaky*—all those words fit better.

She makes her next appointment at the front desk. "Congratulations!" the receptionist says to her, a little more loudly and enthusiastically than Camille would have liked. *Why don't you announce it to the whole waiting room?*

The waiting room itself holds only two people—one a young woman, white, with a long brown ponytail, who is reading a book. The other, a Black woman who is visibly pregnant, her young boy sitting next to her watching some kind of electronic screen. Nobody seems to be paying much attention to Camille.

She returns to her car in the parking garage and heads back toward Hemingway Grove. David set her up with a doctor in HG, but she'd prefer Dr. Morales, who's been her ob-gyn for more than a decade.

She planned the appointment for noon in Chicago so she could avoid rush-hour traffic returning to Hemingway Grove. She travels the ninety miles in less than two hours, mostly highway travel, finally exiting onto the ramp for HG, passing Hemingway's Pub along the way, with its shiny sign and neat landscaping. She turns into the ground-level parking lot in her apartment building.

Waiting there, leaning against a police cruiser, is Sergeant Kyle Janowski.

She gets out of her Jeep and looks at him with raised eyebrows. "Officer Janowski." Using the inferior rank again. "What a nice surprise."

"Afternoon, Ms. Striker," he says. "How was your doctor's appointment?"

FORTY-EIGHT

"LET ME GUESS," CAMILLE says. "The young woman in the ponytail in the waiting room. You had me followed."

"Just doing my due diligence. You're within your rights to refuse to talk to me, as you seem to know all too well." Sergeant Janowski shrugs. "I'm within my rights to find my answers other ways."

"Like... by violating my privacy."

He squints into the sunlight. "See, Ms. Striker, I'm pretty much done fucking around." He levels his stare on her. "There are things happening in my town. Things that aren't right. And I'm afraid they're about to get worse."

"Such as?"

"I have a theory, Ms. Striker. Wanna hear it?"

"Does it matter if I do?" She smirks at him.

"Sure. You could tell me to go fly a kite, which is pretty much what you did the last time I tried to talk to you. You could walk away right now, and I couldn't stop you. But you're not going to walk away." His turn to smirk. "You want to know what I'm thinking."

Maybe she's underestimated this guy. Probably her bias as a city girl, making this guy for a lightweight, a small-town hayseed. Kyle Janowski looks the part through and through—born and raised here, a varsity football player and decent student who never dreamed of venturing far from the place he's always called home. But who is she to judge or make assumptions? Any woman who has had to make it in the professional world should know about stereotypes. That's her mistake. She won't make it again.

"It's a free country," she says. "I've got a minute."

"That's what I thought." The sergeant nods. "Something is happening to the Bowers family. Little things at first. Things being moved around their house. Their dog was stolen but then returned a few hours later. Someone started their barbecue grill one night. Someone dropped a dead rat in the little boy's Halloween bag. Someone's screwing with them, basically. Not hurting them. But screwing with them. Right?"

"Go on."

"Then it escalates to break-ins. Break-ins to their house. This last one, this morning—they sent the Bowers family a message."

"What message?" She catches herself, seeming too eager.

"Oh, I think you know what the message was," says Janowski. He gives her a moment to comment, then continues. "Anyway, this theory of mine—I asked you before if you ever heard the name Silas Renfrow. Care to answer that question this time?"

"No."

"Well, he's a hitman for the mob. Specifically, a hitman for Michael Cagnina. The authorities believe that Silas Renfrow was murdered before he could testify against Cagnina. But there's kind of an unofficial theory circulating that Silas Renfrow didn't die in that detention center. He staged the whole thing and escaped. And my theory? My theory is that Silas Renfrow is alive and well and living in Hemingway Grove."

Jesus, she thinks. *I really did underestimate this guy.*

She looks out over 1st Street. Light traffic, cars on their way to pick up children from school, maybe do some shopping or go to a medical appointment. All oblivious to what's happening in this town.

"My theory says that David Bowers is Silas Renfrow," he continues. "And if there's a wanted assassin living in my town, I kinda want to know that. You understand."

She doesn't answer. She's wondering how good a poker face she has.

"Now, if my sources at the FBI are correct—and I'm pretty sure they are—the word is that Silas Renfrow had a sweetheart. A woman whose ballpark age now would be about forty. Just like you."

She zips up her jacket as the wind picks up. More than anything, it's something to take the focus off her expression. It's getting harder to seem unaffected by what he's saying.

"Forty and never married," he adds.

"Sounds like quite a story you have there, Officer. I'm

forty and single, so I must be the girlfriend of some hitman who's believed to be dead."

Now Janowski goes quiet for a time, waiting for her to elaborate. But she won't. She won't say anything more than necessary.

"Y'know, the feds could never figure it out, how that detention center got raided and all those US marshals and witnesses got killed. It was a top-secret location. Everyone thought there was someone on the inside. A mole. In fact, way I hear it, every agent involved got questioned, and a lot of reputations and careers were destroyed."

"Sorry to hear that."

"Are you?" He angles his head. "Camille, your background is tech support. You're a computer girl, right?"

"Used to be, yeah."

"Yeah, but you didn't work for some big company or some freak internet startup. All that high-tech stuff you did? You did it for the US Marshals Service in Chicago."

She breaks eye contact. She will never look at a small-town cop the same way again.

"All those agents being investigated to see who the mole was, the one who helped Cagnina's boys attack that secret detention facility," says the sergeant. "I'll bet they never once looked at some bureaucrat sitting in a little cubicle in front of a computer in a building on South Dearborn in Chicago."

She finds herself shaking her head.

"You helped him, Camille," he says. "You used all your tricky tech skills, unlocking back doors and breaking through passwords and all that computer stuff—you found the secret location, didn't you? And you told Cagnina. You helped your boyfriend escape. And you found a spot for him to relocate, not too close to Chicago but close enough."

"No," she whispers.

"Why he married Marcie I don't know yet. Good cover, I suppose. And it worked, right? For years. Until David goes and rescues that drowning man and his face goes viral. Some facial-rec software hits on the image. Your boyfriend, Silas, is suddenly exposed—among others, to Michael Cagnina, fresh out of prison. How'm I doing so far?"

You're doing exceptionally well, she thinks. And it's getting progressively harder to play dumb.

FORTY-NINE

HE HAS HER. KYLE knows it. He can read it all over her face, no matter how defiant she tries to appear. She's like a boxer taking blow after blow and not fighting back.

"Tell you what I don't get yet," he says. "Why is Cagnina screwing with your boyfriend now? What beef does he have with Silas? Or, asking the same thing a different way—why is Silas hiding from Cagnina?"

Camille is still putting up her best front, but the look of resignation, if not outright defeat, is all over her. She brushes away a strand of hair and looks out over traffic.

He's not without sympathy here—she's pregnant, for Christ's sake, and David is obviously the father—but he doesn't have time for sympathy. If the mob has come to Hemingway Grove, he needs to know.

"I mean, from my view, Camille—you'd think, after Silas killed all those witnesses against him, Cagnina would want to pin a medal on Silas's chest. But instead, he's screwing with him. Toying with him. All that shit he's pulled. Like he's trying to prompt him or flush him out. He's trying to do it under the radar, low-key, subtle. The mob isn't usually known for its subtlety."

That actually prompts a brief smile, at least a relaxation of her expression. And with that, apparently, a shift in her focus, as if she's shaken out of a trance.

"I have to go," she says. "I can't help you. Talk to David Bowers if you have questions about David Bowers. I'm sorry."

"No." Kyle steps in her path. "This has to stop before there's violence. You're pregnant, Camille. Do you really want violence right now? Tell me I'm right. Or tell me where I'm wrong. Tell me what I'm missing. Tell me *something* before it's too late."

"I'm … I'm sorry, Sergeant. I have to go. I'm sorry." She pushes past him and heads into the building.

FIFTY

SPECIAL AGENT FRANCIS BLAIR opens an extra button on his flannel shirt, revealing more of the black T-shirt underneath. Checks his cover outfit once more in the bathroom mirror. He looks the part of a trucker, a longtime union guy who's now a crook, a thief.

He'll be glad when this is over. All the rigmarole a UC has to go through—living in a different apartment, not his own; memorizing his cover; looking over his shoulder every time he steps out of his cover and returns to his normal life; wondering, every time he enters the FBI building on Roosevelt, whether someone might snap his photo.

It's been eleven months now, living in this shitbox of a rental unit in Ukrainian Village. The heist is next week. He can't wait for the sting to go down so he can return to his normal life and just be Special Agent Francis Blair.

Or does he? He looks again in the mirror—a fifty-five-year-old man, a guy who should be a special agent in charge by now, or at least an ASAC, but he's not even a supervisor. Nothing more than a line agent at his ripe old age, a washout, relegated to undercover on a Customs task force, a promising young agent whose career was derailed by a mobster named Michael Cagnina.

He hears his phone buzz—not his cover phone but his real one, plugged into a charger in the small kitchen area. He's surprised when he sees the name on caller ID.

"Ollie Grafton?" he answers. "How long has it been?"

"Special FX!" Ollie replies.

Right—he forgot that Graf used to use that nickname for Blair, riffing off his initials. They go through some small talk, Graf ribbing Blair about still being in Organized Crime, Blair asking him if he's worn out the rocking chair yet in retirement down in Chatsworth.

"Listen, reason I'm calling," says Graf, "seeing as how you're the only one from the Cagnina team still at the Bureau. There's a cop from Hemingway Grove just paid me a visit the other day. Followed up with a phone call today. Asking some interesting questions."

Hemingway Grove? That doesn't sound good.

"Questions about none other than Silas Renfrow," says Grafton. "Is that a blast from the past or what?"

FIFTY-ONE

"NO, GRACE," I SAY into my earbuds as I pull out of the parking lot. It's Wednesday, and I'm still on edge. "We talked about this. I'm picking you up from school. Don't walk home."

"Why not?"

How about because I said so? Does that ever work anymore?

Better than the real reason—I'm freaked about that car watching our house last week around three in the morning. Because I don't want the kids coming home before I'm there. Because I'd like to have armed escorts follow them everywhere they go until I know what the hell is happening to our family.

"Just . . . wait for me, Grace. You and Lincoln. I'll be there in ten minutes."

My stomach aching, and not from hunger, I navigate around some cars in traffic, being more impatient than usual. I'm halfway to the school when I see flashing lights behind me. A cop pulling me over? Now? Great.

I pull over to the side of the road on 3rd Street. I retrieve my license and registration. Was I speeding? I probably was.

In the rearview mirror, I see a familiar face approaching.

I buzz down the window. "Kyle?"

He leans in, jaw set, his mouth a straight line. Upset at least, if not angry.

"You were speeding and committed improper lane changes, just for the record," he says. "It's a valid stop."

Probably so, but that's not why he's pulling me over.

"I have to get my kids," I say. "Can we make this fast?"

"Can we make this fast? Sure, Marcie, we can make this fast. Here's fast for you. Have you been playing me all along?"

"I don't—huh?" I put the car into Park and shake my head. "I don't under—"

"You know why people are doing things to your family, don't you? You're acting as if all this bizarre stuff is happening and you have no idea why." He makes a show of it with his hands. "But you know why. Right?"

"Kyle." I reach out, but he steps back.

"Put your hands on the steering wheel, Marcie."

"Are you kidding?" I search his face but find nothing suggesting it's a joke.

"That's a lawful order from a sworn officer. Hands on the steering wheel. You're a former defense lawyer, right? You know the drill."

"Um. Oh-kay." I wrap both hands around the steering wheel. "I am no longer a threat to your safety, Sergeant.

Now would you please tell me what you think I've done or what you think I know?"

My concern edging toward anger, too. But my heart is racing. Kyle knows something that I don't.

He leans in again, his face coloring. "You brought this to our town. You brought *him* to our town."

"Brought *who* to our town? Kyle, what the hell are you talking about?"

"Your husband," he snaps. "Tell me his name."

"His name? You mean like his full name? David Christopher Bowers."

He stares at me for what seems like forever, searching my face, while he seethes. I've known Kyle most of my life. He's always been physical—a wrestler and football player, a handyman, later a cop—but his demeanor was always genial. Probably too laid-back for my liking at the end of the day. But in all those years, I have never seen pure rage on his face, as I do now.

"He was an orphan, right?" he says. "Parents died in a house fire when he was a toddler? So any photos of him with Mom and Dad would've burned up. No phone cameras back then, no cloud backups. So no photos of him with his parents. That's convenient."

"Kyle," I say, surprised at the weakness in my voice.

"Then, what, he bounced around foster homes? So nobody he'd call Mom or Dad or Stepmom and Stepdad or any family at all. Probably no photos, or at least no photos he kept. Also convenient. Basically, no evidence at all of his childhood."

I shake my head. "You're saying...you're saying David isn't really..."

Overload. Failure to compute. This can't be right. This isn't true. But he seems so sure of himself.

"Marcie, I am going to give you one more chance." Kyle draws out each word, his voice shaking. "This time, I want David's *real* name."

FIFTY-TWO

DAVID BOWERS BENDS OVER at the waist, hands on his knees. Behind him, the rear door of Hemingway's Pub. "He really said that?" he whispers. "Silas Renfrow?"

"He really said that." Despite herself, Camille is tempted to feel sorry for David, who looks utterly broken and terrified. "Sergeant Janowski has proved to be a pretty quick study."

David straightens up, puts his hands on his head, looks up at the darkening sky. If he's looking for divine intervention, he's out of luck. David made his own bed.

"You've been wishing this away, David."

He nods, finally looks at her. "That's exactly what I've been doing. Hoping if I denied it, to myself and everyone else, it would go away. I figured nobody could prove anything, right? So just deny, deny, deny. Nothing else made sense."

All things considered, she thinks, that probably was as good a play as anything else. But now it's over. David can clearly see that now.

Camille feels a wave of queasiness, takes a step to steady herself.

"Still with the nausea?" David looks at her.

"Still with the nausea."

"How's the baby doing?"

"Fine."

David shivers, rubs his arms. It can't be warmer than thirty degrees out here, and all he has on is a flannel shirt and khakis. But his nerves must be playing a role, too.

"You're going to tell Marcie everything," she says.

He nods. "No choice now."

"Everything," she repeats.

"Yeah, everything. It's gonna...it's gonna kill her." He blows out air. "It's gonna kill her."

"Give her some credit. She's a strong lady."

David heads toward the door, his posture slumped, a defeated, broken man. Then he turns back to her. "How long we known each other, Cam?"

"Oh, jeez." She looks up.

"All that time." He puts out a hand. "All that time, nobody ever knew about our...they never knew about us. They never knew about me. And I swear, I thought nobody ever would."

"And then you had to go save a drowning man in a river."

A grim smirk plays on his face. "No good deed goes unpunished, I guess."

FIFTY-THREE

I LAUGH WHEN I hear the name. Actually laugh. Kyle is obviously not joking, but I laugh anyway. "That's...absurd," I say.

Kyle, still at my car window, holding up traffic on 3rd Street, is having none of it. "I'm done with your crap, Marce, I swear to God I am."

"*My* crap? I think I'd know if I were married to Silas Renfrow."

"My point exactly," he says. "You were his lawyer. You knew him. You're one of the only people who saw his face. He could deny it to anyone else, but you were the one person who would know. So why are you playing this game?"

I blink hard, feeling a jolt. Something sinks inside me.

"What?" Kyle says. "What? *Talk* to me, Marcie—"

"I didn't," I say. "I...never saw his face." I look at Kyle. "He wouldn't let anyone see his face. Not even his lawyers.

We spoke through a solid wall. I saw his eyes. Like, through a peephole. That was it."

I bring a hand to my face. No. It's absurd. Preposterous, right?

Then why is my entire body shaking all of a sudden?

"Silas Renfrow didn't die in that detention center, did he, Marcie?"

Attorney-client attorney-client attorney-client—

"I never—never knew for sure," I manage. "I had my doubts."

"Camille Striker," he says.

"What—who?"

"You don't know that name? Camille Striker?"

I shake my head. "No."

Kyle looks me over, battling with himself, trying to decide whom to trust. "What did you think of that note left on your wall?"

"Note? What note?"

"The note on your foyer—someone broke into your home last Friday."

"*What?*" I almost jump out of my seat. "What are you talking about?"

"You don't know that? David got the call from the alarm company. He didn't—" Kyle's eyes rise, his expression changing. "He didn't tell you."

"No, he didn't tell me. What happened at my house?"

He pulls out his phone. "Nothing was stolen. Nothing was broken. Truth be told, David couldn't get us out of there fast enough."

I don't understand. I don't understand what is happening—

"You said they left a note."

"Yeah, they spray-painted a note on your foyer wall." Kyle holds up his phone. "One of the officers snapped a picture." He hands me his phone.

There it is, in red spray paint across the wall of my foyer, just below the Picasso print:

I know who you are

"Oh, my God," I whisper.

"You really didn't—you didn't know," says Kyle.

"I have to go. I have to go right now." I put the car in gear and drive to the school.

FIFTY-FOUR

GRACE AND LINCOLN BARK at each other in the back seat, something about the PlayStation. Ordinarily, I'd be on them about getting along, about being half as nice to each other as they are to every other person in the world, but right now I feel about as stable as a jug of nitroglycerin next to an open flame.

I pull into the garage and kill the engine. "Wait here," I say. "Wait in the car a minute."

"Why do we have to wait—"

"Because *I told you to wait in the car,* Grace Catherine." I slam the door.

I try to act composed, not race like a madwoman into the house from the garage. It isn't easy. Once inside, I rush to the front of the house, the foyer, and mentally prepare myself as I turn to look at the wall.

It's just a plain white wall, blank except for the Picasso print centered in the middle. A plain white wall—but with a nice shiny fresh coat of paint.

I sink to the floor, a burn rippling through my chest, feeling like up has suddenly become down and down is now up.

David painted over the words. He hid this whole incident from me and covered up the message.

A message from someone who knows who he really is, a category of people that apparently does not include me.

My husband has been lying to me. All these years, my husband has been lying to me.

FIFTY-FIVE

"GRACE, I'M SORRY I snapped at you. Both of you, please clean out your lunch boxes. Lincoln, cello before dinner. Grace, piano."

I say this while gathering my bag from the car so the kids won't see my face directly, won't see the tears, won't notice the makeup smeared on my face.

The kids jump out of the car and head inside. They expect me to follow them. But I do not. Instead, I pull down the ceiling ladder and climb up into the attic above the garage.

Dark and creaky, a cold, open space, filled with Christmas decorations and old boxes. When I reach the top of the stairs, I find the switch to turn on the single lightbulb in the center of the space.

I walk carefully, navigating the haphazardly placed boxes, there being no need for order up here, every footstep producing a groan from the wooden floor. I veer around the boxes marked ORNAMENTS, step over the one marked WREATHS, angle past the faux Christmas tree.

In the far corner of the attic—personal records, placed in long plastic bins with lids, two rows, each stacked three high.

I separate them and spread them out on the floor. The lids identify the contents: GRACE AGES 0–3, LINCOLN AGES 0–3, and so on, all written in black Magic Marker on masking tape. There is one bin marked TAXES/FINANCES.

Since I married David, I have never done our taxes or scrutinized our finances. A box containing this information would be the last one he'd expect me to open.

I don't want to do this. I can't believe the path of my life has swerved in such a way that I need to do this. But I do.

I pry open the top of the bin. Inside are large legal-size envelopes, each fully stuffed, the tax year noted in Magic Marker.

I open the most recent one, pulling out nearly a hundred pages of documents and forms. W-2s and spreadsheets, estimated-payment vouchers, records of charitable contributions clipped together. Nothing. I stuff them back in the envelope.

I work in reverse chronological order, back to the previous year, then the year before that, finding the same sorts of documents, same results.

I comb through the rest of the envelopes and find one marked TAX YEAR 2008.

Years before I knew him. Again, probably the last envelope in this box that I would be expected to check.

I remove the contents. They are not tax forms.

First, inside a plastic sheath, are several copies of his birth certificate. A certificate of live birth, embossed with a seal. David Christopher Bowers, born in Chippewa County Hospital in Montevideo, Minnesota, mother Roberta Ann Bowers, father Edward Orleans Bowers.

A certificate from the Chippewa County Home for Boys, the orphanage where David lived for several years. A certificate of transfer to temporary care, signed by a guardian ad litem after David went to live with the first of several foster families.

All this fake, Kyle would say. The birth certificate, the orphanage certificate, the GAL transfer—none of it real, all of it doctored.

Next, two pages plucked from a photo album, three photos a page, stuffed in individual plastic pouches, three-hole punches on the side of each page.

The first page, photographs of three people at some celebratory event. Seemingly a mother, father, and son, posing for photos.

An older man in a suit and tie with gray curly hair, a roundness to his cheeks, a slight paunch at the midsection. An older woman, probably late forties or early fifties, light-complected with dark hair pulled back, wearing a long sparkly dress. In between them a younger man—a boy, really—maybe high school age or college, wearing a tie pulled down from the collar, his arms around the man and woman.

The young man would pass for a relative of David but not David himself. He is heavyset, with a wider nose, ears that protrude off his head, brown eyes instead of blue, and a mess of curly dark hair.

But David has no relatives. He is an only child, as were his mother and father. No siblings, aunts, or uncles.

I channel Kyle's voice: *How convenient.*

Okay, think harder. Looking at these photos, comparing them to David now: he could have lost weight, obviously, since this photo. And the curly hair? He's always shaved his head, ever since I knew him. He said it was because his hairline was receding and he liked the look of it shaved. Whatever. That's not the point right now.

The added weight and curly hair don't mean this boy isn't David. But the nose and protruding ears—those would require surgery.

But with surgery...yeah, maybe. This could be a childhood photo of David—

"No," I say quietly but firmly. No way. This is all crazy. I may not be able to recognize Silas Renfrow's face, but I would recognize his *vibe.* He was a ruthless killer. David couldn't have faked that away—not completely, not forever.

Have some faith in yourself, Marcie. You'd know the difference between a loving family man and a cold-blooded assassin.

Right?

I know who you are, the spray-painted note said. Am I missing the meaning?

The only other page: three more pictures of the same three people, but earlier in time. The boy younger, maybe eleven or twelve, in a baseball uniform holding a trophy, the mother and father beside him, hamming it up for the camera.

I breathe out a sigh. I'm getting nowhere. Nowhere except a train to insanity.

Then I notice, behind the two pages of photos, a manila envelope. Seemingly nothing inside. I shake it and hear a small rattle. Open it up.

Keys. Keys to safe-deposit boxes. Five in total.

Tiny cards attached to each by a string, bearing the typewritten words `Prinell Bank` followed by a number. `Prinell Bank #323`, `Prinell Bank #324`, and so on.

That's not our bank. I've never heard of that bank.

David has five safe-deposit boxes I don't know about.

FIFTY-SIX

IT DOESN'T HAPPEN ALL at once. It takes time.

Time, first, sitting absolutely still up in the attic in the near dark with that one flickering lightbulb, staring at those safe-deposit-box keys. Keys literally and metaphorically to things unknown, a different world, a different life, perhaps. I don't know, not yet. But I do know this: there is no legitimate reason that a person would need five different safe-deposit boxes. But there are plenty of illegitimate reasons.

Then snapping out of my funk and heading back downstairs. Cooking shrimp and risotto for dinner and chopping broccoli and tossing it into a pan with garlic and soy sauce and burning the absolute shit out of my finger.

Then opening my laptop after dinner, the kids off, more likely than not, to their screens, their phones, texting with friends or playing games or watching videos, things on which I would normally crack down as Cop Mom but that tonight provide me with welcome space, solitude, time to think about what I know to be true about my life and what I do not.

The laptop. Not hard to find Prinell Bank online. It's in Champaign, home of our state's flagship university and just an hour's drive from here. David could easily drive there and back in any given day, sneaking away from the pub without my ever knowing it.

And then typing the words *Michael Cagnina* into a search engine. I don't know why it didn't occur to me that this man, a man I never met, never laid eyes on in the flesh, could be the source of all this crazy stuff happening to our family. I knew he'd been released from prison within the past year. And yes, I always suspected that his former assassin, my former client Silas Renfrow, had escaped that detention center in Rockford.

But no, whether it should have or not, it never once crossed my mind. When I walked away from Howard Shimkus and left Millard Halloway and moved back here to HG, I put anything regarding Michael Cagnina in the rearview mirror. Sure, I heard he was convicted of tax evasion. Everyone in the country heard about that. Beyond that, I had no interest in hearing his or Silas's name ever again. I had no interest in learning another single fact about any of those people.

But now I do. So I type on my keyboard. I learn. And I think. I think about David, everything I know about him, everything I know about us. An hour that turns into two hours that turns into three.

And finally, it clicks. It sends another burn through my

chest, jump-starts my pulse, forces my eyes shut, sends tears slithering down my cheeks once more.

I let them fall for a short time, listening with one ear for any sound of the children coming down the stairs. They can't see me like this. What this will ultimately mean for them I do not know. I will protect them. That will be job number one—doing anything and everything to protect my children. Even if it costs me everything else.

I put the kids down at nine thirty. Lincoln is restless, wanting Daddy to be here to tuck him in. Grace is more concerned with making sure the unreliable power cord to her iPad is working and that the device is charging overnight, because its battery is very low and she has to take a test on that tablet during first period tomorrow.

I hold my breath through all that, shoving everything else out of my mind, determined to make tonight's lights-out a routine one, nothing unusual, just the Bowers family doing what the Bowers family does.

Because something tells me that this may be their last night of normal.

And now I will simply wait. I will sit in the family room with a glass of wine. And I will wait for David—or, more accurately, the man who's always called himself David, who's been lying to me for more than a dozen years—to come home.

FIFTY-SEVEN

DAVID BOWERS LEAVES THROUGH the rear exit, as always, his coat on, scarf wrapped around his neck, watch cap on as well. He closes the rear door but, instead of leaving, lets out a long breath and rests his head against the door. A tough night for him, apparently. It's about to get tougher.

Tommy Malone appears from the shadows, his gun drawn. "Don't move, David," he says. "Don't move."

David jumps at the sight of Tommy, whose face is concealed by a black balaclava—covering him from the neck up, including his hair, leaving only holes for his eyes and mouth. David's eyes move to the gun, an HK45 with a long suppressor.

"Don't move," Tommy repeats. "Don't make me shoot you."

David manages to get his hands in the air, his breathing heavy, exhaling puffs into the frozen air outside.

"Michael Cagnina says hi, David."

David shakes his head. He's not going to give it up easily. "Who?"

"Michael Cagnina. He's hoping to get back in touch with—"

"I don't know that name."

"Speaking of names," says Tommy, "can we stop pretending yours is David? How 'bout I just call you—"

"My name *is* David. David Bowers."

Damn, if Tommy didn't know better, he might buy this act. David's had a lot of practice playing pretend.

"What—what do you want?" says David. "You're here to rob me?"

"You know why I'm here, pal." Tommy takes another step forward. "I'll shoot you if I have to, but I don't wanna."

"Look, you can have my wallet. I have money inside the restaurant. I can open it up. You can have whatever you want. I'll open it up."

He reaches into his pocket for his keys.

"No," says Tommy. "Calm the fuck—"

David tosses a ring of keys to Tommy.

And then, as Tommy's attention is momentarily diverted, David makes his move.

The problem with a suppressor on a gun—it keeps a gunshot nice and quiet, but it doubles the length of the firearm. David pushes down the suppressor with his left hand as he lunges at Tommy. Tommy moves backward instinctively, but not before David manages to connect the crown of his head against Tommy's mouth, a partially successful head butt.

The gun goes off with a *thwip!*

David lets out a grunt as he falls into Tommy. Tommy manages to keep his balance as he steps back, David collapsing to the ground at his feet.

And a pool of blood forming beneath David.

"Look what you—look what you fucking made me do!" he cries.

Then he turns and runs from the parking lot.

FIFTY-EIGHT

MIDNIGHT. MY SECOND GLASS of wine. I won't have another. I could use a little liquid courage for what's coming, but I want a clear head.

My phone buzzes. I pick it up, expecting it to be David. It's not.

"Kyle," I say.

"Marcie, you're okay?" His voice urgent, breathless.

"Yeah—yes, I'm—"

"I'm on my way to you," he says. "I'm bringing Officer Risely with me."

I get to my feet. "What...what hap—"

"Marcie, listen to me. David's been shot. He's in an ambulance on his way to St. Benedict's."

"He..." I search for words. "Is he—"

"He's lost a lot of blood. That's all I know. Officer Risely will stay at your house with the kids. I'm almost to you."

"I..." Through the window, I see the reflections of sirens flashing. On automatic pilot, I grab a coat and head to the front door. A female police officer rushes up the front walkway.

"Two kids," I say.

"Grace and Lincoln—I know," she says. "If they wake up, I'll have them call you first thing. Now go. We'll be fine here."

I race to the car and hop in the front seat.

"Is he alive?" I say to Kyle.

"I don't know. Buckle up," he says before he floors the accelerator.

FIFTY-NINE

KYLE PULLS HIS CRUISER right up to the entrance of the emergency department. I'm out the door of his car before I realize it, feeling my feet running toward the double doors.

People everywhere, a busy night, but Kyle takes my arm and badges his way past a door and security. I feel underwater now, unable to comprehend, unable to process, Kyle's voice to some doctor, and then he pulls me along some more, lots of shouting and bumping, twisting and turning, and then my feet are planted and I'm in front of a doctor.

"Mrs. Bowers, I'm Dr. Grant." Bald, like David, with wild bushy gray eyebrows and a long face, the man who is going to tell me. Tell me, tell me, tell me, *tell me*—

"The bullet nicked the femoral artery," he says, pointing to his inner leg. "He's lost a lot of blood. We've managed to stabilize him, but he's going into surgery immediately."

"Is he...what are...what are his...can you save him?"

"That's exactly what we'll try to do, Mrs. Bowers." He touches my arm. "It could be hours before—"

It could be hours before the surgery will be done. Hours before I talk to him. If I *ever* talk to him—

I snap out of my trance, bat and scratch and claw my way through the cobwebs.

"I want to see him." I look at the doctor, then at Kyle. "I want to see him."

"Mrs. Bowers, I'm afraid—"

"I might never talk to him again. Please."

The doctor's expression relents. "Thirty seconds," he says. "Room 4."

My focus suddenly razor-sharp, I race to the door and look in. Blood everywhere, doctors and nurses and assistants, already turning the gurney toward the door. All I see of David is a heavy bandage over his exposed left leg.

"Stop!" I shout.

"She needs thirty seconds with him!" Kyle says. "The doctor said okay. Everyone out! Thirty seconds."

God bless Kyle. A cop says it, they do it.

I part the sea of white coats and surgical scrubs as they leave us alone in the room. I see David. My David. Not my David.

Not my David at all.

He looks twenty years older, withered and weak. He's been intubated, a thick tube in his mouth, an IV in his neck. His eyelids flutter, struggling to open.

When his eyes focus, when he sees me, he grimaces with pain. I put my face close to his. "I know who you are," I say.

I put my lips against his ear, whispering the name so quietly that only he could hear it. No matter the privacy we've been given, nobody else can hear this name.

Then I lean back again, look at him square. "Blink once if I'm right, twice if I'm wrong."

I already know, but I need his confirmation. I need to see him acknowledge the truth once and for all.

He blinks once.

"It was all a lie," I whisper.

His eyes water up.

"Was I... was I a lie?"

He blinks twice. A tear rolls down his face into his ear. He even manages to move his head side to side.

"Okay." I believe him. I do believe that much. He loves me. He loves our kids. He loves our family, what we've created. That is the only thing allowing my voice to stay strong and steady, my legs to stay functional, my brain to stay focused and alert, even now.

"The detention center?" I ask. "That's when you first saw me?"

He blinks once.

I reach into my pocket, remove the ring of safe-deposit keys. "This is where it is?" I whisper.

He blinks once.

I lean down and press my lips against his forehead. "I love you. The kids love you. Don't leave us. Stay alive, mister, for *us*."

He blinks away another tear.

"Mrs. Bowers, we really have to go."

I put out my hand, a stop sign. But he's right. My time with David is up.

"Don't worry about anything else," I whisper to him. "I'll take it from here."

BOOK II

SIXTY

WHEN I WAS IN high school, our health teacher tried to give us an idea of what it's like to care for a baby. She gave us an egg, and we had to carry it with us for a week without ever letting it crack. Everywhere I went, twenty-four hours a day, I had to make sure nothing happened to that egg. Walking to school, sitting down for a meal, getting ready in the bathroom—always I had to preserve that fragile little oval egg.

That's what it feels like now—balancing an egg in the palm of my hand—as I navigate land mines, as the earth quakes beneath me, as I shoulder the winds of a hurricane, as people known and unknown hurl objects at me and try to force me into a fail.

Except that now the precious cargo I hold in my hands is the lives of my children. Everything I do from this point forward must be with an eye toward Grace and Lincoln. I have to keep them safe. I have to prepare them for the possibility of a life without a father and the fact that their lives will never be the same again.

But first, I need to get through this problem, a problem I do not fully understand, one I must navigate without David's help. I don't know who wants what. I don't know whom to trust. I know a few things, and I suspect a few others. I am flying on a wing and a prayer.

All these thoughts run through my mind as I sit inside a bathroom stall in the hospital with the police outside demanding answers to questions—some of which I can't give them, some of which I won't.

I will not think about the fact that the man I have called my husband has lied to me repeatedly over the years—lies of omission, outright lies, you name it. I will not think about the fact that my entire adult life has been a hoax, a fraud. I will not panic. I will not engage in self-pity. I will not even entertain anger.

Those will be for later. I have to remain completely focused and on mission. I have to have eyes in the back of my head. I have to stay two steps ahead of the police and the people who want to hurt us.

What am I willing to do for my kids? It's a question all parents ask themselves—a rhetorical question usually. Would you give your life for your children? Almost every parent would say yes. Would you lie for your children? Almost every parent would say yes.

Would you break the law for your children? Would you kill for your children?

Questions I've never confronted. Never thought I would have to confront. But now I do.

I leave the stall and face myself in the bathroom mirror.

The answer is yes to both questions. I know it now with a certainty that straightens my spine, that sends adrenaline to my every limb. I would break the law for my kids. I would kill for my kids.

Waiting outside the bathroom for me is Sergeant Kyle Janowski, my old flame, the man I once thought I'd marry. Now, first and foremost, he is a law enforcement officer who may or may not have my best interests at heart.

"Ready to talk?" he says.

I am physically tired, emotionally spent, stressed, and unsteady. I'm about the furthest thing from *ready to talk*.

"Ready," I say.

SIXTY-ONE

KYLE TAKES ME INTO a small room inside the hospital, some kind of lounge. There is a couch and a chair and a coffee station, where an old-fashioned glass pot rests on a burner, the smell of overcooked, stale coffee permeating the room. An old radiator with peeling paint hisses, the air almost overbearingly warm.

On Kyle's phone, I watch the grainy black-and-white security footage from behind David's pub, showing the attack. A man wearing a ski mask accosts David as he's locking the rear door. The gun is long—a suppressor is attached—which must have given David the idea of reaching for it and redirecting it. It almost worked, after David tossed his keys to the suspect. David got his hand on the suppressor and even slammed his head into the attacker's face, but the suspect fired the weapon and ended it right there.

"I don't suppose you recognize the assailant." Kyle, who is holding up his phone, pauses it. "With the balaclava and all—the ski mask."

"Oh. No, obviously I don't recognize the man."

"Any idea who it might be?"

"None." As if I'm on autopilot. I don't know who it is, but I have an idea. "Play it again," I ask.

He replays the video clip from the start. It's no fun to watch, David getting shot and writhing in pain as blood gushes from his thigh, hard to see for the second time. But I had to make sure.

And now I'm sure: the assailant didn't want to kill David. That wasn't his plan. He wanted something from David, but not his life.

I look at Kyle. "You actually thought I might recognize this person while he's wearing a mask over his face or a balaclava or whatever you call it?"

"Worth a shot." Kyle lifts a shoulder. "Whether you can see his face or not, do you have any idea who would do this to David?"

The second time he's asked. I shake my head. But of course I do have an idea.

"Probably the same person who spray-painted 'I know who you are' on the wall of your foyer last week?"

I don't answer. Kyle fiddles with his phone. Closes the video and opens something else before turning the phone to me again.

A photo. A photo of the foyer wall in my house as it currently looks, freshly painted to cover up the spray paint.

"I had Officer Risely, the one at your house babysitting? I had her take a picture ten minutes ago," he says. "Looks like somebody went to the trouble of painting over that spray paint pretty darn quickly. Who painted over it?"

Again, I don't answer.

"Was it you, Marcie? Not wanting your kids to see it? Or was it David, not wanting *you* to see it?"

He touches my arm, but I pull it away. "Don't touch me."

"Fine, fine." He raises his hand. "But see, that matters to me, Marcie. Because I believed you when I pulled you over today and you told me you had no idea about that spray-painted message. David hadn't told you. If it were me, in that situation, I'd have told my wife right away. But he didn't. Did he cover up the spray paint, too?"

I'm following him now. If David covered it up, if he repainted that wall, that makes me still in the dark, innocent. He's wondering what role I've played in this. Am I an innocent dupe or a guilty coconspirator?

I decide it's time to take off the victim's hat and put on the lawyer's.

"Are you questioning the wife of the victim," I say, "or interrogating a suspect?"

"Honestly?" Kyle takes a step back. "At this point, I don't know."

I steel myself, look him square in the eye. "Then maybe you should read me my rights, Sergeant."

But then it hits me, the years as a criminal defense attorney returning. I'm not in custody. I'm just standing in a hospital room, free to leave. So he doesn't have to Mirandize me.

Sneaky.

"I'm done here," I say.

Kyle shakes his head. "I don't think so, Marcie."

"No? You're telling me I'm not free to leave? Then arrest me—"

"Oh, you're free to leave," he says. "But you won't."

"No? Just watch me." But something keeps my feet planted. "Why won't I leave?"

He nods to me, plays with his phone. "Because that video of the shooting? You want to see the rest of it, Marcie."

SIXTY-TWO

KYLE REPLAYS THE VIDEO clip, starting it with David collapsing and the masked assailant running out of the camera's range. David, lying helpless by the rear door, desperate, initially clutches his thigh. But then he reaches into his jeans pocket and removes a phone, looks at it, and tosses it.

"That's his phone," says Kyle. "The one registered to his name, I mean."

David then reaches into his jeans pocket again and wrangles out a second phone.

A second phone. David had a second phone. I'd been wondering about that. That late night call he made downstairs in the kitchen, which I overheard, while his cell phone was charging in the bedroom. The words I heard him whisper in a hiss: *It's not that simple, okay?*

"That's his burner phone," Kyle tells me, stating the obvious.

The video rolls on. David pushes a button on the burner

and raises the phone to his ear. A single button, meaning he had the person on speed dial. He talks into the phone for around ten seconds. Then he all but collapses, his head dropping lifelessly against the concrete as he goes into shock, the phone still clutched in his hand.

"Any idea who he called?" Kyle asks.

I let out a breath, look at the floor as the heat rises to my face.

"Not you," he says, again stating the obvious. Goading me. "He knows he might be dying, and his last call isn't to you—"

"Do you have a point?" I snap. "Or do you enjoy being an asshole?"

Kyle puts his phone in his pocket, trying to control his emotions. "Marcie, I promise you, I'm not enjoying one minute of this. Who was he calling?"

Keep it under control, Marcie. Stay on mission.

"I have no idea," I say, though I do.

"Camille Striker." Kyle looks at me for a reaction. "I told you her name earlier today when I pulled you over. You said you didn't know the name."

I wrap my arms around myself, suddenly cold, even though it's quite warm in this room. "And I *still* don't know her name. Is that...is that who..."

"Is that who he called? I don't know yet. Neither phone is registered—not David's or the one he called. Both are burners. Which is interesting right there." He again looks at me for a reaction. "I just sent some detectives to her apartment. She isn't there. We tried to do a real-time trace on that phone, but now it's turned off, conveniently. In case you're wondering—in case you don't already know—Camille lives in the Hampton Apartments, by 1st Street. On a lease. A lease paid for by your husband."

Stay focused. He's trying to get a rise out of you.

I sit on the couch and bury my face in my hands.

"Marcie, the man in the operating room right now is not David Bowers. It's Silas Renfrow. I can't prove it yet, but I will. And Camille Striker is his longtime girlfriend. She was a computer technician in the US Marshals Service back in the day. She found out where Silas's secret location was in Rockford and helped engineer his breakout. She's his girl. She's always been his girl. And now she's pregnant, by the way."

My hands remain over my face, elbows on my knees, as I take all that in. That was his final punch. He wants me to break. Whatever it is I know, whatever it is I suspect—he wants me to spill it. But I can't. Not yet. Not until I'm ready.

"Am I a suspect?" I ask for the second time, this time through my fingers.

"I already told you. I'm still trying to figure that out."

I draw a deep breath, sit up straight, and pat my knees. "I'm not answering any more questions."

I get to my feet and head for the door.

He steps to the side to block me. "Marcie, no. Don't be like that."

" 'Don't be like that?' This isn't high school, Kyle. This isn't a spat. You're a cop, and apparently I'm a suspect. I have rights."

"What..." He cocks his head, looking at me with a

combination of frustration and abject disappointment. "What happened to you, Marce?"

What happened to me? What happened is that my husband is hanging on to his life right now, and I've just come to learn that he's not the man he's always claimed to be. And my entire family is in danger. That's what happened to me.

"I'm going home," I say. "When my kids wake up, I need to be there."

I walk through the emergency department and let them know I'm going home, making sure they have my cell phone for any updates on David. Then I head through the sliding doors into the open air, far chillier than I remember. I don't have a ride. It would take forever to get a cab or an Uber this time of night. But I don't want to be around the police anymore. I'll walk home if I have to.

I'm two blocks away from the hospital, rubbing my arms for warmth at half past two in the morning, seeing my breath hanging in the air, when a car pulls up alongside me. A Jeep whose shape resembles that of the car that was sitting outside my house the other night.

The window buzzes down. I walk over, but not too close, leaning down to see into the car. A woman, about my age, pretty. Long, kinky hair.

"Marcie," she says. "I'm Camille. Do you know who I am?"

I nod. "I have a feeling I do," I say.

SIXTY-THREE

KYLE HOLDS THE PHONE against his ear and replays the audio from the 911 call made earlier tonight. A woman's voice, urgent but calm, businesslike.

"A man's been shot. He's lying in the back of Hemingway's Pub by the interstate. I don't know the address, but he's bleeding out. Send an ambulance."

The call cuts off immediately afterward. The caller doesn't give her name. No way to be certain, but that voice sure sounds a lot like Camille Striker's. That would make the most sense; David called her and told her what happened, and she called 911 for him. But he could have called 911 himself. Why call Camille first? A tearful goodbye? Was Camille his true love and Marcie just his cover story?

Did Marcie *know* she was a cover story? No. Couldn't be. Marcie wouldn't have lived a lie like that. Not Marcie.

He dials Officer Risely, staying at Marcie's house for now, watching her children overnight.

"Hey, Sarge."

"Hey, Ginny. Is Marcie Bowers home yet?"

"Nope. She's not with you?"

"She left a little while ago. Didn't want to answer any more questions. Not sure...not sure what to make of that."

"Want me to take a run at her when she gets home?"

It occurs to Kyle—he drove Marcie here. She didn't have a ride home. She stormed out so quickly that he didn't think to ask if she needed a ride.

"That's okay," he says. "But do me a favor—keep a squad car outside her house tonight."

He punches out the phone.

"Sergeant Janowski?"

Kyle turns at the sound of his name.

A man, roughly shaved, mussed dark hair peppered with gray, wearing a dress shirt open at the collar and blue jeans.

"Special Agent Francis Blair, FBI," he says. "Chicago office."

Blair—that's the name that Ollie Grafton mentioned. The FBI agent who wondered whether Silas Renfrow really died in that attack on the FBI compound in Rockford.

"Thought I might be hearing from the Bureau. You worked the Michael Cagnina case?"

Blair nods. "You have good information. What can you tell me about what happened?"

Kyle gives his best summary of the events of the night, then he turns to his general suspicions about David Bowers.

When he's finished, Blair looks duly impressed. "So you think the guy in the operating room is Silas Renfrow?"

"That's a guess, but an educated one."

Blair nods absently. He looks tired. He must have rushed down here from Chicago when he heard the news. "Well, it's a damn good educated guess, Sergeant," he says. "Let's get his DNA, test it, and prove it."

"I told the doctors to preserve him as much as possible," says Kyle. "And there's blood all over the crime scene—"

Blair makes a face. "You got the clothes he was wearing?"

"Of course."

"Those clothes have blood on them. My team can extract that easily." He nods. "Better I handle it. I can get the results faster."

Good. It will be nice to have some help. Kyle's felt like a one-man operation looking into these matters. With some-one from the Bureau on board—an expert on Michael Cagnina, at that—his confidence is growing. He's going to solve this thing.

"If he really is Silas Renfrow," says Kyle, "you've got him on dozens of offenses, I assume."

"Oh, he's Silas, all right." Blair lets out a loud chuckle. "And once I prove it," he says, "I'm gonna hang a dozen federal M-1s around his neck and personally sit in the front row while they stick a needle in his arm." He looks at Kyle. "That a straight enough answer?"

SIXTY-FOUR

MY CHEST BURNING, I slide into the passenger seat of the Jeep driven by Camille Striker, a woman who has known David longer than I have, who has known a different person from the one I've known, who has known about me all along while I didn't know about her.

She is wearing a flannel shirt with a winter vest over it, but even through the thick clothing I can see that she's a workout fanatic. Her features are soft, though—long eyelashes and a tiny nose.

"You're in danger," she says. "Your family's in danger. Where are your kids?"

"Sleeping at home, with a police car outside my house and a cop sitting inside."

"Okay, good, good." She blows out a breath. "Good."

"I appreciate your concern, but it would have been nice if someone had let me in on the news a little earlier." My sarcasm isn't helping matters, but it's better than putting my hands on her throat, my first instinct.

She starts driving. "The police must be looking for me," she says. "I thought we should talk first." She glances over at me. "I suppose I should say I'm sorry."

"I don't need your apology."

She nods. "Well, for what it's worth, I told him to tell you. All along, I wanted him to tell you. But David—he made a decision. When all this stuff was happening to you guys—someone moving things around in your house, putting a dead rat in your son's Halloween bag, stealing your dog, all that—David figured they were seeing how he'd react. They weren't sure he was their guy. He looked so different than he did before."

That much I can believe after seeing the photos of him I found in the attic. He went from a chubby, brown-eyed, curly-haired kid, with ears that stuck out cartoonishly, to a bald, physically fit, blue-eyed man with his ears pinned back. A lifestyle change and some plastic surgery did wonders for him.

"So he figured his best play was to act like he didn't know what was happening," she continues. "To play dumb, basically. He figured if he ran, if he took you and the kids and fled town, it would be confirming their suspicions. He'd have to be on the run forever."

"He thought he could bluff his way through it."

"Actually, it probably was his best move. The only mistake he made was not telling you."

Exactly. He was hoping to keep all his secrets just that—secrets.

"He thought you might do something rash," she says.

"That you might insist on running. He thought you were safer not knowing."

That was part of it, I'm sure. The other part—he thought I might leave him if I knew the truth.

"What's done is done," I say. I don't have time for hindsight or sorrow or regret or anger. Not now. Later.

"I take it he's in surgery for a while?" she asks. "That's why you're going home?"

I nod.

"Do they have a prognosis?"

"They don't know." I try to block out that fear, shove it into a separate compartment of my brain and lock it up. If I let everything that scares me affect me, I'll become paralyzed. If I let myself be consumed by my feelings for this woman who has shared secrets with my husband, I won't be able to function. I can't let that happen.

I need to learn what she knows. And, more important, what she doesn't know.

"When did it end?" I ask. "Your and David's...'relationship,' should I call it?"

"About...three years ago. He sent me packing."

"Why?" I ask. "Why'd he do that?"

She shrugs. "He said he just wanted to be alone with his family."

I think back. Three years ago. Yes, that makes sense.

Three years ago was when we decided to build the new house, when I pointed at the FOR SALE sign on the vacant lot at 343 Cedar Lane and said, *Here. This is where we should build it.*

"And yet you're back," I note.

"We...kept in touch over the years. I guess it's hard to let go completely."

A light rain falls, pitter-patter, pitter-patter on the windshield. I look out the window and see that Camille is driving in the direction of my house. This time of night, with no traffic, I'll be home in less than ten minutes.

"The police think David is Silas Renfrow, that you're his girlfriend, and that you helped break David out of that detention facility in Rockford," I say.

"I know. I already had a nice visit from that ex-boyfriend of yours, the sergeant."

"What did you tell him?"

"Nothing," she says.

"What are you going to tell him now?"

A smile briefly plays on her lips. "Nothing. I made a vow, and I'm going to keep it. Why? What do *you* think I should tell him?"

"Nothing."

She pulls the car over to the curb, puts it in Park, and turns to me. "Did they get a video of the shooting?"

I nod. "I saw it."

"Do they know who shot him?"

I shake my head. "He wore a ski mask. A bala-something, they called it."

"A balaclava? Right. But...how'd it go down? Was it a hit? What I mean —"

"I know what a hit is, thank you. And no, it wasn't a hit. He was talking to David. David made a move for the man's gun, and it went off."

Camille shakes her head with a hum. "That sounds like David."

Those words slice through me. Another woman, a complete stranger, talking about my husband in such intimate terms.

"But it doesn't make sense," she says. "They had him tonight. The guy had a gun pointed at David. Why not just pull the trigger? If they've finally figured out that David is who they think he is, if their suspicions are finally confirmed—just pull the trigger. That's how the mob usually works. No conversation. No last words. No explanation. Just wham-bam and get the hell out of there. But that didn't happen. Why would the shooter possibly want to speak to David?"

I shrug my shoulders, like I have no idea. But of course I do. And now I've learned something important.

Apparently, David kept secrets from both the women in his life.

Camille doesn't know about the money.

SIXTY-FIVE

TOMMY MALONE TRUDGES DOWN the side of the hill, almost losing his balance as he skids along the paved running path, currently slick with ice. The wind whips through his hair as he moves forward gingerly—there is no light this time of night. Ahead of him, looming like a great monster rising from the river, is Anna's Bridge, still under construction after the accident.

This spot, he assumes, is almost exactly where David Bowers was standing on the night the car went off the bridge and into the Cotton River. A night when David Bowers almost lost his life. A night that would expose him, ultimately, as being someone other than David Bowers.

He pinches the bridge of his nose. The ibuprofen he took is finally starting to kick in. He should've known how strong David would be. And how desperate, too. Now he has a splitting headache and a fat lip to show for it. Jesus, if Tommy hadn't stepped back and avoided the brunt of that headbutt, if David's head had landed just an inch higher and connected with Tommy's nose — who knows how that would've turned out?

From his jacket pocket, he unscrews the suppressor from the HK45 and tosses it overhand into the center of the river. The noise of the turbulent water and whipping wind drowns out all other sound. He doesn't hear or see the long piece of metal hit the water. It just disappears into a murky mist.

He continues walking as he takes apart the firearm itself, removing the slide off the frame, the secondary and mainspring, the disconnector and control lever, the trigger bar and ejector — Frisbeeing them into the river one by one as he walks.

When he's done, when the firearm's in a dozen different pieces, some sinking down to the bed of the river, some light enough to be whisked away by the choppy flow, he stops. Lights a cigarette. Breathes out. Rolls his neck. First job is done — the weapon's gone.

He squats down, trying to control his anger. "Fuck, fuck, fuck."

Shooting David was the *last* thing he wanted to do. Now what? How is he supposed to get the money now, with David in the hospital clinging to life, with all eyes on him and the rest of the Bowers family? All his work trying to be covert, trying to operate under the radar, and now the whole damn town knows that David Bowers has been shot.

There's only one answer, of course, and it won't be easy: Marcie.

He has to find a way to get Marcie alone.

SIXTY-SIX

SERGEANT KYLE JANOWSKI HOLDS out his hand. Special Agent Francis Blair hands him back the phone after watching the footage from the security camera. "Just like you said, Sergeant. No way to identify the shooter. No facial features, and he was wearing gloves, so no prints."

"We're looking for the weapon," Kyle says.

Blair grimaces. "If that guy works for Cagnina, he wouldn't leave the weapon behind. He wouldn't be that sloppy. He's already dumped it."

"What's your gut tell you?" Kyle asks him. "Is everything that's been happening in Hemingway Grove—is this Cagnina's work?"

"Gotta be." Blair parks himself in a chair and rubs his temples. He looks exhausted, Kyle thinks. He recalls everything he read about the Cagnina case, everything he learned from Ollie Grafton, too—the attack on the detention center where Silas Renfrow and the other two witnesses were kept. And then the fallout. Fingers pointing in every direction, blame assigned, careers destroyed.

Including Blair's, Kyle imagines. True, they salvaged the case with the tax-evasion convictions, but the FBI suffered a real black eye with that attack.

"I lost friends in that attack on the detention facility," says Blair. "And after that, do you know how hard it was to get witnesses to cooperate in any mob case? We'd promise them safety, security, and they'd throw Michael Cagnina in our face."

It takes Kyle back to when he was a rookie on the job, and his field training officer took a bullet during a domestic-disturbance call. He remembers sitting in the hospital, holding the hand of his partner's wife, wondering if he should've done something different during that call, if he could have prevented it. The guilt, the worry, was as heavy as anything he'd ever felt in his life.

And *his* partner survived. Blair, he lost friends that day. Kyle can't even imagine.

"So what now?" Kyle asks.

Blair blinks out of his trance, gestures to the evidence sitting next to him, the sealed paper sack containing David Bowers's clothes. "One step at a time," he says. "We know David is Silas, but we need proof before we can act. So I'll run the DNA and confirm it." Blair clears his throat. Sounds like he's got a cold. "In the meantime, I think it's best we downplay the federal involvement. Downplay, as in, I'm not here at all."

Kyle was wondering if that would be the direction Blair

headed. "So our official statement to the media? You want us to say that for now, all we know is that it appears to be a robbery gone wrong?"

"Exactly. The public would believe that. The owner of a restaurant, accosted at gunpoint as he's closing up? Most people, their first thought would be a robbery."

Kyle nods. "But you're not worried about what the public thinks. You're worried about what Michael Cagnina thinks."

"Exactly." Blair pushes himself out of the chair. "Silas Renfrow has been officially declared dead. The Bureau— we're not looking for him. Nobody's looking for him. Nobody's been looking for him for the last decade and a half."

"Except you," says Kyle.

"Well—he's crossed my mind from time to time," Blair concedes. "Like, every single damn day of my life."

This guy seems okay, Kyle thinks. He can't imagine what it would feel like to have a case torture you for fifteen years.

"What's Cagnina's next move?" he asks Blair.

Blair runs his hand over his hair, paces around on that question. "He's been low-key this whole time, right?"

"Definitely," Kyle agrees. "Seems like he's been sending messages to David with all the shit he was doing to their family."

"Right, because he didn't want to call attention. He wanted to be sure David was really Silas Renfrow before he made a move. He's probably been watching him, baiting him, collecting information. Now he thinks he has his man. Thus the gunman tonight."

"But he didn't just shoot him in the head and leave," Kyle notes.

"Right, that's the weird part. So what's his move now, Sergeant? Think like him."

Think like Michael Cagnina? Kyle lets out a chuckle. "Special Agent—"

"Just call me Blair."

"Okay, Blair—the most excitement we get around here are drug busts, maybe an occasional B and E. We don't even have street gangs down here. I'm not sure I'm the guy to be reading the mind of a Chicago mobster—"

"Yeah, well, you were smart enough to come up with a pretty good theory about Silas Renfrow."

Kyle nods. Thinks on it. "To know what Cagnina will do next, we need to know something we don't know. Or at least *I* don't know."

"Which is?"

"What does Cagnina want?" Kyle says. "He could've easily shot and killed David tonight and walked away. But it didn't look like that was the plan. So what the hell does he want?"

Blair wags his finger at him. "That's the question, Sergeant. That's the question."

SIXTY-SEVEN

FRANCIS BLAIR PICKS UP the evidence bag, the sealed brown bag containing David Bowers's clothes. "I'll rush a DNA test on this," he says. "In the meantime, no mention of the FBI, okay?"

"Got it," Kyle says. "Not even to Marcie?"

Blair rubs his neck. He meant what he said—Kyle's a smart guy. Putting together what he put together about Silas Renfrow and Michael Cagnina—that was good police work.

But Kyle's not all the way there. He asked the question a moment ago: *What does Cagnina want?* Why didn't he just kill David and walk away?

There's an answer to that. But Kyle doesn't know the answer.

Kyle doesn't know about the money.

The real question is, does Marcie? Or did David keep it from her?

"What are your thoughts, Kyle? Is Marcie in on this with David or not?"

"God, I…" Kyle shakes his head, frowns. "I've known her my whole life. I just don't see her being a criminal. But maybe I'm too close to it. Maybe I see the girl I grew up with and can't see the person she's become."

Well, that's an awfully honest self-assessment. This guy's as straight as they come.

Blair puts his hand on Kyle's shoulder. "This is important, Kyle. This is for all the marbles. How we handle Marcie depends on whether she's a victim or a coconspirator. So? Did Marcie know David's real identity all this time?"

"I…I…" Kyle wipes at his mouth. "I told her my suspicion earlier today. I told her point-blank that I thought her husband was Silas. At first she laughed. Then she got more serious about it." He poses a hand in the air, trying to find the right words. "I just can't believe she was making that reaction up. I don't think she knew. All this time they were married, I think she thought her husband was just plain old David Bowers."

"Okay, well—"

"Plus," Kyle adds, "plus I just can't believe that Marcie would ever marry a fugitive who killed dozens of people as a hitman for Michael Cagnina. And raise a family with that man? I don't see it." He takes a deep breath and gives a presumptive nod. "More I think about it—Blair, I'm convinced she didn't have any idea."

That's how Blair figures it, too. But better to hear it from a reliable source.

Now he can plot his next move.

"We have to protect her," says Kyle. "We have to protect that family."

Blair looks at Kyle and nods. "Sure, but low-key."

"Low-key?" Kyle doesn't seem to like that idea. "Keeping the FBI out of it, sure, I get that. But I'm not going to be low-key about protecting people in this town. Marcie Bowers and her kids aren't going to be used as bait for some mobster, no matter how badly you want to catch him."

It's like Sergeant Janowski is reading his mind.

Blair raises his hands. "I wouldn't dream of it," he says.

SIXTY-EIGHT

I SIT ON THE couch in our family room, a child's head on each of my shoulders, Grace and Lincoln still sniffling and moaning as I stroke their hair. When I broke the news, when I told them that "Daddy got hurt and the doctors are trying to fix him," they cried, then calmed, then cried again. The combination of abject fear and hope has produced more shock than pure sadness. Their lives have been turned upside down in the span of those eleven words, and they don't know how to process it.

I don't know, either, but I have to be the rock. I have to hold it together—the phrase that has become my mantra, that I have reminded myself of over and over—*Hold it together.*

Give us good news, I silently pray. We haven't been religious as a family, but I do believe, and I am praying to the God I have neglected all these years to show my family mercy, to bring my children's father back to them.

And to bring my husband back to me? I can't decide that

right now. I have to prioritize, and what all this means for David and me going forward does not even come close to the top of the list. I'm trying to juggle so many other things, trying to stay ahead of what's coming, to make sure the kids get through this alive and with at least one parent.

Is he gonna die? Do you *think he'll live? Why did this happen?*

Each of those questions—and derivations thereof—they have asked me repeatedly, hoping for different and better answers each time. *Your daddy's strong; I think he'll be okay* was the best I could do, unable to channel David's unbridled optimism, afraid to overpromise. In the next few hours—I'm being told the surgery will be completed no earlier than an hour from now—we may be getting very bad news, and I want the children to be as prepared for it as children could possibly be.

I check my phone. It's now past seven in the morning. I want to give the kids as much time in the comfort of their home as possible before we leave. "We should probably get you guys dressed," I say to them, Grace still in her Notorious RBG long sleep shirt, Lincoln wearing a Cubs uniform for pajamas, his matted hair sticking in ten different directions.

The text messages and calls are pouring in now. News travels fast in Hemingway Grove. After the first dozen or so, I wrote a message and copied it so I could answer everyone with the same note: Thanks for your thoughts. It means a lot to us. We are staying hopeful and will speak to you soon.

I leave the couch and walk over to the window. Two TV vans have pulled up, a reporter fixing her earpiece as a cameraman sets up, though the patrol officer stationed outside my house has ordered them to maintain a distance. I assume there will be more reporters at the hospital. It's not every day that someone gets shot in HG. To say nothing of the fact that the victim is the Cotton River Hero, who only recently was featured in a video that went viral online. I can only imagine the headlines, the ledes on the broadcasts: *A man who only months ago was celebrated for a daring river rescue now finds himself clinging to life in a downstate Illinois hospital following an apparent robbery . . .*

An "apparent robbery" is how our newspaper, the *Downstate Sentinel,* has chosen to characterize it after a brief statement was issued by Hemingway Grove police. So it seems like Kyle has not yet decided to go public with his suspicions about David.

But it's only a matter of time. Secrets don't stay secrets in HG.

I'm taking the kids upstairs to get dressed when my phone buzzes. It's Camille, whose number I put into the phone.

"How are the kids?" she asks when I answer.

I don't respond. That's none of her business.

"Let me help you," she says. "Let me help you make sure they're safe."

SIXTY-NINE

"MRS. BOWERS."

I look up, startled, though I shouldn't be. I've been expecting him. I've been waiting more than two hours with my children in this waiting room as they play on their phones.

I try to read the face of the surgeon, still in his scrubs, that shiny bald head of his, as he gestures to the side and walks away, expecting me to follow.

"Hang on one second, guys, okay?" I kiss both my kids. "I'll be right back."

Dr. Grant opens the door to an examination room and holds it while I walk in, the pungent smell of iodine greeting me.

I say a silent prayer and turn to the doctor.

"Well, the surgery went as well as it could have," he says. "We've repaired the arterial damage, and we've oxygenated him."

But. There's a but. The way he phrased that.

"He lost a great deal of blood," he goes on. "When you lose blood volume, you lose blood pressure. Your blood carries oxygen to the brain and other organs. So we've done our best to maintain blood pressure. We've pumped in other substances to maintain the pressure, but they don't carry oxygen. We're transfusing him, giving him blood, but you can only do that so quickly."

"What does that—is he going to live?" I hear the words coming out of my mouth.

"I don't know. It's too soon to tell. It's also too soon to know the extent of anoxic brain injury."

"Brain...he might..."

"He might have brain damage, yes, from the oxygen deprivation. But there's no way to know his neurological state until he...until he regains consciousness. If he regains consciousness."

"If..."

The doctor helps me to a chair. The cushion makes a hissing sound when I sit on it.

"We've induced a coma," the doctor says. "He's stable. But there could be some tough days ahead, Mrs. Bowers. You should probably prepare yourself."

SEVENTY

"OKAY, KYLE, WE DID what you asked." One of the surgeons, whose younger brother Kyle went to high school with, hands him a plastic dish. "The bullet."

"Thanks."

"And we left him intact. Whatever you guys are looking for, under his nails or cuts or abrasions or whatever—we kept him as pristine as possible."

Kyle nods. "How's it looking for him?"

The surgeon's eyebrows rise. "Tough sledding. Odds are against survival, much less functionality."

Kyle puts on a pair of rubber gloves, turns to Officer Risely, his best forensic officer, who is also putting on gloves.

"We need to clean him up for the family," says the doctor.

"I got you. Shouldn't take us more than a half hour or so."

Kyle and Officer Risely enter the room. Kyle tries to

remain clinical, pushing away any thoughts he might have about David and Marcie. But personal or not, part of the job or not, it's never easy to see someone lying with tubes coming out of his nose and mouth, IVs in his neck and arms, machines expanding and contracting, whistling and buzzing.

Ginny goes to work on David's left hand while Kyle looks him over. The nurses and doctors and surgeons did as he asked, cleaned him up as little as possible. David has significant bloodstains caked on his forearms and hands. Otherwise, most of the blood is limited to the regions below the waist, where the injury occurred, and David's backside, as the pool of blood spread beneath him on the concrete.

And one small spot of blood above David's left eye.

"Okay, Ginny, let's start with prints. Get as many as possible."

"Sure thing, Sarge. I'll probably have to clean off his hands. Want me to look under his fingernails before I do that?"

"No, that's okay. There wasn't that kind of contact. Go ahead and clean his fingers if you need to. Whatever it takes for a good print."

He steps back, lets Ginny do her work. Like most people who've been grievously wounded, David looks almost like a different person lying in that bed, all color removed from his face. Were it not for his chest expanding and contracting, in fact, he'd look like someone who'd already died.

Marcie, he thinks. *Boy, has her life taken a sudden turn for the worse.*

"And then one more thing, Ginny," he says. "When

you're done with prints, let's maybe get a couple of samples for DNA."

Yes, he knows Blair already plans to do the DNA testing at the FBI offices. But no reason why he should miss the chance to collect a few more, just in case.

Prints and DNA, ballistics on the bullet—he's going to make sure HGPD does its part of this case right.

SEVENTY-ONE

TOMMY MALONE PUTS ON sunglasses and a COVID mask before he leaves his car. Say what you want about the pandemic, but it normalized the practice of disguising one's face. Especially when you're on the grounds of a hospital, where most people still wear a mask as a matter of course.

In his case, it helps obscure the fat lip he has from last night, from David's headbutt. He needed another round of painkillers this morning, too, though he's feeling better now.

The hospital parking garage is the perfect cover. People are always coming and going. So much easier than going to Marcie's house, which is basically off-limits now with the police car stationed outside.

He finds her SUV on the second story of the covered garage. He keeps walking and looks casually around, pretending to use a device on his key chain to find his own car. But seeing nobody around, he doubles back to Marcie's car.

Another quick look around, then he drops to his haunches

and slips the GPS device under the rear fender, hearing the hard *click* of the magnet.

Just as effortlessly, almost without breaking stride, he heads back to the stairs of the parking garage. He pulls out his phone and sees a nice round orange dot for Marcie's vehicle.

He'll be tracking her wherever she goes.

"Now I just need to get you alone," he whispers.

SEVENTY-TWO

THREE HOURS LATER. THE kids need to get out of this room. They've weathered the initial shock, seeing their father in this state. They've talked to him, told him stories, stared at him. There is a limit, especially for children. They don't want to leave, and they claim they're not hungry, but they need a change of scenery.

I send a text message to Camille, who meets us downstairs in the hospital cafeteria. I get chicken nuggets for Lincoln and some buttered noodles for Grace and put them at a table. Camille is standing at a distance, waiting for me.

"Tough times," she says, nodding at the kids. "I can't imagine."

"You'll be imagining soon enough. Though I hope not under these circumstances."

"Oh, yeah." She puts a protective hand over her belly. "That's right. So how do you want to do this?"

"Stay with the kids at all times," I say. "They won't be going to school for the foreseeable future. Certainly not next week. I'd like them to stay at home or here at the hospital, but...I'm not sure kids can be cooped up like that 24-7."

"If they want to get out—like, to a park or something—I'll go with them."

"Good. I'll be around a lot, too."

She cocks her head. "A lot, but not all the time?"

I look back at the kids. "A lot, but not all the time," I say. "I can't completely give up my law practice. People are counting on me."

"You need protection, too, Marcie."

Maybe. But not the same kind of protection as the kids.

"David would want me to protect you, too," she says.

I pivot, looking directly at her. But this is not the place for a scene, so I take a breath and lean into her ear. "Don't ever tell me what David would or would not want, as if you know him better than I do. You don't. Got it?"

She draws back, chastened. "Okay. Sure; fine."

"David would want me to work through this as best I can. And that means I may have some things I have to do without the children. So promise me that when I'm not around, you'll protect the children."

"I promise. I swear."

"Good. Now come meet the kids. They'll like you."

"You think? Why?"

"Because you won't talk down to them. They hate that."

She seems to appreciate the comment. She's about forty

and soon to be a first-time mother. I know from experience that she's wondering what kind of mom she'll be.

"And when does this going-off-and-doing-things-without-the-kids begin?" she asks me as we walk.

"This afternoon," I say. "I have to be gone for an hour or so."

SEVENTY-THREE

I LET CAMILLE SPEND time with the kids in the children's room of the hospital before I leave. It's not age-appropriate for them, this room—it's more for younger kids, its walls painted with images of barnyard animals wearing goofy smiles. But there's a TV that occupies them, and it's better than a regular waiting room. Beggars can't be choosers in a hospital.

As I thought, Camille's good with the kids. She's not a coddler, not sugar-sweet, but sincere and straightforward.

I let out a nervous breath and check my watch. It's getting close to four. This time of year, that means it will be dark very soon.

Time to go.

The kids aren't happy about it. I tell them they can see Daddy again if they prefer. But Mommy has to run an errand, just for a little while, and Camille will stay with them.

I head to my SUV, parked on the second level of the hospital's parking garage. I start it up, back out, and drive toward the exit. My headlights come on automatically as dusk falls.

The Community Bank of Hemingway Grove is on the other side of town. The parking lot is small, and that's not where I want to park anyway. I choose a remote location down the street, taking the last spot of on-street parking, located in front of a Japanese restaurant that closed during COVID and is now shuttered and vacant.

But three doors down is a travel store. A little bell rings as I enter. I don't have much time. But it's not hard to find the section for luggage, prominently highlighted in the rear of the store.

I buy every oversize duffel bag they have—eleven of them in total—plus a couple of luggage pullers. The saleswoman is so thrilled that she offers to throw in a free travel wallet.

I carry my purchases to my car, where I stash them in the back.

Then I hustle across the street and walk to the Community Bank. I'm there at nearly half past four, just thirty minutes before closing time.

I walk up to the teller. "I'd like to open some safe-deposit boxes," I say.

She sends me down a flight of stairs to the lower level. A woman is waiting there for me. She asks me if I meant to couch my request in the plural.

Absolutely I did.

"Three safe-deposit boxes in total," I say. "The largest size you have."

SEVENTY-FOUR

WELL, THAT DIDN'T TAKE long.

Marcie's SUV leaves the hospital just after four o'clock. Tommy uses his monocular to see into the vehicle from his spot across the street. As far as he can tell, Marcie does not have her kids with her.

He puts his car into gear and follows her. She keeps to main roads. She drives past the Community Bank—for a moment, Tommy was sure she was turning in there—and ultimately does a U-turn, finding a parking spot a block away on the opposite side of the street.

Where is she going? She's parked next to a boarded-up restaurant. Next to that is a convenience store and a travel store.

She gets out and heads into the travel store. Tommy parks his car a block down from Marcie's and waits for her to come out.

She isn't in there long. She knew what she wanted,

which apparently was a bunch of large duffel bags and a couple of luggage carriers to pull them.

Interesting.

Marcie returns to her vehicle and tosses her new purchases in the back. Then she crosses the street on foot, navigating through traffic. She walks down a block, and—yes, she's headed to that bank after all.

She could have parked in the bank's lot. But she chose not to. Instead, she chose to park far away. And enter the bank after dark.

Tommy can't help but smile. Hiding something, Marcie?

He parks his vehicle a block farther still from Marcie's. Then he jogs over to her car and jumps into the back seat.

He puts on his balaclava and waits.

SEVENTY-FIVE

"UNO," CAMILLE CALLS OUT, setting down a card in the pile.

"You're down to one card?" Grace looks over her cards at Camille. "Are you sure you're playing right?"

"Why, are you accusing me of cheating?" Camille winks at her.

"I'm just saying..."

"You won't have *this* card." Lincoln sets down an ace into the pile.

"Camille Striker?"

Camille turns and sees a man, roughly shaved and middle-aged, wearing a button-down shirt and jeans.

"Wondering if I could have a word with you."

Looks like law enforcement. She's ready with a response— no comment—but not in front of the kids. "I'm watching these kids."

"Understood. We'll step over here. They'll never leave

your sight." The man walks over to the threshold of the room and leans against the wall.

Presumptuous of him, but okay. "I'll be right back," she tells the kids.

The man has his credentials open as she approaches. "Francis Blair, FBI." He quickly tucks away the wallet. "Wanted to have a word with you."

"Shoot," she says. "Doesn't mean I'll have one with you."

"I understand. Sounds like Sergeant Janowski hasn't had much luck with you."

"But you think you will?"

He smirks, nods at the kids. "Funny—Sergeant Janowski told me that just the other day Marcie Bowers denied knowing who you were or ever hearing your name. And now here you are, babysitting her kids."

"Maybe we just met," she says, trying to stay on top of this but feeling like this conversation is going to be different from the others.

"Maybe. Yeah, maybe." Blair works his jaw. "Sergeant Janowski also told me that you used to work for the US Marshals Service in Chicago as a computer technician. He thinks you're Silas Renfrow's girlfriend, and you hacked into some secret information and found out where Silas was being held. You helped him escape. Which would put you in the soup for the murders of everyone who was killed that day."

"If that were true, yeah."

"Is it true?" he asks.

She looks this guy over. Typical Bureau guy, in her

experience—one part cocky, one part self-righteous, but competent. In his case, she suspects, more than competent. "I'm not sure I want to answer that question," she says.

He smiles, too ready of a smile. A smile that isn't a smile. "Looks like you're carrying," he says, nodding to the bulge at the ankle area of her pants.

"I have a permit."

"Not for a hospital you don't. You can't have a firearm in here. Unless you're law enforcement, like me. And I'm pretty sure you're no longer law enforcement, Camille."

Shit. He's right. She didn't think of that.

Dammit. He has her, and he knows it.

"One call to Sergeant Janowski and you're on the hook for—what? What's the state charge on this? Unlawful use of a weapon? We'll figure something out. Is that what you want, Camille? Right now, in the middle of all this shit, you have to spend the better part of a day, if not overnight at this point, in a local jail?"

She steels her jaw. "What the fuck do you want?"

"I want the truth," he says. "The local cops can chase their tails all they want. I prefer it that way for now. But you and I both know you're no computer technician. So tell me everything I need to know, and do it now."

SEVENTY-SIX

I LEAVE THE BANK just as it's closing, at five o'clock. They were nice enough to put my three new safe-deposit keys on a chain with a little plastic tag bearing the bank's logo.

It is now full-on dark, and, like clockwork, the temperatures have dropped at least ten degrees. I pull my collar up and walk down the street until I reach the spot where my car is parked on the opposite side of the street.

I don't know if what I just did is the smartest thing I've ever done or the dumbest. But I have to settle this problem, and I have to do it on my own terms.

I use the key fob to open the car doors, but I don't hear the familiar crunch of the doors unlocking simultaneously. I pop inside the car and start it up.

And then I feel cold metal pressed against my neck.

I freeze.

"Hi, Marcie. Remember me?"

I look in the rearview mirror. The man is wearing a black ski mask. *Balaclava* is apparently the right term. To me, it's just a black ski mask. Meaning it covers his entire face, save his mouth and his eyes.

It's not the first time I've seen those eyes. Nor is it the first time I've been able to see his eyes and *only* his eyes.

Still a piercing blue color. Still cold as ice.

Silas Renfrow.

SEVENTY-SEVEN

FOR A MOMENT, I think I'm dead—or will be any second. The barrel of his gun remains pressed against my neck, his eyes still on mine in the rearview mirror.

"You don't seem surprised to see me," Silas Renfrow says to me. "Are you starting to figure things out? Or have you known all along?"

I can't yet speak, my breath whisked away by the rush of adrenaline, the abject terror of seeing those eyes staring into mine.

I figured out enough last night, researching a man and a case I'd put behind me—the prosecution of Michael Cagnina. I figured out David's identity, and I knew he wasn't Silas Renfrow, that he couldn't be a cold-blooded killer.

"Put your hands on the steering wheel, Marcie, so I don't have to keep this gun pointed at your head."

I do it quickly, wrapping my trembling fingers around the steering wheel. I'd do anything to get that gun away from me. The gun that shot David and may have killed him.

Silas removes the gun from my neck but stays close, leaning forward from the back seat.

"I should've figured he'd try to find you once he rejoined the world as David Bowers," he says. "He'd ask me about you after you'd come for our attorney-client visits. His cell was down the way from mine. He couldn't hear us, but he could see you. He thought you were beautiful, of course. But he said you seemed 'formidable.' He was positively smitten with you, Marcie."

I try to picture it—David in a cell of his own, looking through the eye slit at me while I sat outside Silas's cell, talking to him.

"But enough about the past," he says. "Let's talk about now. I couldn't help but notice you just bought a bunch of duffel bags. And I see you've got a ring of safe-deposit-box keys around your finger. You're moving the money, aren't you?"

"I…no…no…"

"There's no time for games," he snaps. "I know David has that money. Don't play dumb with me."

"I…" I don't know what to say. I don't know what to do. I'm trapped, cornered, without any help—

"Tell me his name," he says. "Tell me your husband's real name. Because I'm getting tired of this wide-eyed innocent routine of yours. And if Michael Cagnina doesn't get his money back, your entire family is dead. Instead of a dead rat in little Lincoln's trick-or-treat bag, I'll put a bullet in—"

"Wesley!" I shout, bursting into tears, losing it right there in the car in front of a man who would kill me without hesitation. "My husband's real name is Wesley Price. The accountant for Michael Cagnina. The man who risked everything to take down a mobster!"

SEVENTY-EIGHT

AFTER HE'S FINISHED LAYING out his theory to Camille Striker, Special Agent Blair glances over at the children in the play area, Grace and Lincoln Bowers, arguing over a game of cards. The boy, he takes after his father—or at least how his father looked when he was Wesley Price, before plastic surgery and a shaved head altered his features and he became David Bowers.

"I'm not confirming or denying anything you've said." Camille looks him straight in the eyes.

"Yeah, I get it," he says. "You're sworn by law not to give up his identity. Even to an FBI agent. Even after you've retired. I respect that." Blair sighs. "Look, no reason we have to be at loggerheads here. We want the same thing."

She takes a step back. "No, we don't. I want the Bowers family to live to see another day. And another after that."

"So do I—"

"No, you want Cagnina. You don't care how you get him."

Blair's head drops. He blows out a sigh. "Look, this can

turn out okay for everyone. We can catch Cagnina *and* keep the Bowers family safe. You want to help Marcie? Persuade her to help *me*."

Camille studies him. "Marcie as bait. I don't think so."

"Hey, the situation is what it is." He opens his hands. "I didn't create it. But if Cagnina's got a guy making a move on them, no reason I can't be there to catch him. I catch his guy, I catch Cagnina."

"If he hasn't skipped town," says Camille. "He shot David—maybe killed him. Why on earth would he stick around?"

Oh. It hits Blair just then.

Camille doesn't know about the money. Of course. David—Wesley Price—wouldn't have told her about it.

"Okay, let's make this easy," says Blair. "I'm going to bring Cagnina in. And you're gonna stay out of my way. If you obstruct a federal investigation, you're gonna be giving birth to that child in a federal penitentiary."

SEVENTY-NINE

I WIPE MY FACE after that breakdown, after saying David's real name—Wesley Price—aloud.

"Marcie," says Silas from the back seat, "much as I love a good cry, I don't have time for it. Here's what's gonna happen. Listen and listen good."

A police cruiser rolls down the street, heading east, the opposite side of the street. Do I flag him down? Lay on my horn? What happens then? A shootout? Silas would probably take the officer out before he or she knew what was going on.

The cruiser drives past without incident, my heart rate decelerating.

"Where's the money? In a bank, I assume. Safe-deposit boxes. That's what I'd do."

I take a deep breath and nod.

"Where? Here in town?"

"Champaign," I say. "You can have it. You can have every penny. Just leave my family—"

"Do what I say, and your family will be fine. Now, what's the name of the bank?"

"Prinell...Prinell Bank."

"And you have access to the money? You have access to the safe-deposit boxes?"

"I...I don't know."

"Marcie—"

"I don't know!" I shout, panicking. "I've never been there. I just found out about all of this, okay?"

"I swear to *God,* Marcie, if you're—"

"I don't *know!*" I shout, punctuating each word with a pounding of the steering wheel. "He—knowing David, he would have given me access."

A pause. He's thinking this over. That detail, access to the boxes, never occurred to me. What if I can't get into the bank's vault?

"Tomorrow morning, first thing, you drive to that bank," he says. "I follow. You take out the money in those duffel bags, and you put them in your car. You drive your car to some parking lot nearby. You leave your car unlocked. And you walk away. Got it?"

I nod my head—and silently wonder what will happen if I can't get that money out.

"Good," he says. "Now—"

"Wait." I turn to him. "First thing in the morning, I'm at the hospital. I meet with the doctors first thing at eight, when visiting hours—"

"I don't care about your schedule. The doctors can wait—"

"No," I say.

No. I have to go to the hospital tomorrow morning. I have to see David.

It may be the last time I see him.

"It…everyone will wonder if I'm not there," I say, thinking quickly. "The police might get suspicious. They might go looking for me."

He doesn't answer right away. But what I'm saying should make sense to him.

"Well, I guess an hour more won't hurt," he says. "Fine, Marcie. Go to the hospital at eight and leave at nine for the bank. I'll follow. And while we're on the subject of the police," he says.

He jams the gun against my neck again.

"If you get some clever idea about involving the authorities, just remember. Michael Cagnina has unlimited resources. If I walk into a police sting operation tomorrow, you won't be any safer. He has plenty more people like me out there."

"I know. I…I won't, I promise—"

"Promises don't mean shit. Get that money tomorrow, Marcie. Your life and your children's lives depend on it."

The back door kicks open. Silas jumps out and disappears around the corner.

EIGHTY

I RACE BACK TO the hospital, violating any number of traffic laws, distracted, unnerved, so many thoughts flying through my head.

The money. I protect my family with the money. It's our only saving grace.

Or our downfall. The end of everything.

I park in the hospital's garage and run into the building, texting Camille that I'm coming, wondering if she's in the kids' playroom or David's hospital room or the cafeteria. I jump into the elevator and wait for the doors to close.

Before they do, a hand blocks the doors.

Kyle steps into the elevator.

"I don't have time for you," I say.

"Too bad." The doors close behind him. As the elevator begins to rise, he hits the Stop button. The elevator rocks to a halt.

"I don't have to talk to you."

"Yes, you do!" He grabs me by the arms. "I was wrong,

Marcie. I was wrong about David. I just ran his prints and DNA. We got the rapid results. They're not admissible in court until they're confirmed, but we usually rely on them—"

"I know police procedure," I say, rolling my hand. "Get to the point."

"I ran David's prints through AFIS. Know what they came back as?"

I don't answer.

"I had this all wrong," he says, stepping back. "I thought David was Silas Renfrow and Camille Striker was his girlfriend and a former computer analyst for the marshals' office who helped him escape. That's all wrong. David— he's here under witness protection, isn't he? And Camille was never his girlfriend—she was his supervising agent in the WITSEC program. Right?"

Right on all counts. Though the correct term for Camille's job, according to what she told me last night, is *witness inspector*—the primary point person on a witness relocation. But the US Marshals Service is so secretive that they give the inspectors varying official titles, so anyone doing research won't know. To all the world, Camille appeared to be nothing more than a computer techie, not the person responsible for keeping David safe under witness protection.

"David can only be one person, then," says Kyle. "There was only one real witness against Cagnina after he killed all the others. His accountant. Wesley Price."

So he figured it out. But I can't involve Kyle. Silas was right. Cagnina won't stop until he gets that money.

"Let me go, Kyle—"

"The DNA?" he says, flustered. "David's sample came back inconclusive."

"Let me out—"

"But we sampled a spot of blood on his forehead. *That* came back for Silas Renfrow."

Dammit. He's figuring everything out. I can't have that.

"When David headbutted his attacker? He connected with the attacker's mouth, which wasn't covered by the mask. He must have drawn blood."

"I have to go see my kids, Kyle. Unstop that elevator."

He draws back. "Did you not hear me? Silas Renfrow is here in town! He tried to kill David. You don't have anything to say—"

"I am trying to hold my family together," I say, choking up as the words spill out. "My kids need their mother right now. I am hanging on by a *fucking* string here."

"Okay, all right." He moves back, gives me space. "But I'm bringing Silas in. I'm going to find him—"

"Don't. Just please—don't do anything, Kyle. Please."

"What? Why in the hell not?"

Because he doesn't understand everything. He thinks Silas and Cagnina are after David for revenge. He doesn't know that this is about money.

And if I tell him—if I do anything other than what Silas specifically wants—more people will die.

EIGHTY-ONE

"MOMMY!"

Grace and Lincoln rush to me when I walk into David's hospital room. I bend down, and we do a group hug. My eyes immediately fill, tears streaming down my cheeks. How much I want to go back. How badly I want to rewind and change so many things. No matter what happens— life for these kids will never be the same.

Camille, recognizing her place, steps outside but makes eye contact with me before doing so.

We all break down, everyone's emotions at a high boil. I have to remember what they know, what they think— that Daddy is hurt badly, but nothing more. They have no idea how much danger we're all in, and I can't tell them.

David looks exactly the same, hooked up to all the tubes. No change, the doctor told me before I got to the room. Wait and see. I kiss David's forehead.

Then I place my hand on his cheek, cold to the touch.

Oh, David.

"I don't care what your name is," I whisper. "I know you. I love you. I love that you risked your life to testify against a mobster, that you risked your life to jump into a freezing river to save someone you've never met. That you mist up when you look at our children. That's the man I know. That's the man I love. Come back to us, David."

I press my lips against his, then walk away.

Outside the room, Camille is waiting for me. We step away from the police officer guarding the room and move down the hallway.

"I just got a visit from the FBI," she says.

"Oh, you're kidding. Oh, that's just..." I fall against the wall. "That's just great."

"An agent named Blair," she says. "He knows, Marcie. He's figured it all out—David's identity, my role. He worked on the original Cagnina case. Sounds like he's never really let go of the case."

"Let me guess," I say. "They want Cagnina. They don't give a shit about David or me or the kids."

"That...pretty much sums it up. He's coming over tonight to the house."

The FBI is going to sink its claws in me and make me do whatever they ask.

Meaning that the very thing Silas specifically instructed me *not* to do is going to happen whether I like it or not.

EIGHTY-TWO

HERE WE GO. I better be on my game.

He follows me into my basement, past the backup refrigerator and paint closet and into the game-room area, finished and carpeted, a large flat-screen TV on the wall, a comfy couch.

Special Agent Francis Blair—fiftysomething, I'd guess, handsome in a rugged sort of way, the five-o'clock shadow and mussed dark hair. "Very nice basement," he says, which sounds more like an accusation than a compliment. "Must have cost a fortune," he adds, as if I didn't get the hint the first time.

He knows about the money. That changes everything about this conversation.

Blair rubs his jaw. "Your friend upstairs, Camille, she doesn't know, does she? About the money, I mean."

I don't answer. I'm under no obligation to. My silence feels guilty, though.

"No, she wouldn't know." He answers his own question. "David couldn't tell her. She was a deputy US marshal."

I sit on the couch. Maybe I don't have the strength for this after all.

"The local guy, Sergeant Janowski—he doesn't know, either, I suppose." He shakes his head. "So the only people who know about the money are Cagnina's guy, David, you, and me."

I steel myself, staying in character as part defense lawyer, part protector of my family. "Is this an interrogation?"

He loses his smile. "I want you to help me catch Michael Cagnina. The man who wants to murder your whole family? Remember that guy?"

I look away. Just hearing that. It's not exactly news, but—hearing it.

"You want to use me as bait," I say. "And I would do that why?"

"Why? Because your husband never reported the cash as income," he says. "And he's been laundering that cash through his restaurant. And of course let's not forget the way he got the money to begin with."

"So what is this, then? You're offering me a deal?"

Blair sits on the couch, the other side of the L.

"You know how this works, Mrs. Bowers. I can't promise anything. I can only promise that if you help me catch Cagnina, I will recommend to the US attorney that you not be prosecuted for tax evasion or money laundering."

"Me or my husband?"

"For tax evasion and money laundering? Fine—I'll recommend that David isn't prosecuted for *those* two crimes."

I don't like the way he qualified that.

"Or embezzlement," I add.

Blair double-blinks, jerks his head. "Embezzlement? Theft? Is that what you think happened? That David *stole* the money?"

I draw back. That's what I thought *he* thought—that before David went into WITSEC, he stole twenty million dollars from a secret account belonging to Cagnina.

"Tell me," I plead, my nerves jangling, so tired of secrets, so sick of learning things about my husband from strangers.

Blair's face changes, something dark coming over his expression. "David didn't steal that money," he says. "He earned it."

"He...he earned..." I get to my feet, not understanding, or maybe not wanting to understand, walling it off because it couldn't, it could not be true.

Blair slaps his knees with his palms, then stands as well. He cocks his head, chuckles, runs his hand over the scruff on his cheek. Then he wags a finger at me. "What do you know about your husband and that detention center, Mrs. Bowers?"

"That...he was there voluntarily. He wasn't a criminal, wasn't suspected to be a criminal. He was...he was just a witness."

"That's true." Blair nods. "That part's true."

"But he was there temporarily. He didn't want to stay behind bars like a criminal."

Blair nods. "Right. He transferred out."

"Yes. About two weeks before the attack on the detention center."

Blair points his finger at me, holds it there. "Sure seems like your husband got awfully lucky, doesn't it? Leaving just before the attack?"

And then it happens. The house of cards I've been balancing, suddenly toppling over. My world spinning upside down.

My legs almost give out. I fall against the wall, closing my eyes, as if doing so will prevent the words from leaving Agent Blair's mouth.

"How the hell do you think Michael Cagnina discovered the location of that detention center?" he says. "We investigated everybody. Everybody. Every federal employee who got within a mile of our case. Every deputy marshal, every agent, every employee. But nobody thought of our one remaining witness, our prized possession, our golden goose, our only chance at taking down Michael Cagnina, even if it was just for some lame financial crime that wouldn't put him away forever. It was better than nothing. It wiped a little egg off our faces. So nobody looked hard at Wesley Price."

"No...no," I whisper. *"No."*

"And then it was over, and he was whisked away into witness protection, and nobody would let me within a *fucking* mile of him. You know how secretive WITSEC is, right? I didn't even know his new name. And I could never *prove* my suspicions, right? Well, now I'm here, and now I can, and now I damn sure *will*."

"No," I whisper. "No, it...it can't..."

"That twenty million was a *payoff,*" he says. "A payoff from Cagnina after your husband gave him the location of that detention center."

I slide down the wall, crumpled into a ball.

"He's responsible for the murder of half a dozen federal agents," says Blair. "And I'm not giving him immunity for that. Not ever. But you, Marcie? You wanna avoid going to prison with him and sending your children to orphanages? Do you? *Do you?*"

"Y—yes," I manage. "Yes. Please."

"Then you'll tell me everything you know right now," he says. "And you'll help me catch whoever Michael Cagnina sent to town."

EIGHTY-THREE

DAWN. THE SUN PAINTS the sky a bright orange out my bedroom window. Not that I'm asleep or even in bed. I gave up any hope of that hours ago.

My phone buzzes. I tiptoe out of the bedroom, where my kids and dog are sleeping, all nestled together like one ball of vulnerability and love and heartbreak. I answer Blair's call in Grace's bedroom, staring at a poster of Taylor Swift looking up into the rain.

Blair. He broke me last night. Over these last days, as I've started to learn and suspect things about David, my imagination traveled to various places, but never to the place Blair took me last night. My husband, responsible for a mass murder. No, he didn't pull the trigger, but he gave up information that directly led to a massacre.

I have tried it on, but it doesn't fit. Not with the man I know, the man I love. Can someone really walk away from a past like that, lock it in a dark dungeon, and become a completely different person? Were the kids and I his repentance, some internal promise to do better this time, to be a loving father and husband?

I don't know. But Blair broke me. I told him everything.

"I think we're all set," he says to me now. "You're going to the hospital at eight in the morning?"

"Correct."

"And at nine, your car pulls out of the hospital parking garage and heads down to Prinell Bank in Champaign."

I told him where the money is.

"And Silas will be waiting for you."

I told him about Silas, too. He wanted a physical description, peppered and hammered me for one, but all I could see was those eyes. Those eyes.

"We'll be following, too," says Blair. "From a distance. Don't worry. Silas won't make us."

"And what if he does?" I ask, my voice flat, unrecognizable to me. Who am I now? I'm just a puppet. Do what you're told, dancing puppet, and maybe, possibly, there will be some semblance of a life left for your family.

"He won't make us. Don't worry."

Don't worry. Sure. Why would I worry?

"There's a store down the street from Prinell Bank on Springfield Avenue called U-Move," he says. "You can't miss it—a big black-and-yellow sign. One of those places where people rent moving trucks and moving supplies. There are rental trucks all over. Silas will like that choice. After you've loaded the money into your car, drive to U-Move and park in the customer lot. Park midway in the lot. Not too close to the street, because Silas wouldn't like that. But not too far back, either, because we want to see everything."

"Midway in the lot," say I, the dancing puppet.

"Right. After you park the car, and remember to leave it unlocked, you get out and walk westbound. There's a little diner called Dino's. Go sit there, have some lunch or coffee or whatever. Someone will come get you. That's it. We'll take care of the rest."

Same plan we discussed last night, minus the details of the particular places he wants me to go. But simple enough.

"You didn't talk to Camille about this, right?"

"Right." The dancing puppet did as instructed. I kept Camille in the dark.

"Okay, well, so—we good?" he asks.

I hiccup a chuckle.

"Okay, put it another way—are you and I clear?"

"Clear," I say.

"Just do what I say, Marcie," he says, "and this will all be over soon."

EIGHTY-FOUR

IT'S TIME. CHECK IN with David and the doctors, then dance for the FBI.

We drive two cars to the hospital, Camille following the kids and me. In what's become our routine, I first visit David's room alone, while Camille takes the children to the kids' room, a few floors away from the ICU. If there is difficult news, I want to hear it first.

David. My thoughts scattering in every direction. The things I know about him—how he dotes on the kids and me, his work ethic, his decency, his selfless, life-risking rescue of a man he'd never met. But now the things Blair said, too. They don't just paint my husband in a new light—they rip the canvas in half and toss it in the dumpster. A modern-day Jekyll and Hyde, responsible for a mass murder. A con man who buried his lies, who used his wife and children for redemption, a reboot on life.

I don't believe it. I can't. My mind can't go there, can't

find any footing, simply cannot accept that the man I love, the father of my children, is a monster.

So. Deep breath. One step at a time, right? I'll do my job for the FBI today. Then we'll figure the rest of this out. There has to be a different truth from the one staring me in the face.

I won't give up on you, David.

I get off the elevator and walk past the nurses' station, ready for my perfunctory greeting from the police officers stationed outside the room.

But the guards aren't there. Where... where are the officers—

I break into a sprint toward the room, my chest filling with dread. I burst through the door and find David in the bed, looking exactly the same, almost like a mannequin in his immobile state, with the machines whooshing and whirring and burping, the tubes entering him from all directions. I let out a sigh of relief.

"Good morning, Mrs. Bowers."

I jump as I see the doctor seated in the corner, a medical chart in his hand. Dr. Thaddeus Grant, with the wild, unkempt eyebrows and long face.

"Where's the guard for the room?" I ask. "And why are you... sitting in here?"

"We need to talk," he says in that annoyingly calm manner.

"First, I want to know why the police are no longer guarding this room, why David's life is suddenly not worth protecting." I pull out my phone and start dialing numbers. "What the hell suddenly happ—"

And then it hits me, like a slap across the face.

I look into the doctor's eyes. The phone drops from my hand.

"Mrs. Bowers, your husband isn't registering any cortical or brain-stem activity. I'm afraid there's...I'm afraid he's gone."

I turn to David, lying just as before, his chest expanding and contracting, kept alive only by artificial means.

"He's...he's..."

"He's suffered brain death. I'm so very sorry."

I move to him, feeling like I'm floating. I put my trembling hand on his face, cool to the touch.

"Can he...can he hear me?" I manage, my throat choking on the words, knowing the answer already. "Can I talk to him?"

"It sure can't hurt, Mrs. Bowers."

I pull down the bed rail and lean over my husband, my face nestled into his, my hand caressing his face.

"Oh, my sweet David," I whisper. "I will always, *always* love you. The kids will always love you. You're not gone. You'll never be gone. You'll always be in my heart. You'll always be their father. Always, David."

You never got the chance to see the kids graduate from college, to walk Grace down the aisle, to watch them become parents themselves, to hold and love their children, our grandchildren.

You never got the chance to clear your name.

"I know...you wanted to tell me everything. But you didn't have to. I know you. I *know* you. Your name doesn't matter. What happened a long time ago doesn't matter. It doesn't change who you are to me. To us. To our family. Nothing will ever change that, David. Nothing."

Time passes as I cry, as I hold David tight and whisper to him, all the memories, all the moments so precious beyond words. The first time we met, on the running path. Our first kiss, under the red maple tree in Potter's Park. The birth of Grace, all twenty-one hours of it. The vows we wrote for our wedding. And of course when David proposed, dropping to a knee under a bright sunny sky in Loon Gardens. *I have one question for you,* he said, his voice shaky, emotion clouding his eyes, as he opened the box with the engagement ring in it—only to have a bird drop a load on his shoulder at that very moment, *kersplatting* right onto his polo shirt. *Marcie Dietrich,* he went on, not to be outdone, *you got a towel I could borrow?*

But then it's time. Time for me to leave. I can't bear the thought of releasing him, of not touching him, but I have no choice. The rest of our family is depending on me.

"I don't want you to worry about us," I whisper in his ear. "We're going to be fine. I can handle this. I promise. I promise I'll make it through this for the kids."

I pull back from him, wipe my face, and look down at the love of my life, expressionless and emotionless. At peace, I hope.

I lean down one last time and gently press my lips against his. "I'd do it all over again," I whisper. Then I pick up my phone and leave the room.

EIGHTY-FIVE

KYLE WALKS INTO THE room and closes the door behind him. We're in an office that Dr. Grant let me use. I am sitting in a chair, trying to hold still, probably looking as messy as I feel.

But I don't have time for messy.

"Dr. Grant told me," he says. "Marce, I'm so sorry."

I nod. The tears have dried now, after I let it all loose for half an hour. The time is now 8:50 a.m. I have to leave in ten minutes.

"He said you wanted to see me," he says. "How can I—what can I do?"

"My kids can't know, first of all," I hear myself say, my cashed-out voice sounding more like a croaking frog's than a human's. "Not yet. Not today. He's on life support. He needs to stay that way for now. For today. Until I get back."

"Okay, sure." He looks at me with a question. "Get back from where?"

"I met Agent Blair. He wants me to help with something today."

"Today? Well, c'mon, Marce, he'll understand that something came up."

I get to my feet, my legs still shaky, trying to maintain my composure. "Today is not a day for 'something came up.' Not even this."

I have to comply with the FBI and help them catch Silas, or my kids, in a twenty-four-hour span, will lose both parents.

"They're dropping a net," he says. "Aren't they? And using you to do it."

I've been instructed not to tell anyone. Not Camille, not Kyle, not anybody.

I take a deep breath, emotion rising to the surface. "Kyle, I have to ask you something. I know things between us haven't been . . . well—"

"That's not your fault," he says. "I had all kinds of suspicions about you."

"You were doing your job. You were trying to protect your town."

That was always his dream. To stay here forever, to be the one who kept this nice little town as nice as possible. I used to think that was small, unambitious. I used to think a lot of things.

"I never said this before, but—I'm sorry for how everything turned out. I said we couldn't be together because I didn't want to spend my life in HG, and then I ended up marrying someone else and doing that very—"

"It is what it is," he says, playing the hardened, emotionless cop, though he is anything but. "Yeah, it was hard at first. Maybe it still is sometimes, if I'm honest. Every time I drive down the road and see that damn Hemingway statue staring at me." He chuckles.

It couldn't have been easy for Kyle. And yet he's making it easy on me now.

"Okay, here goes," I say, clapping my hands together and then locking my fingers as if in prayer. "I don't have any family. No siblings, no living parents. Neither, as far as I can tell from Camille, does David. We're both only children with deceased parents. And now David's gone, leaving only me for my kids."

Kyle's chin rises, as if alerted.

"And even though we've hardly spoken to each other in sixteen years, I still know you better than anyone else in the world. I know this sounds crazy—"

"Marcie," he says, touching my arm. "Everything's going to turn out fine today. I'm sure of it." He nods, and I see his eyes fill, his mouth working to stave off emotion. "But if you're asking me, if something happens to you, will I..." He swallows hard, unable to finish the sentence. He clears his throat and makes an effort to look me in the eyes. "Of course I'd take care of Grace and Lincoln—"

I rush into his arms, overcome with emotion. I can feel him breaking down, too, the thumping of his heart, the trembling of his body. How did things get so turned around that the man I jilted will now come to the rescue and raise my kids if need be?

Finally, when my voice returns: "We have plenty of money. It would all be yours."

"Why do you think I said yes?" he whispers back.

I laugh. It feels odd to laugh. We separate, each of us wiping our faces, keeping a distance. Using humor to defuse tension, always a tool in Kyle's toolbox.

"I have to go," I say, noting the time. It's almost nine. I start walking backward.

"I know you'll make it back," he manages. "I know you will."

I nod, because I have to believe that. But I don't speak, because my throat is clogged with emotion.

Then I turn and leave the room.

I had to get that covered. Now it's time to do the job.

EIGHTY-SIX

NINE O'CLOCK. I PULL out of the parking garage of St. Benedict's Hospital, looking both ways before I turn onto the street, taking an extra glance, wondering if I'll spot Silas Renfrow—not that I know what he looks like.

He might be close. He might not. I surely don't want to lose him. That wouldn't make anyone happy—not Blair, not Silas. But Silas knows where I'm headed.

I drive toward the interstate, passing Hemingway's Pub along the way. A number of makeshift signs—GET WELL, DAVID!—are planted in the lawn outside the pub, surrounding the Ernest Hemingway statue.

That statue, another memory: how much David and I fought over it when he had it built, just two years after the pub opened, while it still struggled financially. *It would catch people's eyes,* he said. *But the cost,* I replied.

Little did I know he just had to grab some cash from a safe-deposit box to pay for it. One of so many lies he told me. His parents dying in a fire, growing up in orphanages—

300

No. Stop. Overload. I have to get through this. I am the only parent now. I have to do what the FBI wants me to do so I can return to my kids. *Cry later, Marcie.* Vent and fume and mourn when this is over.

I'm on I-57, motoring south to Champaign. Traffic isn't bad at all for a Friday morning. But it's heavy enough to prevent me from noticing anyone following me. Silas is back there somewhere; that's all I know for certain.

It's not long before I get off at the exit and roll into Champaign, heading for Prinell Bank on Springfield Avenue.

I reach it easily enough, a two-story building of brick and glass, nestled on a street corner. I pull into the parking lot and get out. I pull out the two luggage carriers I bought, stacking one on top of the other. Then I put the eleven empty duffel bags, still folded neatly, on top of the carriers and pull them behind me to the front of the bank.

I pause a moment at the front of the bank, just outside the entrance. Somewhere out there, Blair and probably a dozen agents are watching. I want to make sure they see me, the dancing puppet, doing their bidding.

I can't believe I'm doing this. I can't believe any of this.

I walk in, greeted by an elderly man trying to convince everyone that he still has dark brown hair. Behind him, tellers to the left, cubicles to the right.

"Good morning!" he says.

"Good morning," I say. "I'd like to get inside my safe-deposit boxes."

This will be the first hurdle. Do I have access to the boxes?

And if I don't, what in the world am I going to do?

Don't panic. Don't panic until there's reason to panic.

A woman, young, Asian, with a name tag that says JEN-NIFER, escorts me to her cubicle. I show her my identification and give her my name.

She types something on her keyboard and looks at the screen. I'm holding my breath, thinking of my next line if she says, *No, sorry, you're not on the—*

"Got you right here, Mrs. Bowers." She looks up at me and smiles. Relief floods through me. I could kiss her.

"Five of them?" she asks. "Five of our large ones."

I nod. I'm not capable of speech, my body charged with electricity.

She grabs another employee, a young man who looks like he's straight out of college, presumably to help with lifting the safe-deposit boxes. I follow them down a long hallway, past some bathrooms. At the end of the hallway, an EMERGENCY EXIT sign.

Can I exit out of my life?

Near the end of the hallway, a set of stairs. We take the stairs down, and we're inside the vault. The woman, Jennifer, unlocks a door. We walk into the safe-deposit room. We stop at the first of my boxes, number 323. She turns a key, I turn a key, and the drawer slides open.

We then repeat the process for boxes 324 through 327.

"Would you like a private viewing room?" she asks.

"Please," I whisper.

"Would you like us to help carry these?"

From what I read online, a million dollars, in denominations of hundreds, weighs around twenty-two pounds. I have no idea how many millions can fit into one of these huge safe-deposit boxes.

"Please," I say again.

I step back. The first box is low to the floor. The two employees pull it out and lift it together. "Oh, not bad at all," the man says. They move it into an adjoining room, a room without windows. I hear the box land on the table with a clank.

Huh.

They repeat the process with the other four. I try to act nonchalant, as if this were all standard and routine, as if the fate of my family were not hanging in the balance. But when they tell me that they'll leave me now, and the room is all mine, I rush in and close the door behind me, my heart pounding so hard I can't breathe.

The boxes are made of steel, around five feet long and three feet wide, a few feet deep.

I unlatch the first box and pop it open.

It's completely empty.

I open the second box — empty.

The third, the fourth — empty. Not even a speck of dust inside.

I open the final box. Nothing inside except a large manila envelope.

I step back, dumbfounded, flattened.

Where the hell is the money?

EIGHTY-SEVEN

FOUR EMPTY BOXES AND one with nothing but a manila envelope inside. My nerves rattling, my heart slamming, my hands shaking so hard I can barely use them, the white noise inside my head drowning out all sound, I open the envelope, bearing one word, *Marcie,* on the outside.

I carefully dump out the contents.

A cell phone.

A handheld remote, small enough to fit in my hand, with two buttons.

A thumb drive.

And then a series of papers.

The first one is a single page. It reads, in David's handwriting:

Marcie—

If you're reading this, either I'm dead, you know my real identity, or both. Regardless, I'm sorry. I'm so very sorry. Please read what I've enclosed here. I hope it will explain everything.

I've loved you since the first time I laid eyes on you at the detention center. And I always will. You and the kids are everything to me.

The second is a thick set of papers stapled together—David's explanation to me of "everything," apparently. But now is not the time for a trip down memory lane. There is a trained assassin waiting outside for me to deliver him money, a man who will kill me if I don't. There is an FBI agent expecting me to deliver that money who will put me in prison and make my kids orphans if I don't.

The one thing I don't have is the money.

I put that document to the side. That leaves a third document—like the first one, just a single page. Only six words.

I read it and reread it. Six words.

Six words that change everything.

The note drops from my hand, leaving me frozen for a moment, silent.

I look around the room, as if there's anything to see, any clue to what I'm supposed to do next.

I pick up the note from David. It's ten pages in length. His life story, looks like. I want to read it in full, digest every word, but I have little time, so I flip and scan, flip and scan for the stuff I need to know right now.

...an only child, born in a town near Lake Minnetonka, in Minnesota...

...moved to Naperville, outside of Chicago...

...accounting degree from U of I in Champaign...

...alcoholic, dead-end job...

...suspicious bookkeeping, should have recognized sooner...

...I didn't know my client was a front for a mobster...

...I had to know, I had to be sure...

...I followed him to the warehouse...

...I didn't know what else to do, whom to trust...

I slow down for the key parts at the end—what David did once he discovered that his client, an industrial warehousing company, was really a front for the mob. Then I reread those parts, just to make sure, realizing that I'm on a short clock.

And then I make a decision.

I'm going to believe you, David. I'm going to trust you.

I pick up the cell phone, some fancy-looking one, probably a high-end burner phone, and power it on. I get a small signal. I'm in an underground vault. The fact that I can get any signal at all tells me that this is a very sophisticated phone.

Well, here goes. If I do this, there's no turning back.

I gather up my things. The empty duffel bags stacked flat on the luggage carriers. The new phone, the small handheld remote—remote for what?—and the thumb drive go inside my purse, along with David's thick ten-page note to me.

I walk carefully back up the stairs, stepping gingerly on my tiptoes. When I reach the top of the stairs, the hallway is empty. I look to my left. The emergency exit. But no. If I push through that door, it will scream out an alarm. I won't get twenty yards.

Maybe a fire alarm. But I don't see any in this hallway.

The bathroom. I walk down the hallway into the women's bathroom. It's empty. I go inside one of the stalls and leave the door to the stall slightly ajar. I put down the toilet seat and sit on it.

And I pull out the phone David gave me. I don't have a directory of numbers, but I don't need a directory for this number. I punch the three digits and wait.

"911," the operator answers. *"What is your emergency?"*

No more dancing puppet. It's time for an audible.

EIGHTY-EIGHT

IT'S NOW 10:31 A.M. Blair, standing in the shadows of the gas station across the street from the bank, blows into his hands. Gloves would have been smart.

But it shouldn't be long now. Marcie's been inside a half hour.

That front door will open any minute now. Probably one of the employees will hold the door for Marcie while she lugs hundreds of pounds behind her in duffel bags, using those luggage carriers she brought.

As if on cue, the front door opens. A man in uniform, security, holds the door, pushes a kickdown to keep it open.

Here we go.

A woman rushes out. But not Marcie. A younger woman, college age. Then another person. Then another. People flooding out of the bank.

He takes a step forward, listens. An alarm of some kind coming from inside the bank?

"Marcie, what the hell did you do?" he whispers.

EIGHTY-NINE

THE ALARM SHRIEKS OUT as I sit on the bathroom toilet, my feet off the ground, knees touching my chin, holding the luggage carriers and the duffel bags up with me, straining to keep them above the bottom of the stall walls. It shouldn't be long. Don't be long.

The sounds of footfalls around me, outside the bathroom. The door to the bathroom pops open.

"Anyone inside? Anyone in here?"

A man's voice. He's probably looking down low for any feet in the stalls. He won't see any.

"Bathroom is clear!"

I breathe out.

I make myself count to twenty. This is the rear of the bank. There's nobody down in the vault. I was there alone, and now I'm not there. In the confusion and chaos, they probably figured I ran upstairs and got out with everyone else.

...eighteen, nineteen, twenty.

I don't want these luggage carriers. Too heavy and too cumbersome. I can't run with them. But I keep the duffel bags. This is all about the money. It's the only thing keeping me alive. They're a handful, collectively, but at least they're light. I hope I can run with them.

I peek my head out into the hallway, the shrill of the alarm exponentially louder now that I'm not cocooned inside the bathroom.

I turn right and head for the emergency exit. It will sound an alarm, but now it won't be noticed. Everyone's heading out the front door.

I bang through the door and into the cool morning air, the bright sunlight.

My car is around on the other side, not far from the front entrance, parked by a side street. I am all alone here in the rear. I can hear the commotion outside, by the front of the bank, Springfield Avenue.

If the FBI has this place surrounded, or if Silas is positioned just so, I'll be spotted. But I'm in the least visible part of the bank, the hardest part for them to cover. And they won't be expecting this.

Anyway, screw it: this is my only shot.

I leave my car there in the lot.

I start running north, slipping through the hedges that border this end of the bank's parking lot, scratching my face, but I get through, duffel bags in hand. Into another parking lot, but instead I turn and start running down an alley, heading east. I have to get clear first.

Get clear first, get away, lose them entirely.

And then figure out what to do next.

And keep the duffel bags. Somehow, in some way, this will be about the money.

NINETY

"WHERE IS SHE?" BLAIR shouts into his earpiece. "Do you see her?"

Blair creeps forward as a mass of people spill out of the bank, stopping briefly on the sidewalk outside, then moving farther down the sidewalk, away from the bank.

Then sirens—from both directions, east and west. Police squad cars screeching to a halt in front of the bank, a fire engine pulling up right in front, blocking the bank completely from Blair's view.

"Do you see her? Her car's still there. Do you see her?"

"I don't see her," he hears back.

"Shit. *Shit.*" Blair runs across the street, holding out his badge. "FBI!" he shouts.

A firefighter, decked out in heavy coat and helmet, turns to Blair. "Someone called in a bomb threat."

Dammit. That was Marcie. She's ghosting him.

But she couldn't have gone far.

Keeping his credentials up, Blair works his way through the crowd.

"Sir, you can't go in here," says a uniformed officer.

"FBI. I have to go inside."

"You can't, sir."

"I can and I will—unless you want to obstruct an FBI investigation."

The officer steps aside. "There might be a bomb in there, sir, but you're the FBI, I guess."

Blair rushes into the bank. He looks around frantically. The vault should be downstairs. He takes the first set of stairs, winding around in the center of the ground floor, but no—it's not the vault. It's a bunch of damn offices.

He runs back up the stairs. "Where's the vault?" he shouts to an officer.

"What?"

"The vault. The—the safe-deposit boxes!"

"I have no idea."

Great. Blair finds the back hallway. Runs down the hall and finds a flight of stairs. He takes them down in double time, landing with a hard thud.

The vault. He finds the private viewing room. Five safe-deposit boxes. All of them empty.

Nothing. Not a single dollar.

Only one piece of paper that he finds lying under the long table. He picks it up and reads it. Just one sentence, all of six words.

"Oh, no," he says. "No, no, *no!*"

Blair stuffs the paper in his pocket and runs back up the stairs. Looks to his left down the hallway. An emergency exit.

He pops through and looks around outside. He jogs over to the side of the lot and sees Marcie's vehicle, still there. He cups his hand against the window and looks inside.

No duffel bags, no money. No way she got very far on foot with all that weight.

Did she have another car waiting? Has she been playing him all along?

Either way, she's adiosed. Probably with a good ten minutes' head start.

He pulls out his cell phone and dials the number for Marcie's phone carrier.

"This is Special Agent Francis Blair, FBI, Chicago field office," he says. He reads out his authorization number. "I need a domestic real-time location on a cell number. The subject is a fugitive and a material witness. This is an exigent circumstance."

Those magical words at the end, meaning he doesn't have time for paperwork—he'll do it later. Just track the damn subject for me now, and I'll justify it afterward.

He waits. Wherever Marcie is, if her cell phone's on, he'll be able to track her.

She won't get far.

His phone buzzes again. He's still waiting for the cell-tracking operator, but he looks at his phone. The new caller isn't listed. Which means it's Tommy Malone.

Also known as Silas Renfrow.

Blair answers the phone. "She's in the wind," he tells Silas. "But we'll find her."

NINETY-ONE

"SO WHERE THE HELL did she go?" Silas shouts into his earbud as he puts his car in gear. "We have to find her!"

"Yeah, Silas, I know," says Blair through the earbuds. *"The question is how."*

Silas pulls out of the U-Move parking lot down the street from the bank just before police barricades go up, cordoning off the entire block because of the bomb threat.

"Well, you're the FBI! Can't you—I don't know—block the highway exits or something?"

"On what ground? Can't exactly advertise what I'm doing, can I?"

"Can't you track her?"

"I just tried. Her cell phone's off."

"So she definitely thought this through." Silas punches the steering wheel. "Are we sure she took a car?"

"I'm not sure of anything," Blair says. *"But it's the only thing that makes sense. With all that money and those luggage carriers, how far could she expect to get on foot?"*

"Do we—I mean, do we even know she took the money?"

"The safe-deposit boxes are empty, and the duffel bags are gone. So you tell me."

Right. Right. "So what the fuck do we do now?"

Blair doesn't immediately answer. Silas grips the wheel with white knuckles, ready to pull it off its mooring.

"Best guess, she's taking her kids and making a run for it with the money," says Blair. *"I'm heading to the hospital. That's where the kids are. She won't go anywhere without those kids."*

Silas races his car around the streets north of Springfield Avenue, looking for anything out of the ordinary, any car speeding, someone running on foot. "What about me? What do I do?"

"Take a look around there locally. I doubt she's still in Champaign, but take a look around the surrounding neighborhood. Who knows?"

"Roger that."

"Don't do anything stupid if you find her, Silas," Blair says. *"Remember, the money's the important part. Marcie I can deal with later."*

"Easy for you to say."

"I'm telling you, I have her spooked."

"Is that right, Frankie? Does she seem spooked right now?"

"I don't know what's going on with her, okay? She surprised me. But I know this much—her husband might not survive, and she can't go to prison and leave her kids high and dry. She'll gladly trade the money to avoid that. I have all the leverage. If you go and kill her, you create a lot of headaches for me. We can still salvage this."

Silas doesn't respond.

Salvage this? Sure, Blair can just go back to his shitty job and his shitty life. His reputation will be intact. He'll have a pension. Maybe not his half of the money, but something, at least.

But Silas? Silas doesn't have shit. He's been on the run for the last fifteen years. He needs this money or it's game over for him.

And Marcie? She knows he's alive.

"Are you listening to me, Silas? Don't fucking kill her!"

Silas disconnects the phone call.

"Not until I get the money I won't," he says to himself. *"But then she's all mine."*

NINETY-TWO

I RUN STRAIGHT THROUGH the alley, due east, but turn north at the first street, so anyone looking down the alley from the bank won't see me. I zigzag through alleys and streets until I'm five or six blocks north and east from the bank, in a park.

The park is all but empty in the middle of the day on a weekday, with temperatures in the thirties or forties and the sky gray. I spot a gazebo not far away and make my way to it.

My heart pounding, chest burning, I collapse to the gazebo's floor, catching my breath and giving myself time to think.

I have no idea how close behind me they are. How much of a head start did I get? Are they a block away or three miles off in the wrong direction?

Where am I, and where do I go from here? I can't use my phone to call an Uber; if I turn it on, they'll track me.

Wait—David's phone, the burner he gave me. I pull it

out and do a search. I find what I'm looking for—it's not too far away, eight-tenths of a mile.

Okay. It's now or never. I peek around me, looking for speeding vehicles or people running, listening for sirens. It's as good a time as any.

I can hardly run with these duffel bags. Should I abandon them? Something tells me I might need them. But they're too numerous, too clunky to run with.

I decide to leave them here. If I really need them, I'll come back for them. What are the odds, in the middle of a cold November day, that someone will take them off this gazebo?

Whatever. I have to move, and I have to move now.

I take off, a flat-out sprint when nobody's around and a controlled jog when a car approaches along the street or I pass a pedestrian. At least there aren't a lot of people out now. The fewer people who see me the better.

The downside: I'm far more exposed if someone looking for me happens along. But I'm committed to a hard run. There are no guarantees. My best bet is to get where I'm going as fast as possible.

I stop, bend over at the knees, and catch my breath. I can jog three miles easily, but an all-out sprint for half a mile has burned my fuel down to empty. I take desperate gasps of air, my chest heaving, my head woozy, nausea surging to my throat.

How do I get out of this? No brilliant plans, no get-out-of-jail-free cards spring to mind. Nothing that guarantees I'll live. No guarantees that David or I, should we manage to survive, will avoid prison.

Cars travel past me along this north-south street. I try to keep my face down as they pass. There's no good cover here. I'm out in the open.

Go, Marcie, go.

My chest burning, my legs like rubber, I motor on, spotting a major thoroughfare up ahead. Is that it? I run like I'm running for my life. I'm running for two young lives.

There. I reach it, a four-lane road, congested. I take violent, heaving breaths. The dizziness and nausea overcome me; I bend over and retch, having no food in my stomach to vomit. More deep breaths, one eye on the street, looking for gaps in traffic.

When one comes, I race across the street, feeling very exposed, then down two storefronts until I'm finally, miraculously, at my destination: J. T.'s Sportswear.

Never thought I'd be so happy to see a store that sells Big Ten sweatshirts.

I wipe sweat from my face and draw a few more deep breaths before I walk into the store, filled from wall to wall with clothing, mostly orange-and-blue apparel of all sorts. I grab a blue Fighting Illini sweatshirt and a matching blue hat. I throw in some sunglasses to boot. It isn't perfect, but even a little concealment helps.

"You doing okay there, ma'am?" asks the clerk, a young kid with a goatee and bad acne. I can only imagine how flushed and sweaty and disheveled I look.

"I'm having one of those days," I say.

"I feel *that.*"

Yeah, do ya, sport? Wanna trade places?

Something catches my eye in a display near the

register—a Fighting Illini Swiss Army knife. "I'll take this, too," I say.

While inside the store, I do a search on David's phone for my next stop, confirming that it's only three blocks away. *Okay. Let's go.*

In the parking lot, I pull the sweatshirt over my head, don the cap and sunglasses, and slip the knife into my pocket. I start down the street for my next destination. Again, I feel exposed, walking on the sidewalk along a busy thoroughfare, but at least I've changed my look. I hold my cell phone to my ear, even though I'm not using it—it's not even powered on—as an excuse to lower my head as if in concentration.

I reach my destination a few minutes later. The lobby inside is empty. A man in a yellow shirt is smiling at me as I enter.

"Hi," I say. "I need to rent a car."

While they process my information, I step out and call Camille on David's phone. She doesn't answer at first—unrecognizable number—but picks up the second time I call.

"Camille, it's Marcie," I say. "Take the kids and run."

NINETY-THREE

FIFTEEN MINUTES LATER, I get into the rental car, a blue Dodge SUV. I feel instant relief, now inside a car and dressed differently. I search on David's phone for an internet café, expecting several in a campus town. The nearest one is only two miles away, a place called Screens & Beans.

I'd be heading backward, in the general direction of Prinell Bank. But it's by far the closest café, and I wouldn't be tangled up on the campus itself, where it seems like it would be hard to make a quick exit.

Screens & Beans it is.

I find the internet café easily enough and parallel park my rented SUV. My head down, I briskly walk in.

I'm hit with the overpowering aroma of ground coffee. The place is divided into thirds—on the left, seating where customers can enjoy their drinks; in the middle, the coffee bar; and to my right, rows of computers available for rental by the hour.

A ponytailed cashier who does not seem to be enthusiastic

about his job takes my credit card and assigns me to a spot in the "connect" room, as he calls it.

Nobody pays me any attention as I walk in, their eyes all glued to the screens in front of them, just like my kids when they're on their phones.

My kids. I have to do this fast and get back to them.

I sit down and start up the computer. I reach into my purse and remove the thumb drive David left for me in the safe-deposit box.

The computer recognizes the thumb drive. The menu pops up. I'm expecting documents, maybe photographs. Instead, a single icon appears, one I don't recognize.

An audio file, best I can tell. An audio recording.

I double-click on the file. A long rectangular box appears, in the middle of which is a small triangle, a Play icon. I click on the icon, and the sound comes on.

Static at first, and very loud, loud enough to elicit a reaction from the man sitting next to me. I quickly adjust the volume in the corner of the screen. I wish I had earbuds or headphones, but I don't. I put my ear up close to the speaker at the top of the screen so I can listen with the volume down.

Still static, nothing but white noise.

And then a voice. A man's voice I recognize.

Bent over my computer station, my ear up to the speaker, looking like a crazy person, I listen to the whole thing.

Then I replay it, take one more listen to the whole recording.

I sit back in the chair. Okay. Now I know.

Now I have a plan.

NINETY-FOUR

"I'M SORRY, AGENT BLAIR, that cell phone is still turned off."

Blair, racing back to Hemingway Grove on the highway, says into his earbud, "Keep trying. The moment that cell phone pings, call me at this number."

"Will do, Agent."

He dials the number for Kyle Janowitz.

"This is Kyle."

"Kyle, it's Blair. I've been calling you."

"Sorry—been occupied. Is Marcie okay?"

Careful, now. Careful how you handle Kyle.

"Something went haywire this morning. Marcie took off. Her phone's turned off, and we can't find her."

"Oh, no. I mean, Blair, what did you expect from her today? That she'd be in the right frame of mind to perform some task for you, after just finding out her husband died?"

Blair jumps in his seat. "David is *dead*?"

"She didn't tell you?"

"Uh, no—no, she didn't."

That's not good news. Emotional as she must be, Marcie will be even less predictable now. All the more reason he needs Kyle.

"I need you to help me with something, Kyle."

"Then you'll need to tell me why."

"I can't get into that right now. I wish I could, but I can't."

"I need more than that, Blair. I'm not your errand boy. I will cooperate with a federal investigation, but not in the complete dark."

Blair feels his frustration boil over. But he needs Kyle. Keep it cool.

"I promise I'll tell you, but not now. All I can say right now is there is more to Marcie than you know. And I'm afraid she's on the run. And if she is, she'll take her children."

"Why would she run? I thought she was cooperating with you."

She was, or so Blair thought. Until she read that hand-written note from her husband in the vault, that six-word note Marcie left behind in her rush to leave. Blair glances over at it now, resting on the passenger seat:

Don't trust anyone from the FBI

"You have two choices, Sergeant," Blair tells him. "You can secure those children, who I'm sure are at the hospital. Or you can ignore my request. If you ignore my request, lives will be at risk, and probably your career, too. So do us both a favor and help me. Find the kids, secure them, and call me when you do so."

He punches out the phone and unleashes all the rage he'd suppressed in one primal shout. Then he takes a breath and dials Silas. "Talk to me."

"You can't track her by phone?" Silas asks. *"Or by her credit card maybe?"*

"Her phone's turned off. And I'm pushing it as it is — you have any idea what I'd have to go through to track her credit card transactions in real time? I'm not actually performing Bureau work right now, Silas, in case you hadn't noticed."

"Okay. Well, so where am I looking down here? Feels like a waste of time."

"If she's still in Champaign, she's hiding," he tells Silas. "So think like her. Think of places she could do that. Places she could blend into a crowd. Nothing small like a convenience store. Probably not even a restaurant. A bar, maybe — hiding in a dark corner by the exit. Or maybe a coffee shop, where she could cocoon herself in a corner. Probably lots of bars and coffee shops around a college campus. I'd focus on those."

"Bars and coffee shops. Will do."

"Keep your eye on the prize," says Blair. "Money first, revenge second."

NINETY-FIVE

FIRST STEP OF THE plan: blast this audio file.

I pull up my email at the computer station and run into a username-password prompt. I remember my username but not my password. On my laptop at home, I'm never asked.

I have an option for *Forgot your password?* I click on it, my heart racing. Now that I have a plan, I can't wait to execute it.

It says it will send a password reset to my phone. But my phone—I can't turn it on. If I activate it, Blair can find me. The feds use that real-time cell-site location capability all the time.

I breathe out. This is the only email I have.

I try passwords I've used: *Dietrich0414*, my maiden name and birthday. *MDB0414*, with my married-name initials. *GraceLincoln343*, with our street address on Cedar.

No, no, and no. And it's telling me that with one more wrong password, I'm locked out.

"Shit," I mumble through gritted teeth.

Fine. No choice. I need my email server to send me a new link. And it will only send it to my cell phone. So here goes.

I turn on my cell phone and wait for it to awaken. It lights up and shows me a screen saver of the kids and David lying in the grass and hugging.

It takes a moment to refresh, makes me type in my phone password to open it.

C'mon, c'mon, c'mon . . .

Then the text messages kick in, several of them. I go straight to the one my email provider sent me. I click on it to reset my email password. It opens to a new page. I type in the new password and press a button. There.

Then I shut off my phone immediately. And pray it didn't ping a cell tower in the roughly forty-five seconds it was turned on.

NINETY-SIX

"IT KICKS OFF A range from the cell-tower ping, an approximate area," Blair says into the phone. "It would—just tell me where you are, Silas. Find some address and tell me where exactly you are."

Blair, pulled over on the side of I-57, listens as Silas reads him a street address.

"Shit, you're right in the range!" he says. "She's right there around you somewhere, within, like, a six-block radius!"

"Okay, but where?"

"I don't know—you're on a busy street. There can't be *that* much commerce. It's not Chicago—"

"Right. I'm on the busiest street around here. By far."

"Good. Then tell me what you see."

"Shit, you want me to—okay. A laundromat, a Chinese restaurant, a yoga place, a something, I don't know, whatever 'screens and beans' stands for—"

"Wait!" Blair shouts. "Screens and beans? That's gotta mean—is that one of those internet places? Computers and coffee?"

"Fuck if I know."

"Go check it out. Now!"

Why didn't Blair think of that before? She wants access to a computer. She can't use her phone—she's had it off this whole time, other than the forty-five seconds she used it for some reason. So she's using a computer. Email?

"Okay, I double-parked, and I'm heading over."

"Remember what I said, Silas—money first."

This feels promising. This could be it. Blair's phone buzzes. Another call. Kyle. "Hold the line, be right back," he tells Silas.

He hits a button to connect the second call. "Yes, Kyle."

"I found the kids. They were with Camille. She was leaving the parking garage, but we stopped her."

Blair pumps his fist in the air. Thank Christ. "Did she say where they were going?"

"No. She clearly doesn't want to tell me. She was very upset that I stopped her."

"Okay, but you have them."

"I just took them to the station. We're holding them there in protective custody. And nobody's moving them—including you, Blair—until I know what's going on."

He feels relief flood through him. The kids are stashed away. Marcie can't run now.

"Totally understood, Kyle. I gotta go." He kills the call, flipping back over to Silas. "Anything?" he asks.

"I'm on her," Silas whispers. *"I fucking see her."*

Blair pounds the steering wheel. They've got this back under control.

Feel the walls closing in, Marcie? You're not going anywhere.

NINETY-SEVEN

WITH MY NEW PASSWORD, I pull up my email and hit Compose. A new email pulls up. I put my own email in the To field. I search through my emails for another address and find it, too.

Then I click on Attachments to append the audio file. But I don't know where to locate the file. My kids could probably do this in two seconds, but I search directories. There—it's on a D drive, apparently. I find the audio file and double-click on it. Now it should attach to the email.

But it doesn't. Instead, a big hourglass appears on the screen.

An hourglass? I don't need a freakin' hourglass right now. *Let's go, let's go!*

It spins and twirls, deciding whether it wants to let me attach this audio file to my email.

C'mon, c'mon, c'mon…

The front door to the café opens. In walks a man wearing sunglasses, with red hair, a phone to his ear as he looks around—

I flinch. I know that man. That's...that's...yes, the creepy redheaded sunglasses guy I met in downtown HG the day my dog, Lulu, went missing.

That must be Silas.

I duck my head low, pretending to be typing while I watch his movements in my peripheral vision. He moves to his left, toward the other side, where patrons are drinking coffee and talking. It won't take him long to clear that room and come to my side.

I'm out of time.

The hourglass spinning, mocking me.

There. The audio file attaches to the email. I hit Send.

The screen goes blank.

Huh? Did it send? Did it crash? Was there something sophisticated about that audio file that I couldn't—

Silas is back at the middle of the store, by the coffee. Holding very still. Speaking into the phone. Then switching the phone into his left hand, tucking his right hand into his coat.

My computer screen still blank—no idea if the email went through.

Silas takes a step in my direction.

I grab my bag and turn to my right, for the rear exit, trying not to seem obvious but panic taking over, my walk turning into a sprint, hoping the sweatshirt and hat I bought will conceal me.

But I'm pretty sure they don't.

NINETY-EIGHT

"I'M ON HER. I fucking see her."

"Keep me on the line, Silas. Get her alone and tell her I want to talk to her."

With his sunglasses still on, standing over by the coffee roasters by the front door, Silas switches the phone to his left hand. He tucks his right hand into his pocket, where his handgun resides. Marcie doesn't know what he looks like. He's always worn the balaclava. All she knows is his eyes, concealed now by his shades.

But he can't get this wrong. He's not wrong, is he? College sweatshirt and hat, but that sculpted face. That's Marcie.

One way to find out. He moves toward her.

She jumps from her seat and rushes toward the exit.

He tries to be subtle—*Don't attract attention*—moving into the "screens" area, picking up the pace, walking down the aisle of computers as she reaches the exit.

He glances at her computer station. Screen still open,

computer still in use. She's leaving in a hurry. The hallway to the exit door is long. Good. Once they're outside, nobody will hear what he does to her from the inside.

He sees her open the exit door, notices something on the back of her collar.

A price tag. The sweatshirt is newly purchased. As if he had any doubt it was Marcie.

He hits the exit door hard, a solid door that doesn't push, it pulls. He pulls it open, swinging it toward him to the right, stepping through the exit on the left.

Nothing in the alley but a large dumpster. He approaches it slowly.

"Come out, come out, Marcie," he taunts, reaching for his gun.

In his peripheral vision, a blur, and then a sharp, stabbing pain, something piercing through his cheek, stabbing the gums in his mouth.

He cries out and instinctively reaches for the wound, just as another stab lands, this time puncturing the back of his right hand. As he crouches over in pain, he is shoved to his left, straight into a wall, smacking his head.

He hits the pavement hard, unable to focus, as he hears the primitive panting of a woman cornered, a woman he underestimated.

NINETY-NINE

SILAS, CROUCHED IN A ball, puncture wounds on his cheek and hand, blood dripping off his face, looks up at me. I drop the Swiss army knife to the ground. I have something better now. I am holding the gun that fell out of Silas's pocket.

And I am pointing it at the man who killed my husband.

The gun is heavy in my hand. I can't hold it still. I can't hold my body still, overtaken by adrenaline.

"You fucking bitch..."

I wind up and kick him in the chest. He has nowhere to move and absorbs the full brunt of it, curling deeper into a ball. I kick him again and again and again, feeling all the rage and desperation break loose from me.

Then I stop. He is no immediate threat. But I am. I have this gun. I could kill him right now. I have every reason to.

Do it, Marcie. He wants to kill you. He wants to kill your kids.

He killed David.

I raise the gun and aim at him. My chest heaving, my thoughts swirling, fear and desperation and fury, because I did nothing to deserve any of this, my children did nothing to deserve any of this, not one single thing—

"You won't do it," he says, wincing. "You don't have the stones, kid."

"No?" I say, my voice surprisingly even and cold. My finger curls around the trigger.

"Marcie! Marcie!"

I blink and snap out of the trance, feel a shudder run through me.

"Marcie! Listen to me, Marcie!"

I turn. The phone. Silas's phone, resting on the pavement. Sounds like Blair wants a word with me.

But first, I give one more swift kick to Silas, somewhere no man wants to be kicked.

Then I pick up the phone to incessant protests, desperate shouts of my name, and move away from Silas down the alley.

The back door to the café pops open. "What happened?" someone shouts.

"That man needs medical attention!" I shout, my back turned, walking away. "Call an ambulance! No, call the police! Call the police now!"

I get some distance, then bring the phone to my ear. "Blair," I say.

"Marcie, listen to me. We can work this out."

No, we can't. If I didn't know that before, I do now. We are past working it out. It's all about the money. They won't stop until they get their money.

And once they get it, they can't let me live.

"You've got nowhere to run, Marcie."

He's right about that. But neither does he.

"Just listen to me, okay?"

"No, you listen to me, Blair," I say. "You want the money? Come get it."

I drop the phone and leave the alley.

ONE HUNDRED

I'M READY NOW, READY for this to end.

Ready to retrieve my kids and get as far away from Hemingway Grove as possible.

My heart pounding but my mind clear and focused, I jump in my rented Dodge SUV. I return to the park where I rested after first fleeing the bank, the gazebo where I left the duffel bags. This time, I park in a lot close by and run over to the gazebo. I'm back in the car in less than a minute with the bags.

Then I drive west toward the interstate, checking David's phone for directions. Keeping a lookout for Blair or evidence of law enforcement—a helicopter overhead, a police checkpoint barricading access to the highway. But finding nothing. As if I didn't already know—Blair isn't law enforcement, not today. He has no team behind him. He never did. It's just Silas and him.

I take the ramp onto the interstate, heading north to Hemingway Grove. I mind the speed limit. No reason to draw attention to myself, though the only contraband in this car is the gun I took off Silas.

Did Silas get away? Or is he busy explaining himself to Champaign cops right now? One fingerprint off that guy, and he'll spend the rest of his life in prison.

I remember the store from when I was driving down here earlier today. A superstore, a recognizable one, with a tall sign peeking high in the air for visibility from the highway. I see you. I'm coming.

I pull off the highway and into the parking lot of the superstore. I park between two other SUVs, just one extra layer of concealment. As far as I know, Blair doesn't know what car I'm driving, and I haven't turned on my phone, which I know he's tracking, so I can't imagine how he could locate me here. But you never know.

A greeter, an old man, smiles and waves to me when I walk in. "Hope you're having a great day, now!"

Not the word I would use to describe my day.

I find a store clerk, a young woman in a visor and a company vest. "I just need to buy a few things," I tell her. "But two of them, I need to buy in bulk."

Twenty minutes later, I'm at the cash register with a young clerk who looks high school age, who'd need to call someone else to ring up a sale of liquor (which I seriously considered buying for courage).

"Run this," says the woman who first helped me, showing him a ticket with a barcode on it. "Ma'am, pull around to the back with a receipt, and we'll unload the boxes."

The kid at the cash register aims his scanner at the barcode and checks the register for the price. "Holy shit," he says, doing a double take. "Is that right?"

I look at the screen. More than fourteen hundred dollars. "That sounds right," I say.

"Uh, okay. And then you have..." He looks into my cart. "How many..."

"How many life jackets? Twenty-four," I say. "I think they were all the same price, but we should probably be sure."

I dump them out of the cart. He scans them one by one, then I throw them back in the cart.

"Okay," he finally says. "Is that everything?"

"Don't forget these," I say. I hand him four pairs of kids' toy handcuffs.

"Ohhh-kay, sure, why not?"

He rings me up. I pay my bill.

"And you're going around back for your pickup," he says. "You'll need this receipt for"—he shakes his head—"a hundred and fifty reams of paper."

"I won't forget. Thanks."

He looks at me with a question.

"Don't ask," I say.

ONE HUNDRED ONE

AROUND AN HOUR LATER, I take the exit off the inter-state to Hemingway Grove with a flutter in my chest. I don't know where Blair is or how much he knows, but I assume he's here in town, probably with Silas, ready to pounce the moment they see me.

I pick up David's phone and do a search for the Hemingway Grove Police Department. I click on the number and wait for an answer.

"I need to speak with Sergeant Kyle Janowski," I say. "This is Marcie Bowers. It's urgent." I stay on the outer rim of the town, opting for a route that outsiders like Blair and Silas wouldn't know.

"Please hold."

My stomach knotted up, my back and shoulders aching, I feel like I'm tapping my last reserve of energy. But we're almost at the end, for better or —

"Marcie?"

"Kyle."

"Where are you? Are you okay?"

"I'm okay. Listen. Do something—"

"Don't run, Marcie. Don't run, okay? Whatever it is you did—"

"I'm not running, Kyle. Listen—do something for me. Check your email."

"Check my . . . email?"

"Check your email and wait for my call."

I punch out the phone. I'm almost there.

I drive down a two-lane road in my rental car, seeing in front of me a clearing, and then the Cotton River. The road slopes downward as I descend the bluff, as I pass a sign saying ROAD CLOSED AHEAD, though I keep driving. A second sign again telling me ROAD CLOSED, though this time it's blocking the road. I navigate around that sign, tires crunching rocks on the shoulder, and continue driving until I reach another sign, the reason the road is shut down:

Bridge Closed

DO NOT ENTER

Anna's Bridge, named for Anna Hemingway, the daughter of the fur trader who founded this town, still closed after a man suffering an epileptic seizure lost control of his vehicle and broke through the guardrail, plunging into the Cotton River.

Had this not happened, we would still be one happy, if blissfully ignorant, family. I would continue to live a lie that I didn't know was a lie. However long I live, another fifty minutes or another fifty years, I will always wonder if believing a lie would have been preferable to knowing the truth.

I wipe a tear off my cheek, as if I have time to cry right now. I don't. I won't.

It's not easy getting around this last sign, but having an SUV helps as I maneuver along a sloping shoulder and get back onto the road. A road that quickly becomes the bridge.

The bridge rocks ever so slightly as my SUV climbs onto it. I feel a rush, the sensation of not knowing whether the ground beneath you will hold, whether you will plunge fifty feet into freezing, turbulent river water. But this bridge was always a little creaky. It always held, and it holds now. The truss's guardrail is what gave way, smack in the middle of the bridge, the area I slowly approach.

That portion of the guardrail has been removed entirely, replaced with nothing, a gaping hole. A section of the bridge's roadway is gone as well, leaving only the beams below it.

I'm alone out here for the time being. I won't be for long. I reread the last paragraphs of David's letter, left for me in the vault.

...didn't know what the money was for...

...didn't know which agent...

...didn't know whom to trust...

...didn't feel safe telling anyone...

I release a long, trembling breath. *I believe you, David.* If this is it for me, if this is the end, at least I know I'm doing what's right.

"I love you, David," I whisper. "I love you, Grace. I love you, Lincoln."

I pop the trunk and get out of my SUV. There is wind, probably more so on a bridge, threatening to blow the baseball cap off my head. I Frisbee the hat through the gates of the bridge until it disappears out of sight. I close my eyes and let the wind lift my hair.

Then I go to the trunk and pull out the duffel bags. I drag them along the grated floor of the bridge, away from the SUV.

I remove the four pairs of handcuffs, open them from their packages, make sure I know how to work them.

Then I reach into my pocket and pull out my cell phone, my personal one. I power it on and watch it come to life. This tiny little device, providing so much information, desperately searching for cell towers to ping. Which FBI agents use to locate you.

"Here I am, Blair," I whisper. "Come get me."

ONE HUNDRED TWO

BLAIR DIALS THE PHONE as he drives. Silas finally answers.

"Her cell phone's back on," he tells Silas. "I got a location. Where are you?"

"By the hospital, like you wanted."

"Okay, well, best I can tell from the cell-site location — you're not gonna believe this. Remember the bridge that guy drove off of? How this whole thing start —"

"Yeah, yeah, I know."

"That's where she is. She's on the fucking bridge!"

"The bridge? She's just parked on the bridge?"

"Far as I can tell. That or she's smack in the middle of the river."

"Why? Why would she drive to the bridge?"

The same thing Blair's been asking himself. "Maybe she has a sense of irony."

"Or she's feeling sentimental. Does this broad have a death wish?"

"I don't know. But listen up," says Blair. "You're north of her. I'm south of her. Let's pin her down. You enter the bridge from the north, I'll come in from the south. She'll be trapped. Can you find your way there?"

"I think so. I'll map it. What's the name? Anna's Bridge or Old Anna's Bridge?"

"That's it. I'm only a few minutes away. Call me when you get there, okay?"

"Will do. But what's her angle?"

"That's what I'm trying to figure out. She turned her phone on for a reason. She wants us to find her. She's waiting for us."

"She wants this to be over. She's giving up."

Maybe. But so far, Marcie Bowers has been anything but predictable.

"Let's not break out the party hats just yet," says Blair. "Get to the bridge, Silas. And talk to me before you do anything."

ONE HUNDRED THREE

BLAIR DRIVES TO THE top of the bluff overlooking the Cotton River. He pops the trunk and gets out of his car, the wind smacking him, blowing open his coat until he zips it up to his neck. He pulls a pair of binoculars out of his trunk and walks over to the edge of the bluff, raising the binoculars to his eyes.

Marcie is standing in the middle of the bridge. Behind her is a sizable gap in the bridge, a missing piece of the roadway. Right—it's the spot where the motorist busted through the side and went into the river below. The truss bridge, a series of interconnected triangular steel beams forming the sides, is missing one of the triangles where the vehicle blasted through it, and they've removed a portion of the road at that juncture, leaving only the underlying zigzagging structural supports of the roadway.

Marcie is standing just in front of that gap, right at the precipice. Beneath her, the roiling, raging waters of the Cotton River.

And next to her, lined up in a row, one after the other, right beside her—the duffel bags. He does a quick count. Eleven. That's what Silas said—Marcie had eleven duffel bags. Eleven bags, meaning...eleven million dollars? Who knows how much of the twenty million has already been spent. But even if it's down to eleven—that's a lot of retirement money.

But why so close to the edge of the bridge, Marcie?

He focuses on her again. Her eyes are down, looking at her phone, cradled in her hands, as the wind tosses her hair in all directions.

What is this?

He pulls out his phone and dials Marcie's number while watching her through the binoculars. She recognizes the number and punches a button, raises the phone to her right ear while covering her left ear with her other hand.

"Where are you?" she shouts, the wind rippling through the phone connection.

"I'm on the bluff above you."

She looks up, finds him. *"I want this to be over!"* she cries.

"What are you doing, Marcie?"

"What am I doing? I'm doing what I should have done the moment I realized we had all this money! I just wanted you to witness me doing it, so you'll know."

He doesn't understand. "Witness you doing what?"

"You can't put me in prison for money I don't have," she says. *"You can't kill me for money I can't give you!"*

Huh?

Oh. Oh, shit—

"Marcie, wait!" he shouts, but the line goes dead.

He keeps his binoculars trained on her. Marcie walks to the far end of the row of duffel bags, squats down, and with both hands shoves a duffel bag forward until—

"No! No!"

—until it disappears off the edge, through the gap in the bridge, tumbling end over end into the tumultuous waters of the Cotton River, where it smacks the surface and bobs along the waves, the current carrying it downstream.

And then she pushes the next one over the edge, another *splat* as it hits the river water.

He races to his car and jumps in, moving down the sloping road too fast, nearly losing control as he navigates around one of the ROAD CLOSED barriers, knocking the other one away. With the bridge in sight, he sees another bag tumble into the waters below, bobbing for a moment before the current carries it downstream.

He looks across the river and sees Silas's car on the opposite bluff, beginning its winding descent toward the bridge.

He dials Silas's number as he drives. "She's dumping the money!" he yells into the phone. "She's dumping all of it!"

ONE HUNDRED FOUR

THE CARS COME SPEEDING toward me from both directions as I finish pushing the seventh duffel bag over the edge, watching it smack the perilous water below. The previous six bags have begun their trip down the river like a small armada, bouncing and bobbing. If my quick online research holds, each of those bags will eventually sink to the river bottom. But I don't really care.

The car coming from the north end, which must be Silas, won't be able to reach me, what with the large gap in the roadway. But Blair, coming from the south end and traveling north, won't have that problem.

I finalize my preparations, one click of the handcuffs, and slowly rise to my feet as Blair's car—the first to reach me—skids to a halt about ten yards away, not far from my rental SUV.

Blair pops out, shuffling toward me, his gun up and trained on me, the wind instantly pummeling his coat and whipping his hair in his face. "What the fuck are you doing?" he yells.

"Don't come any closer!" I yell to Blair. "You shoot me, and I take the rest of the money with me into the river!"

Blair looks down and registers what I mean. Each of the remaining four duffel bags is joined to its neighbor by handcuffs. And the last of them is handcuffed to my right wrist. We are one long chain, the four bags and me.

Blair holds up a hand as I hear, behind me, another car skidding to a stop. I glance back at Silas as he jumps out of the car, looking worse for wear, the right side of his face badly swollen and a makeshift bandage covering the wound, holding a firearm two-handed. He stops at the gap in the road, separating us by around ten yards.

Blair's hand signal is for Silas's benefit. *Hold off*, he's saying. *Let me handle this.*

Blair's in charge. That's what I figured.

"Be smart, Marcie!" Blair says. "We can work this out. Everyone can win."

"The police are coming!" I shout through the swirling wind at Blair.

"Yeah? Fine with me. I can explain everything. Including how you and David stole that money. And David won't be here to deny it, will he?"

The mention of my dead husband sends something spiraling inside me. "Are you sure you can explain everything to the cops, Blair? Including what your buddy is doing here?"

Blair blinks. Glances at Silas.

In the distance, finally—later than I expected—the faint sound of sirens. Blair's head turns slightly when he hears it, squinting as his hair whips into his eyes.

Then he looks at me. "This was all just a ruse, right?" he says. "Luring me and Silas onto a bridge so we'd have no escape?"

I shrug. "Afraid so."

He nods, almost grudgingly. Then he pivots and fires the gun three times in rapid succession.

Silas staggers backward, three gaping holes in his chest, before hitting the roadway hard, the gun skittering from his hand.

Finally, Silas Renfrow is truly dead.

That was for you, David.

"I just saved your life!" Blair shouts, pushing hair out of his face. "Silas was going to kill you, and I stopped him!"

"Oh, you're the hero now?"

"And so are *you*," he says. "You lured him in. Our plan worked, Marcie, don't you see?" The call of the sirens grows louder, Hemingway Grove's finest on the way.

"Our plan," I repeat.

"Yeah, our plan. You come out of this like a hero. You and I both. We forget about any criminal charges. You and the kids stay together as a family. And when this is over, we split what's left of that money."

The first squad car appears up at the bluff, followed by another, as the police begin their journey down the road to the bridge.

Blair sees it, too. "Make this deal with me, Marcie. You

go back to your happy life and keep a couple million. No prison. Why not? What's the alternative—you tell your story and I tell mine? I'm pretty good in those situations. You really wanna roll the dice on a he said, she said when I'm giving you a happy ending?"

"How about just a he said?" I open my phone, which has the recording pulled up. I play it on speakerphone for Blair, two men conversing:

"Nice to meet you, Mr. Cagnina."

"Yeah, well, I had to see it for myself—an FBI agent willing to be helpful. I can make you a rich man. But I wanted you to hear it straight from me—you fuck me on this, I kill you and everyone you care about."

"We understand each other. I have twenty million reasons not to fuck you."

Blair looks at my phone like Superman looks at kryptonite. David, when he heard this recording so many years ago, only knew that the person speaking was an FBI agent. He didn't know Blair, didn't recognize his voice. But I do. And I did.

"I sent this to the Hemingway Grove PD, if you thought this was the only copy," I say. "You didn't know Cagnina recorded your conversation, did you, Blair? I guess he wanted an insurance policy. He left a thumb drive of this recording with the stash of twenty million so you'd know, if anything went wrong, that he had you over a barrel."

"And your husband stole the thumb drive when he stole the cash."

True. An insurance policy of his own.

The police squad cars are on the bridge now, their sirens

blaring, lighting up the darkening skies as they head toward us.

Blair sees it, too. He looks back at me, the wind rippling his coat and tossing his hair, and makes one final plea. He holsters his weapon and shuffles toward me. "Fine—keep all the rest of the money, then. Every nickel. But you and me, we stay square. We're both heroes. Nobody ever bothers you again. That recording—I can figure that out. But you and I stay square." He puts out his hand and shuffles closer. "What do you say, Marcie? I'm much better as a friend than an enemy, I promise."

"Let me think about that," I say, wanting to back up but knowing there's no room behind me. "What are you doing?"

"What am I *doing,* Marcie?" Blair says. "I'm taking your sarcasm as a no. And I'm reaching for you, trying to get you back from the edge, but...oops!"

He lunges for me, making a show of reaching for me in a protective way, but also making sure his front foot, as it lands, gives a swift kick to the duffel bag to which I'm handcuffed.

He'll have a story, I realize in that moment when the bag flies backward, my hand with it, that moment when I lose my balance. *Marcie wanted to commit suicide out of shame...I tried to talk her off the ledge...I reached for her to save her.* With David and me out of the picture, he'll have a story that covers everything.

I fall backward off the bridge and through the air, the chain of duffel bags sailing downward with me.

In that last moment, while I spiral through the air, a

moment before I plunge into the icy, tumultuous waters of the Cotton River, I think of my screen-saver photo of David and the kids in a pile together in our backyard.

I did this for you, I say to them. *In some way, in the flesh or not, we'll always be a family.*

ONE HUNDRED FIVE

GRACE, YOU ARE FEARLESS. You strive for perfection. That will serve you well, honey, but life will not always be easy. There will be setbacks, but they won't make you a failure. Show me someone who has succeeded, and I will show you someone who failed but kept trying. Smile, sweetie, remember to smile, to let some light shine into your life. Always remember that happiness is not a destination but part of the journey itself.

Lincoln, you are your father through and through. You are outgoing and warm and happy. Don't ever change that. Just remember that hard work and perseverance will get you what you want in life. Nobody will hand it to you . . .

My eyes pop open into a dark green blurry nothingness, no sound but the thump of my pulse. Where—which way is up, which is down—

I can't feel my limbs, can't move, panic setting in as I feel my lungs contract, as I thirst for air—

Light. Light above. The water's surface. So beautiful.

My arms. I move them, flap them, try to wiggle my legs, any movement to propel me upward, but I can't make them work, can't make them move enough, but I see you, the light, I see the light and I want to kick, I want to flap my arms and then yes, I'm moving upward but I'm fading, too, fading in this foggy water, and I want so badly to swim to see Grace to see Lincoln because I have so much love left to give them so many things to teach them so many hugs and kisses and tears to wipe from their faces but the one thing I don't have is breath and I'm fading, I know it now, and I am in your hands, I am in your hands to do what you will with me—

Light coloring my eyelids, then a blast of cold air, sweet, pure, delicious oxygen, and I let out a gasp and I'm thrown against a person, a man gripping me in a bear hug as we swing from a ladder—

"I got you! I got you, Marcie!"

—the water rising and crashing against us, the helicopter hovering above me.

"Hold on to me, Marcie! Hold on tight—"

Kyle.

"—they're bringing the raft over! Hold on tight, and we'll get you to safety!"

I hold on to him as best I can, my right wrist weighed down by the duffel bags full of life jackets handcuffed to me—an impediment now but probably the reason I made it back up. The wind blowing us in every direction, the ladder twisting and turning, the cold, the bitter cold so numbing and stinging—

"You're crazy, you know that?" he shouts. "You could've died!"

I may be crazy, but I'm alive. I could've died, but I didn't. I made it through.

Just like I promised you, David.

ONE HUNDRED SIX

"MARCIE...DIETRICH...BOWERS," I say, my teeth chattering, my body in an uncontrollable shiver as I sit on the cot in the ambulance, swaddled in a heavy blanket.

The paramedic shines a light in my eyes. "And what day is it?"

"Fri—Friday. Don't...know the date." A vicious coughing spasm follows.

She clicks off the light. "We're putting in an IV of warm saltwater solution. Keep coughing. It's good to cough."

Well, that's good, because I've already regurgitated around half the contents of the Cotton River. Now my lungs, my abdomen just ache. But however stinging the cold, however beaten I feel, I can't deny an overwhelming feeling of relief, even euphoria.

Kyle, sitting in the corner of the ambulance, covered in a blanket of his own, punches out his phone, shaking his head. He looks over at me. "How's the patient?"

I try to smile.

"It was a stupid idea, Marcie. It was way too risky. If you'd given me more than ten minutes' notice of what you were doing, I never would've let you do it."

I cough again. I glance at him but don't respond.

"Which is why you didn't give me more than ten minutes' notice," he says. "I know, I know." He lets out a hard shiver. He's soaking wet, too. He was in the river, with one hand on the ladder, pulling me up to the surface one floating duffel bag at a time. They used something to cut the handcuffs, freeing my wrist from the bags.

"Anyway, he's dead."

"Si—" I try to finish his name but can't, overtaken by another coughing spell.

"No—well, yes, Silas is dead. But I was talking about Blair. You were wrong about him. He didn't try to talk his way out of it."

So when push came to shove, he realized he couldn't bullshit his way past that audio recording. "Su—sui—suicide?"

Kyle shakes his head. "No, but close enough. Suicide by cop. He drew his firearm. He had a dozen officers training their weapons on him, ordering him to raise his hands. He was never gonna shoot his way off that bridge. The sergeant on the scene said Blair made no real effort to fire. He just wanted the return fire from us."

Both Silas and Blair, dead. A tremor of cold slices through me.

"What did they want from you?" he asks. "What were they after?"

That's the right question. And the answer is easy. But

maybe not so easy. Because it suddenly occurs to me that, with Silas and Blair both dead, the only living person who knows about the money is...

Me.

"Long story," I manage before breaking into another coughing spasm.

"We can talk about it later," he says. "You'll need to rest. Just be glad you survived."

I nod, take a couple of deep breaths. Never again will I take for granted the sweet joy of breathing, the simple act of inhaling oxygen and expelling carbon dioxide.

"Or did you?" he says.

I look at him with a question.

"Maybe you didn't survive, Marcie Bowers."

I don't catch his meaning. But he fixes his stare on me, raises his eyebrows.

"Oh," I say. "Right."

EPILOGUE

ONE HUNDRED SEVEN

I KILL THE ENGINE, the boat coming to a rest on the bobbing water. Our dog, Lulu, jumps off my lap as I get up and head to the back of the boat, reach down to the hitch, and start pulling the thick rope toward me.

Slowly but surely, the fancy red-and-black tube float in which Grace and Lincoln are nestled moves toward the boat. Grace, her wet hair blown back by the wind, her cheeks sunburned, is beaming. Lincoln raises his skinny arms in the air around his life vest. (Life vests are our friends.) Lulu, she just barks at them until they climb aboard.

"Had enough for today?" We've been at it for nearly two hours, Captain Marcie driving the speedboat in zigzags and circles, the kids squealing as they get tossed around the lake.

Which lake? I'm not supposed to tell. Let's just say that where we live now—well, it's warm and lush and green. We don't live on the beach, but we are close to this lake.

Inside the boat, the kids dry off with towels and sip from juice boxes, comparing notes on their favorite parts of the last two hours, while Lulu tries to lick the water off their legs. Me, I sit in the front of the boat, watching the sun's reflection off the rippling water, enjoying the warm breeze.

I wish he could be here with me. That was the plan, someday, to retire on a lake to a quiet life with children and grandkids. I will think of that every day now. David still comes to me, but only in dreams. I wake up with a wet pillow and a hollow feeling.

I start the engine, the quiet hum as I slowly edge the lever forward and drive toward the dock. The slow rides along the lake are my favorite part of where we live. The apartment we're renting—well, it's not much to look at, and the AC is dicey, but the kids think the elevator is cool, and the view from the fourth floor is something to behold, beautiful and serene. I could do with serene for a while.

A man is standing at the dock as we approach. You might think I'd react with fear. I thought so, too—that I'd be jumpy, suspicious of every stranger, guarded in every interaction, flinching at shadows, living in constant fear that our new cover will be blown. But paranoia has not followed me here. For one, I was declared dead from complications after my spill into the Cotton River. There was an official press release, news coverage, even a funeral—a joint memorial service for David and me—in Hemingway Grove.

And two, from what everyone can tell, Michael Cagnina is not hunting for us and never was. He's old and sick and doesn't want any part of anything that could send him back to prison. Cagnina wasn't behind what happened to my family. It was all about an FBI agent who never got the twenty million he was promised for disclosing the location of the secret detention center and an assassin who wanted a cut of the action in exchange for helping him track it down.

"That's Sergeant Kyle!" Lincoln shouts, joining me at the wheel. "Right? Isn't that him?"

Indeed, I see as we get closer, that is Kyle on the dock. I bring my hand to my forehead and salute him. He salutes back and waits for us as I tie off the boat in our docking space.

"Howdy, stranger," he says, squinting into the sun. I've become so used to seeing him in his uniform, buttoned-up and alert, that it's a bit startling to see the T-shirt and sandals.

I give him a quick hug. Nothing that might give him ideas.

"You staying the night?" I ask him as we walk to my car.

"Nah. I'll probably drive back to the convention tonight. I have to speak on one of the panels early tomorrow. It's a two-hour drive from here."

That's probably for the best. Kyle holds up a phone, showing me a newborn with an anguished look on her face. "Camille had a girl," he says.

I take the phone. "She's adorable."

"She named her Marcie."

I turn to him. "Really?"

"No. I just wanted to see the look on your face. Her name is Emily. Get over yourself."

I punch his arm. "Not nice, sir. Hey, what about the father of the child?"

"Still married to his wife. Sounds like Camille's given up on him. She's raising the baby herself."

The kids run up ahead and jump into the car.

"On another note, I hear there might be a taker for the pub property," Kyle says. "Maybe they'll take down that damn Hemingway statue."

Yes, there is a taker, someone looking to start another restaurant. I'm negotiating through a lawyer and a trust—considering that I'm "dead" and all. And they won't take down that statue until I say so. Because within the base of that statue, hidden from view by the shrubbery, is a secret compartment that opens only via a tiny handheld remote that David left me in the safe-deposit box. That hollow interior currently holds the sum of around fifteen million dollars—the entirety of the twenty million David stole, less what he spent over the last fifteen years between building our house and slowly laundering some through his business, with me oblivious to the whole thing, letting him handle the financials. Eventually, when we sell that property along with the pub, I will have to do something about that money.

For now—well, I took a little bit with me just to get adjusted here. What I do with the rest of the money, I'm unsure. I'll be generous with charitable donations. I will stash away some for the kids' college education and maybe keep a little for the family. After all, it kinda feels like "hazard pay" for me, too.

"I could see it," Kyle says, riding in the front seat, his

elbow out the window, as we drive to our apartment building. "I know I'm a hometown kid, but I could see it, living somewhere like this."

Is that more than a casual comment? Sure feels like it. But I won't follow up. Not now. All my attention, my entire focus at present, is on two beautiful and promising kids who seem to be finally coming out from under a major shock to their systems. They've had good days and bad. Today was a good one. The best I can do right now is try to fit as many days under "good" as possible. And hope and pray for the arrival of that day when mourning turns to loving memories, when tears turn to smiles. It will come. It's hard to imagine it, but I know that day will come. The kids will be okay. Never the same, always with a piece of their hearts missing, but okay.

So that's it. That's how I lost David. There were moments when I didn't know how we'd carry on without him. But we will. We hit rock bottom six months ago. It's nice, at least, to feel like the path we're on leads to a good place, a place that's real, a place we will eventually call normal.

ABOUT THE AUTHORS

JAMES PATTERSON is the most popular storyteller of our time. He is the creator of unforgettable characters and series, including Alex Cross, the Women's Murder Club, Jane Smith, and Maximum Ride, and of breathtaking true stories about the Kennedys, John Lennon, and Tiger Woods, as well as our military heroes, police officers, and ER nurses. He has coauthored #1 bestselling novels with Bill Clinton and Dolly Parton, and collaborated most recently with Michael Crichton on the blockbuster *Eruption*. He has told the story of his own life in *James Patterson by James Patterson* and received an Edgar Award, ten Emmy Awards, the Literarian Award from the National Book Foundation, and the National Humanities Medal.

DAVID ELLIS is a justice of the Illinois Appellate Court and the author of nine novels, including *Line of Vision,* for which he won an Edgar Award, and *The Hidden Man,* which earned him a 2009 Los Angeles Times Book Prize nomination.

For a complete list of books by
JAMES PATTERSON

VISIT
JamesPatterson.com

Follow James Patterson on Facebook
@JamesPatterson

Follow James Patterson on X
𝕏 **@JP_Books**

Follow James Patterson on Instagram
@jamespattersonbooks